Please return this book on or before the due date stamped below

Snake in the Grass

By the same author

Aunt Letitia

Snake in the Grass

Dominic Luke

ROBERT HALE · LONDON

ISBN 978 0 7198 0668 1

Robert Hale Limited
Clerkenwell House
Clerkenwell Green
London EC1R 0HT

www.halebooks.com

2 4 6 8 10 9 7 5 3 1

Typeset in 10.5/14 Sabon
Printed and bound in Great Britain by
Bodmin Limited, King's Lynn

ONE

'Oh shiiit!'

Something had darted out into the road in front of him: a dark shape picked out momentarily in the glaring headlights. Dean swerved and braked, acting from instinct. His car skidded wildly across the road and onto the verge, where it paused for a second before slowly tilting forwards to end up nose first in the ditch. Dean was flung towards the steering wheel. The seat belt cut into his shoulder. It hurt. It hurt a lot. He would have yelled with the pain of it, had he not already been yelling with terror.

It was all over in the blink of an eye. Dean stopped yelling. He turned off the engine. Suddenly it was eerily quiet, except for his thumping heart and panicky breathing. He felt as if he'd been picked up and given a good shaking by a disgruntled giant. He'd never been more scared in his life.

What was it that had run across the road in front of him? Dean pictured the dark shape as he had seen it spotlighted by his headlights: a sleek black creature with glaring green eyes. The creature had given him a look as if to say: get off *my* road.

But that couldn't be right. It had to be down to his overactive imagination. It was true that there had been an item on Radio 5 a few weeks back about beasts which lurked in the countryside, killing sheep and eating them, terrorizing dog walkers in secluded woodlands and savaging their pets. The police knew all about it but kept it quiet. Dean, however, scoffed at such rubbish. There was not a shred of evidence, just hearsay. You had to be scientific about these things or you'd end up believing anything. What he'd seen just now had probably been an ordinary-sized cat made enormous by his unruly imagination. It was highly unlikely that panther-sized

5

creatures were roaming the English countryside undetected. There was nothing dangerous about the countryside – unless you brought that danger on yourself, as he had just done by having this stupid accident. Now he needed to decide what to do next. He couldn't just sit here staring down at the bottom of the ditch. What if his car exploded? He wasn't sure if cars really exploded or if that only happened on TV, but it was better to be safe than sorry.

He kicked open the door and scrambled out, making a mental note as he did so not to use such a hackneyed phrase as *better safe than sorry* in future: it was the sort of thing his mother would say.

There was water in the ditch. His trainers got soaked. He crawled up onto the verge, slipping and sliding in the mud. What next? He looked all round. Thin clouds were scudding across the sky, lit from behind by bright moonlight. Moonlight also lay coldly across the soggy fields. He must be miles from home and he didn't have his phone with him. Why oh why had he left the party in such a hurry? He'd have to walk now. In the dark. With wet shoes. He'd get trench foot. Or hypothermia. Or worse.

Some night this was turning out to be.

He was shivering: *shaking like a leaf*, as his mother would have said in her hackneyed way. The effect of shock, perhaps. A normal reaction? Or was he being a wimp? Richard would say wimp; and his stepfather would go on about teenage drivers and what a menace they were. But who cared what his stepfather would say? The man was only interested in money, the cost of things. And as for Richard: well, Richard was a bastard.

Headlights flicked across the moonlit fields. A car was coming. That was a stroke of luck, on this little-used lane. No need to tramp in the dark. He could get a lift home.

Then again …

His overactive imagination was off once more. He couldn't rein it in.

What if the driver of the car was a serial killer?

It was a ridiculous idea, he told himself. What were the odds on meeting a serial killer? Millions to one. On the other hand, serial killers – unlike wild beasts – were real: it was a well-documented fact, there was evidence. It would be just his luck to meet one, a serial killer who picked up hitchhikers and took them back to his grotty flat (serial killers always had grotty flats: the ones on channel 5 did, anyway). Once in the killer's lair, Dean would be strangled with an electric flex, his body dismembered and dissolved in acid....

No, no, no! Shivering and shaking, Dean cursed his imagination as the hum of the car grew ever louder in the still, cold air. Other people didn't have this problem. They didn't let their imaginations run away with them. It was just him. There could be no two ways about it: he was a freak.

The car slowed as it rounded a bend, then accelerated on the straight, bearing down on him. The headlights were like piercing eyes – but at least they weren't green, like the panther's. The panther didn't exist. It was a figment of his imagination. As was the serial killer.

All the same, it was better to be safe than—

Dean stepped back from the road, crouched down behind the upended boot of his car. 'Don't stop, don't stop, please don't stop.'

The car slowed, pulled over to the verge, stopped. The engine revved once, twice, then fell silent. Nothing happened. Slowly, Dean straightened up, blinking in the glare of the headlights. The lights suddenly snapped off, plunging him into darkness. The moonlight seemed very dim after the glare. All was quiet.

The driver's door opened. Two legs swung out. A woman's head appeared. She stood there looking at Dean with the door between them.

'Hello there! Need any help?' Her breath smoked in the cold air.

'My car's in the ditch.' Dean added, 'Something jumped out into the road. I swerved ...' as explanation, justification.

'Fox or pheasant?'

'It was black and looked like a cat. It wasn't a cat,' he added hastily: it sounded silly, to have driven into a ditch for the sake of a cat. 'It was big, enormous.'

'A panther?' The woman's voice expressed amusement, curiosity and scepticism all at the same time. 'There are beasts lurking in the countryside. I heard about them on Radio 5.'

'It did look rather like a beast,' Dean admitted. 'It had green eyes.' He was rather doubtful now about the colour of the eyes, but felt it would be too much like shilly-shallying to change his story at this late stage.

'Gosh! How exciting!' The woman closed her car door and walked towards Dean, placing one foot precisely in front of the other, heels clicking on the tarmac. 'You seem harmless enough. One has to be careful, you understand, in my position: a woman on her own at night …'

Dean was greatly insulted at being termed *harmless*. He was not sure that the same could be said of the woman. She had black hair, was dressed in black. He skirt was very short, her legs looked very long: Dean was fascinated by them. She seemed very sleek and athletic, like the beast. The beast, though, had been a figment. This woman was most definitely not.

She was near at hand now, scrutinizing him carefully. He could not guess at her age in the moonlight. Not old. But not young, either. She seemed very self-confident – reckless even. Dangerous. He could no longer see her legs, but her breasts were … oh my … her *breasts* …

Dean gulped, made an effort to look away. Not that he was doing anything *wrong*. It was her own fault. She was asking for it, wearing a top like that. Wasn't she freezing?

He didn't like the way she was looking at him. Speculative. Acquisitive. *Hungry.*

'You are shaking like a leaf.' A hackneyed phrase, *shaking like a leaf*; but the way she said it was anything but.

'It's cold.'

'Shock makes you feel cold.'

'It's December. It's cold.' Dean refused to admit to shock.

'Your poor car!' The woman laid a pale hand on Dean's arm.

'What are you doing?' he asked in alarm.

'Treating you for shock.'

He backed away but there was nowhere to run. She had him trapped against the upended boot of his car. Her hands were all over him, fingers probing. His knees buckled, his heart was going haywire. Every time she touched him, it was like an electric shock. He jerked and flinched and gasped.

Whatever she was up to, it wasn't murder.

'Oh, ah, oh!' He gulped. 'Do you really – ah, ah – do you really think this helps? Why are you undoing – ow, ouch, oh – undoing my – ah, ah, shit, ouch, shiiit...!'

She stepped away from him. It was all over.

Had one minute passed, or many? He had lost all sense of time. He pulled up his jeans with shaking hands, fumbled with the zip. It was a lot darker now. Thicker clouds had come across, covering the moon, drawing a veil over the scene of the crime.

Crime? Well, that was what it was. He'd been assaulted. Molested. And he'd just stood there and let her get on with it. And to think he'd been worried about being strangled and dissolved in acid. However weird things got in his head, real life always turned out to be far, far—

As he struggled with his belt, his brain went into overdrive, firing off questions like sparks from a Catherine wheel. Or was *that* what all the fuss was about? Or had he missed something? Did she know that it had been his first time? Could women tell? Had he made a fool of himself in some way? What if she was laughing at him? Why did he now feel so jittery, so spaced out? Was this normal? Or was it the first sign of some horrible disease? What if she'd given him warts or crabs or scabies or herpes or gonorrhoea or syphilis or AIDS or—

Shut up! Shut up! Leave me alone!

'Well?' The woman was standing by her car, her clothes back in place, smoothed down. She was holding the passenger door open. 'Can I give you a lift anywhere?'

'No thanks.'

'Are you sulking?'

'No.'

'You are.'

'Am not.'

'Then get in the car.'

What else could he do? If he refused, she would just go off and leave him there, and he had no idea how to get home. He'd probably freeze to death long before he found his way, or he'd fall into a ditch and drown. This woman was his only hope – and she knew it.

With great reluctance, he got into the car and pulled on the seat belt. He sat tensed up, scowling.

He watched out of the corner of his eye as she drove. Her pale, long-fingered hands stroked the steering wheel, caressed the gear stick – the same hands that had been stroking and caressing him a matter of minutes ago: invading his personal space, toying with him. His overactive imagination had not been too far out after all. There *had* been a wild beast lurking, waiting. It was *her*. *She* was a panther. *He* was her prey.

'Are you going to say anything?'

'No.' Dean clamped his lips together. Why should he talk to her? Why should he be cooperative? It was bad enough that his body had cooperated just now, betraying him – not that he wasn't used to it. He was used to being scourged by spots, having muscles that never got any bigger, feet that smelled, hair with a mind of its own, reflexes he had no control over. But he could still choose who he talked to and who he didn't.

'Why were you driving so fast?' Her words probed intrusively, the way, just now, her fingers had done.

'I don't know what you mean. I wasn't driving fast.'

'Don't try pulling the wool. If you hadn't been speeding, you wouldn't have ended up in that ditch.'

'I told you, there was a—' He stopped, frowning. He wasn't going to tell her anything. 'You're a weirdo,' he muttered.

'Quite possibly.' The woman changed gear, driving uphill. She added, as if to herself, 'This is where too much gin gets you.'

Dean seized on this. 'You're *drunk*? A *drunk driver*?' No wonder she seemed dangerous, reckless. She was out of control, sozzled.

'Never mind me. I asked you a question. Why were you out driving?'

'If … if you must know—' Dean couldn't help himself. It all came spilling out. '—I was pissed off. *Really* pissed off.'

'And why was that?'

'Because of my party.'

'Oh?'

'I had the house to myself. I decided to have a party. A Christmas party.'

'What went wrong?' She glanced across at him. 'You might as well tell me. I can see that you are dying to get it off your chest.'

'Smart arse,' muttered Dean. But she was right. He simply couldn't hold it in. 'Richard turned up, that's what happened: Richard, my stepbrother. I didn't invite him but he turned up anyway. Everything had been going to plan until *he* came along. He had a vodka jelly. All the girls went, "Ooh, Rich, how clever, what a great idea!" They were well impressed. Like it's anything special, a poxy vodka jelly.'

'He stole your thunder?' the panther suggested. 'You had hoped to impress the girls yourself?'

'No,' said Dean, meaning *yes*. He tried to turn his back on the woman, which was not easy in the passenger seat of the car. He hated her. She was too clever by half. And she seemed to think it was amusing to mock him. She could talk to herself from now on.

His shoulder was killing him. He'd probably dislocated it in the crash. He'd be crippled for life. And as if that wasn't bad enough, he couldn't stop thinking about the party. Rage boiled inside him.

Finally, he couldn't keep a lid on it any longer. Words came spouting out like steam from a pressure cooker. His party had been perfect, he insisted, everything in place: he'd researched it on the internet. It hadn't been boring, naff or a pile of pants: that was just people trying to be clever at his expense. But then Richard had arrived. Richard had gatecrashed. Richard had brought a vodka jelly and a whole bottle of tequila. He'd turned the music up full; he'd monopolized Sandra Hays; and, as if that wasn't bad enough, when he was drunk he'd started to dance on the kitchen table, stripping off at the same time. Dean ground his teeth, remembering how his party had veered out of control as Richard gyrated on the kitchen table in nothing but a pair of boxers. The boys had whooped and guffawed. The girls had watched with wide eyes, giggling. It was at that point that Dean had stormed out in a rage, venting his spleen by driving at dangerous speeds along the country lanes – but the panther didn't need to know about that bit: he kept quiet about the speeding.

'He sounds like quite a character, this Richard,' she said as she negotiated a crossroads.

'Well, he's not. He's a bastard.' Dean gave the woman a sidelong glance. Just who was she, this raving lunatic? Even *his* imagination had never come up with something this bizarre. 'I hate people who just barge in without being invited,' Dean muttered darkly, thinking about his trousers as well as his party.

The woman gave a bark of laughter. 'I take it you don't get on with your brother?'

'He is *not* my brother. He's my *step*brother. I hate him. Everything was fine until my stupid mother decided to get remarried. I *liked* being an only child.'

'But you're not an only child. What about your sister?'

Dean was jolted out of his sullen mood. He glanced at the woman with some trepidation. Was she more of a witch than a panther – a witch who could read your mind? 'How do you know about my sister?'

'I see her around. I saw her the other day, shopping in Waitrose with your mother.'

Dean blanched. His sister *and* his mother. What else did this witch-woman know? He'd thought she was a complete stranger.

His heart was pounding. He couldn't breathe. He was having one of his panic attacks. (*Don't exaggerate, darling, they're not panic attacks. It's teenage angst, perfectly normal.* His bloody mother: what did she know?)

'Your mother used to attend an evening class I taught. Painting for beginners. That, of course, was in the days before your father ran off with his secretary.'

'She was not his secretary.' Dean spoke through gritted teeth. 'She was his business partner's wife.'

'Oh? They say secretary in the village, but the gossips are not always accurate. I suppose it *is* less of a cliché to run off with one's business partner's wife.'

'Why don't you just shut up and mind your own business!' Dean shouted. He was feeling faint. It was one thing being ravished by a total stranger, quite another when she turned out to be someone who shopped in Waitrose and knew your mother. And now, not content with having rooted about inside his trousers, she seemed to want to root through his family's private affairs. She had no sense of decorum. Was off her head on booze. Was probably a loony too. She certainly acted like one.

He did his best to ignore her.

They drove on in silence. The car purred into the village, turned into Dean's road.

'H-how ... how do you know where I live?'

'It's a small village. I live here too.'

'But I've never seen you before in my life!'

'I find that hard to believe. We live only a stone's throw from each other and I've been teaching at the college in town for years.'

'M-my college?' Dean squirmed in his seat. This was getting worse and worse. She had to be playing tricks on him. Or maybe the whole thing was a hallucination caused by the shock of the accident. He didn't know her, he didn't, he didn't ...

On the other hand ... (*Oh, Dean, you live with your head in the clouds. You never see what's right under your nose.*)

'Here we are.' The car pulled up outside Dean's house, which was all in darkness. 'Looks like the party's over.'

'Humph!' He got out and slammed the door.

'*Auf wiedersehen!*' The woman waved out of the window as she drove away.

'Nazi,' muttered Dean.

The partygoers had gone. They had turned off all the lights before they went but had left the front door wide open. There was no sign of Richard. Dean ventured indoors, turning the lights back on, surveying the wreckage with a sinking feeling as he passed from room to room. The place was littered with empty and half-empty glasses, cans and bottles. Crisps and nuts had been trodden into the carpets. Cheap cider had been poured lavishly over the polished surface of the dining-room table. His mother's best saucers had been used as ashtrays. There was a definite whiff of marijuana in the air. The vodka jelly, however, had vanished.

Dean knew he ought to make an effort to tidy round, but he did not want to risk being up and about when his mother and Basil got home. Best to hide in bed now and face the inevitable recriminations tomorrow. By then he'd have had time to get it straight in his mind. He'd have some explanations ready. It was all Richard's fault: this must somehow be made clear. Richard had hijacked the party, enjoyed himself, then cut and run, leaving Dean to cop the flak. Richard should be the one tidying up; he should be the one getting it in the neck. *And,* thought Dean as he stomped up the stairs, *I bet he got off with Sandra Hays, too, the bastard, the bastard, the bastard*!

Twisting and turning in bed, Dean groaned, unable to find sleep. He kept thinking about the accident. He broke into a sweat, reliving the blind panic he had felt as his car swerved and skidded; experienced once more his abject terror as it slid into the ditch. All because of the beast: the enigmatic black beast with green eyes. But as the accident grew more and more real in his memory – making him go hot and cold in turn, shivering under the duvet – the beast grew more and more hazy and dreamlike. Perhaps it had never existed in the first pace. Perhaps there had not even been a small cat. There *were* such things as optical illusions, not to mention the Heisenberg Uncertainty Principle. You could not always believe the evidence of your own eyes.

So the beast had been an optical illusion. But that panther, that succubus, that witch on a broomstick (or Fiat Brava, to be exact): she had been real, all right. Dean curled up, clutching his knees to his chest, trying to blot out the panther, but he couldn't. Was sex always like that, so mechanical, so fleshy and rudimentary, so slap-dash? Were the lads at college lying through their teeth when they went on (and on and on) about how brilliant it was? *Or,* Dean asked himself, *is it just me?*

He groaned some more, grinding his teeth. *It's just me. I know it's just me. Oh God, why am I such a freak?*

He tried to calm himself down. He'd be having another of his panic attacks if he wasn't careful. He had to get a grip, look on the bright side.

Look on the bright side. Another of his mother's phrases. Why did she have to talk such rubbish?

It was all Richard's fault.

Dean yawned as his mind finally slipped into a well-worn groove. Hating Richard was comforting and soothing. Its normalcy induced sleep.

He slept.

TWO

LYDIA TAYLOR BACKED her car slowly along the narrow drive, craning over her shoulder to see where she was going, taking care not to ride over Mr Wetherby's neat lawn (heaven forbid....) Her home lay back from the road. Two new villas flanked the driveway, almost blocking from view her little old sandstone cottage.

As she opened her front door, she listened from force of habit for Prize's welcoming bark, but she listened in vain, for her dog was dead and the cottage was cold, dark and empty. She closed the door. The clicking of the latch marked the moment when she was cut off from the land of the living, trapped once more in a limbo of ghosts and memories and deafening silence.

She turned on lights, stoked the fire, warmed herself in front of it (what had possessed her to go out dressed in such flimsy clothes?). She looked down at the sofa, strewn with the daily newspaper and several library books. She had thought the books might help in some way. She had read in them that loneliness and grief were part of the healing process, a natural stage in mourning, but they were talking of human deaths, not canine. Nobody had anything to say about the death of one's dog. The books were useless.

Going through to the kitchen, Lydia reached for the gin bottle, glugged a generous measure into a glass, searched for tonic (*surely I must have some somewhere....*). Delving into her cupboards, she wondered if she was being silly, hysterical, making a fool of herself. The vet had not exactly said so, merely hinted at it by the tone of his voice, the roll of his eyes. She seemed to remember him saying, 'It's only an animal', but that might be putting words into his mouth.

She gave up her search. There was no tonic. Curses. Perhaps the pub? She glanced at the clock, squinting to bring it into focus. As late as that. Chucking-out time had come and gone. But they might still be up and about, the landlord and his wife, clearing up. If she telephoned, would they let her pop down to fetch some tonic? The landlord was always eager to please, especially where women were concerned. But it might be his wife who answered the phone. Lydia decided not to risk it.

Gin and lemonade it had to be, then. And a slice of lemon. She sliced a lemon, slicing her finger at the same time. Blood ran onto the chopping board. The lemon juice got into her cut, made it sting. She hopped up and down, sucking her finger, wincing.

Rinsing her finger under a tap, drying it, applying a plaster, Lydia winced again as she caught a glimpse through the kitchen window of her car parked outside. What had she been thinking of, driving in her state? She was absolutely plastered, couldn't even walk straight. Nor was she dressed for December. She could not imagine why she had dressed up in these old clothes. She had barely looked at them in years – not since the days of Nigel, in fact.

Going for a drive must have seemed like a good idea at the time, but that time was now lost in an alcoholic haze. It made her blood run cold, thinking what might have happened, how she might easily have killed someone – or killed herself. And as for what had *actually* happened....

'Oh God. Oh please no. No, no, no.' Every inch of her cringed at the memory, the young man – the *boy* – by the roadside.

'Shameful, that's what it is.'

The disembodied voice made her jump. 'Oh, it's you, is it?'

Her mother's ghost tut-tutted. 'What a performance. And to think you're nearly forty. You really ought to know better at your age.'

'I am not nearly forty. There are still two years before I'm forty.'

'Nineteen months.' The voice was as irritatingly precise in death as in life. Lydia ignored it.

She picked up her drink, went back to the main room, took up a position in front of the fire. Goose pimples rose on her arm as she saw in her mind's eye the wide-eyed stare of the boy caught in her headlights. She had stepped out of her car and straight into the role of a femme fatale, as if it was a part she'd been playing all her life. Where had it come from? More to the point, why? Another manifestation of grief? Or was she going round the twist? It was not as if the young man had been handsome or personable. Pale-faced, spotty, inarticulate – like one of those impermeable blank-faced clods who always sat at the back in her classes. It had been like making love to a lump of dough. She had found it necessary to prod, poke, pull and guide him. The femme fatale had been amused. It seemed to Lydia now more like a nightmare.

Back in the kitchen, Lydia slopped more gin into her glass. Mother's ruin, they called it. Perhaps a good measure of it would blot out her mother's ghost – not to mention the boy by the roadside; and, of course, her dog.

Curses! Here she was, back to thinking about Prize. But why shouldn't she? Poor old mutt. It was not his fault if he'd grown decrepit and riddled with disease (it had never occurred to her that dogs got cancer: it seemed an unnecessarily cruel stroke of nature). She had put off and put off the inevitable visit to the vet; but when all was said and done, she could not see the dear thing suffer in any way.

'I'm afraid there's not a lot more we can do, Mrs Taylor,' the vet had said. It was what, in her heart of hearts, she'd expected.

'*Miss* Taylor,' Lydia had corrected him: a bald vet, she recalled, with a huge bushy beard. The hairless pate and hairy chin had given his face a topsy-turvy appearance. She had quite liked the vet to start with.

'Would you like to hold him one last time?' the vet had asked.

'Oh yes. Thank you.' Lydia had thought him very perceptive and sensitive. She remembered looking down at Prize. How thin he'd gotten! He'd been half the dog he used to be. His trusting rheumy eyes had stared into hers.

'Now then.' The vet had produced a hypodermic needle.

Lydia had watched in mute horror as the vet plunged the needle deep into Prize's body. The poor hound had twisted and jerked, nearly wrenching himself free of Lydia's grasp. He had tried his best to muster a bark, but all he had managed was a whimper as he expired. It had all been so quick, so unexpected. She could have sworn that the vet had given her no indication of what he was about to do.

Lydia, gulping gin, wandering from room to room, experienced again the shock and rage she had felt at the surgery.

'You have murdered my dog in cold blood!'

'Now, now, Mrs Taylor: his time had come, it was all for the best. Would you like us to dispose of the body? Yes, I think that would be best. Much less fuss for you. There's a van that comes, collects all the carcasses, takes them for incineration.'

Finding herself in the kitchen once more, Lydia sloshed another helping of gin into her glass, thinking of her final glimpse of Prize, recumbent on the vet's table. She had been in a daze, hardly aware of what she was saying, of what she was agreeing to. Prize had been taken away to be burnt. She didn't even have a grave to visit, somewhere to take flowers. The vet, in her memory, showed no remorse. Had he really said something along the lines of *all major credit cards are accepted*, or was she making that up after the fact?

Lydia dropped another slice of lemon into her glass. The lemon was spotted with blood, turned her drink a rather pleasing pink colour. She concentrated on the colour, tried to forget the topsy-turvy-faced vet.

In the main room she sat down heavily on the sofa, books and bits of the newspaper cracking and crackling beneath her.

'My word! Look at the state of this place!'

The disembodied voice of her mother caught her off guard as usual. She jumped, spilling gin. It slowly soaked into her short, black skirt.

'Problem with you, my girl, is that you're too wrapped up in yourself. You always have been. You should spend less time contemplating your navel and make more of an effort with your housework.'

'Stop bossing me around. I am not a child.'

'Speaking of children: that poor boy. What *were* you thinking? He'll be scarred for life, I shouldn't wonder.'

'Oh, shut up, you interfering old bat.'

Lydia silenced the ghost, but could not silence the doubts and fears crowding into her mind as she stared at the flames of the gas fire. What if the boy told his friends? Teenage boys always boasted about things like that. It would be all round the college in no time. It might even come to the attention of the principal. And what about his mother? What if he told his mother? It would be impossible to ever look her in the eye again.

'My life,' said Lydia, 'is over. In tatters.'

She sipped her pink drink and tried to pull herself together. No good wailing and beating her breast. If she was heading for a crash, then at least she could face it full on, make Prize proud of her. She must take the bull by the horns. Her first task would be to go and see that woman – the boy's mother, whatever her name was: she'd forgotten. The best plan was to march up to the woman's door, ring the bell – some legitimate excuse would come to her when sober – and look straight into the woman's eyes. Yes. That's what she would do.

Leaving her drink unfinished on the floor, Lydia wobbled up to the bathroom, brushed her teeth, splashed water on her face, swayed and stumbled into her bedroom where she divested herself of her clothes. She attempted to put on her nightie, gave up, crawled under the duvet from the bottom of the bed and collapsed onto her back.

I must stop drinking so much, she told herself as the room spun round.

There was no heavy weight warming her toes, no sound of snuffling. Prize was gone. Dead.

'He was only an animal,' she muttered as she tumbled headlong into oblivion.

She snored.

THREE

DEAN LOITERED ON the stairs in a state of suspense, listening to his mother talking at the front door.

'Do you really think they'd be good enough? To tell the truth, I haven't looked at them in ages. They're buried under the stairs.'

Dean could not make out what the woman on the doorstep was saying.

'Well, if you're sure....' Dean's mother expressed doubt. 'I'd like to help, naturally, but I was only ever a very amateurish amateur.'

'Mumble, mumble,' said the woman on the doorstep.

'Do you really think so? I *was* quite proud of that one, if I do say so myself. I'll tell you what I'll do. I'll unearth them all and bring them down to you, then you can decide if they'd be suitable. Would that be all right?'

'Mumble, mumble.'

'Don't mention it. It's no trouble at all. Goodbye, then!'

His mother shut the door. Dean descended.

'Who was that?' he asked.

He knew who it was. Peering from his bedroom window through a chink in the curtains, he had seen her approaching the house, walking purposefully up the drive towards the front door: the panther. The blood had drained from his face; he had felt a panic attack coming on. Why was she here? Was she stalking him? Just how dangerous was she?

He had been ensconced in his bedroom all morning, too ill for college. He really did feel ill, he wasn't just trying to avoid the fallout from his party. His stepfather, of course, had suggested otherwise, bellowing up the stairs at the top of his voice, demanding Dean *show himself*. Dean had taken no notice.

He now faced his mother in the hallway. She looked harassed, was wearing an apron, holding a tea towel. The wreckage of the party was clearly keeping her busy.

'Who was that?' Dean repeated.

'It was only Lydia Taylor.'

'Lydia who?'

'Lydia Taylor. You know. She lives in that little cottage down Well Lane.'

'I don't know. She's a complete stranger.'

'Oh, Dean, you live in a world of your own! She teaches at the sixth-form college in town – your college.'

So it was true. She did work at the college, like she'd said. 'What did she want?'

'She's organizing some sort of exhibition for village artists, wants me to contribute.'

'You?'

'Yes, well, I *was* rather surprised, I must admit. And it seems a bit off-the-cuff, this exhibition. A bit vague. But I suppose it's early days. Lydia thought of me because of those classes I took. I did art, if you remember. She was the tutor.'

Dean said, 'I don't remember that,' but he did. His father had been enthusiastic. 'Of course you must do evening classes, Gwen! It will be good for you, get you out of the house.' *Get her out of the way, more like*, thought Dean sourly. That had been back in the days before his father's defection. They had often run out of milk in those days. 'Dean, I have to pop to the shops. Your mother's at her evening class, so you'll have to look after Amanda for half an hour, all right?' It must have been going on even then, Dean realized in retrospect: his father must have been carrying on with his business partner's wife all that time ago. His father, Dean affirmed, was a lying, cheating scumbag. But Dean was forced to admit, in the name of scientific accuracy, that the business partner's wife had in fact worked as the company's – and hence his father's – secretary.

His mother put the tea towel aside on the hall table. 'I think I'll root out those paintings now, before I forget. It's rather a nuisance when there's so much else to do, but one doesn't like to let people down. You can give me a hand, Dean.'

21

'Do I have to?'

'They're in the cupboard under the stairs. You know what a jumble that is. I need a man to move the heavy things.'

Buttering him up by calling him a man, thought Dean, was not a ploy that was going to work. He was wise to her ways. She ought to realize that by now.

She sighed. 'Of course, you don't *have* to help. I just thought, as I'd spent all morning cleaning up your mess—'

'Richard's mess.'

'It wasn't Richard's party.'

'Richard was in charge. I wasn't even here.'

'No. You were out in your car, driving into a ditch. Which reminds me: if you're not going to help with the paintings, you can phone the garage and see if they've finished with your car.'

'Can't. Got to study.'

Dean beat a retreat to his bedroom, slammed the door, threw himself on the bed. The curtains were closed, the radiator on full blast. Usually it soothed him, lying in the heat and the half-light and thinking about important things such as the history of the universe; but today the trivia of daily life kept intruding. *I've spent all morning clearing up*, his mother had said, like it was a big deal or something; but what was one morning when the universe had been around for thirteen billion years? Did she actually realize how *petty* she sounded?

He hadn't heard the last about his party, that was clear. And there was his car as well. His mother wouldn't say much, of course. She'd just wear that martyred look as if you were the world's biggest disappointment. But his stepfather – his stepfather was another matter. No one could shut Basil Collier up once he got going. It never helped to point out that it was none of Basil's business. Dean had grown weary of repeating, 'I'm not your son, you can't tell me what to do!'

And now, as if he didn't have enough on his plate, the panther had turned up to torment him. She had to be up to something. It was too much of a coincidence that she had come calling today. And that story about an exhibition: as if anyone in their right mind would want to look at his mother's paintings!

He sighed, sat up, decided he'd better at least *look* as if he was studying in case his mother barged in. He reached down for a book from amongst the untidy heap of clothes, trainers, pens, notebooks and magazines strewn over the floor. Geography. That would do.

As he flicked through the textbook, he wished that Lydia Taylor was as mythical as those Radio 5 beasts. But she wasn't. She was real. He had very good reason to know just how real.

He shuddered, but there was no shaking her off. Very well. He'd think about it logically. He'd go through it point by point. To start with, in the plus column—

Plus column! Oh my God! He was turning into his stepfather, adding and subtracting, balancing the books, looking at the world in a mealy-mouthed, pedantic way.

The textbook slipped to the floor as Dean turned on his side, facing the wall. Never mind plus columns. Just concentrate on facts. And the fact was, he was no longer a virgin. He would no longer be the odd one out at college. He could hold his head up at last. There was no need to tell anyone who he'd actually done it *with* – although, come to think of it, wasn't there a certain cachet in snaring an older woman? (He needn't mention that she had been the one doing the snaring.)

But what was the use? He'd never be able to tell anyone what had happened. It was too embarrassing – too humiliating.

He threw himself onto his back, stared up at the ceiling. It seemed very low today, pressing down on him, boxing him in, leaving him no room for manoeuvre. The thing was, he'd thought he was up to speed on the subject of sex. He'd done his research, been meticulous about it. He'd even lowered himself to buying certain top-shelf magazines – in a spirit of scientific enquiry, naturally. But nothing in all his research had led him to expect the actual act to be so ... well, sticky, smelly, *messy*; so very crude and mechanical. The panther had taken control. 'Not like that, like this ... let me show you.' He should have known she was a teacher, the way she'd carried on, knowing best. He knew what to do, he wasn't stupid! But the problem was, he'd been in no position to think about anything as she poked him and prodded him and squirmed against him, squashing him against the upturned boot of his car.

Had it been exactly ... manly ... to let himself be pushed around like that?

He turned on his front, buried his head in the pillow, wishing the panther had left him alone, wishing he was still a virgin. Life was tough enough already, a daily rollercoaster taking him up and down, up and down, doing his head in until he wanted to scream. Now there was even more to torment him.

It was all Richard's fault, this latest debacle. Richard had started it, gatecrashing the party.

Richard was the bane of his life.

FOUR

So FAR, so good.

Walking through the village, enveloped in a charity shop Burberry and knitted red bobble hat complete with matching scarf, Lydia experienced a sense of relief, knowing from their brief conversation that Gwen Collier was unaware of the seduction of her son. Nor had there been any hint of it at college today: no nudging or winking, no whispering amongst the boys in the back row. *I might*, thought Lydia pulling up the scratchy scarf to cover her nose and mouth; *I just might have got away with it. In any case*, she added stubbornly, *I did nothing wrong. The boy is an adult, of legal age. He is eighteen.*

Eighteen! 'Why oh why did I do it?' she wailed out loud, startling the vicar who was just coming through the lichgate from the churchyard.

He peered towards her through the gloom, made a tentative identification. 'Miss Taylor, is it? Good evening.'

'Evening … er … evening.' She was never sure how one addressed a vicar. *Vicar? Reverend? Your worship?* His name was Garth (it would be) but he was known in the village as Dick Emery on account of his buck-toothed appearance. Whatever form of address one adopted, *Dick Emery* must be avoided at all costs. 'Lovely evening.'

'Cold,' said the vicar as he hurried on his way.

Lydia cringed. Lovely evening! What was she thinking of? There was nothing lovely about it. Not only was it cold, as the vicar had correctly pointed out, it was dark and dismal too; and Christmas was looming menacingly on the horizon to add to the misery.

25

'I am going round the twist,' Lydia muttered as the vicar disappeared into the night. 'Talking to myself. Hearing voices. I am on the slippery slope to hysteria.'

Her brief sense of complacency shrivelled and died in the cold, clammy evening. She drew her scarf tighter, shoved her hands in her coat pockets. The boy – the boy whose name she couldn't even remember – had not yet given the game away, but he wouldn't keep quiet for ever. Boys of that age were loud, boastful, facile. The contents of their minds were endlessly disgorged in a stream of dirty jokes and puerile comments. But the boy was not her only problem. She was also beginning to have second thoughts about the ruse she had just used to call on Gwen Collier. All that talk of an exhibition had seemed to spark some interest in Gwen. Against expectation, she had agreed to cooperate. But perhaps she was simply being polite. Perhaps she would forget all about it.

'Please God,' muttered Lydia as she approached the bright lights of the pub.

She hesitated under the thatched eaves. The pub had just opened for its evening session. Breathing in the icy air, the cold and damp working its way through her multiple layers, Lydia looked through a window that had been sprayed with lavish amounts of aerosol snow, saw the flickering glow of the tempting log fire inside (real, not plastic). She listened. There was not even the faintest echo of her mother's ghost, no strictures on the evils of drink, no disapproving tut. The wide, dark December evening was empty and silent.

She thought of her cottage, desolate without Prize.

With a decisive movement, she opened the pub door and walked in.

'Ah! I'm sure this beautiful young lady would like a drink!'

Lydia's elderly neighbour Mr Wetherby was at the bar. His wife was sitting by the fire with her coat on. The only other people in the lounge were the barmaid and a mechanical polar bear in a Christmas hat, jerking wildly (dancing?) on a metal stand. Tinsel glistened, Christmas baubles hung from the ceiling. Warm air wrapped Lydia round like an embrace.

'That's very kind, Mr Wetherby. I'll have a gin and tonic if I may. Good evening, Mrs Wetherby.'

'Hello. Yes. We're just ... Hmm.' Mrs Wetherby was her usual vague self. She had a scrawny neck, sunken cheeks, looked half dead. Her husband was much more robust; red cheeked and white haired. He was rather on the short side, looked (thought Lydia) rather like a gnome – a particularly pernicious gnome.

Lydia shrugged off her coat but kept it close at hand, ready for a quick getaway. How soon could she make her escape without seeming rude?

'It's a cold evening,' Lydia offered up as she poured tonic into her gin.

'Cold. Yes. Hmm.'

'Not as cold as it used to be.' Mr Wetherby sat down with his pint of real ale. 'We used to get snow.' He glanced at his wife and bawled, 'We used to get snow, didn't we, Jeannie?' Turning back to Lydia, he went on, 'We don't get proper winters now. Everything's changed. This country's changed – and not for the better.' (Lydia braced herself.) 'I blame the unions. Ruined this country, they did.'

'Nothing to do with Mrs Thatcher, then?' Lydia muttered.

'What was that?' Mr Wetherby looked at her suspiciously. 'What did you say?'

Lydia, who knew better than to begin an argument with Mr Wetherby, smiled beatifically and sipped her drink.

'You wouldn't know, my dear; you're too young to remember. The unions held this country to ransom in the sixties and seventies. It was a disgrace, an utter disgrace!' Mr Wetherby banged his glass on the table to underline just how disgraceful it was, took a breath at the same time and continued. 'And now it's immigrants. You can't move for foreigners. They come flooding in through the Channel Tunnel. They get houses, jobs, handouts, no questions asked. We get nothing. If you're English, you get nothing. Isn't that right, Jeannie? If you're born here, you're ignored.' (Why, Lydia wondered, did he feel it necessary to raise his voice when speaking to his wife? Mrs Wetherby wasn't deaf.) 'Second-class citizens: that's what we are. Second-class citizens in our own country.'

Another pause for breath, another bang on the table. Lydia, who had heard this litany several times, tried to remember what came next. Sex offenders, perhaps ('they should be castrated, the lot of them, and have done with it'); or one-parent families ('whores and spongers spawning delinquent bastards'). After that, he might go on to outline his scheme for combating the spread of HIV by culling the victims ('works with foot-and-mouth, why not AIDS?').

At that moment, however, there was a welcome interruption as the landlady came moseying into the lounge bar: a rather plump woman, no more than thirty.

'All right, Donald. All right, Jean. All right, Lydia. A cold one this evening. Do you think we'll have snow? Might get a white Christmas for once, ha ha ha!' The landlady cackled. She always found herself most amusing.

'Ah, it's you, is it.' Mr Wetherby's watery blue eyes slowly focused on the landlady's breasts. 'I never see you do any work, you know,' he said silkily.

'What do you mean? I'm always working, ha ha ha!' The land-lady moved to stand in front of the fire, blocking the comforting glow with her ample posterior. 'I'm not like you pensioners, living it up. I daresay you've forgotten what work's like. Isn't that right, Lydia?' The landlady's eyes swivelled round to focus on Lydia. 'Not often we see you in here at this time of day. But I suppose you'd have been out walking your dog normally. Such a shame about your dog. You'll miss him, I expect.'

This brutal reminder of Prize – hearing mention of him on someone else's lips – brought involuntary tears to Lydia's eyes. The library books said it got easier with time, that the wounds began to heal; but Lydia's experience so far was that it got worse. She usually prided herself on being level-headed but right now she felt like that dancing bear on the stand, going through jerky mechanical motions, unthinking, pointless.

The landlady was eyeing her inquisitively. 'Prize. Such an unusual name for a dog, I always thought.'

Lydia gulped her drink, steadying her nerves; managed to wipe her eyes surreptitiously at the same time. 'Yes, it is an unusual name, isn't it!' She spoke brightly, shielding her grief from the land-lady's probing eyes: her grief was private. 'He was given to me by an ex-boyfriend who, on dumping me, said that he was sorry to deprive me of his obvious and superior charms, but I could comfort myself with his gift, a sort of consolation prize.'

'I had a goldfish once,' said the landlady. 'It died too. I overfed it. Killed it with kindness, my dad said. I buried it in the garden in a matchbox, but the cat dug it up and ate it, ha ha ha!' Her eyes zeroed in on Mrs Wetherby. 'Did you ever have a pet, Jean?'

Mrs Wetherby blinked. 'Oh. Well. I. No.'

'No pets! No thank you very much!' Mr Wetherby levered himself back into the conversation. 'Dog hairs all over the furniture, it's unhygienic. And the way dog owners let their animals *shit* all over the place: a disgrace! Wouldn't happen in Singapore. If you drop litter in Singapore, you go straight to jail, no questions asked. We should take that line here.'

'We could have electric shock therapy for litter louts,' Lydia suggested.

'Electric chair, more like. Why should taxpayers foot the bill for *their* mess? It's a disgrace!'

'Disgrace,' muttered Mrs Wetherby. 'Litter. Electricity. Hmmm.'

Lydia wiped her eyes again. The tears wouldn't stop. Even pulling Mr Wetherby's leg – a favourite pastime – didn't make her feel any better this evening. Now that she had finished her drink, she had nothing to fall back on. And the landlady – of course – had taken note of the empty glass. It would be the talk of the pub later. *You know that Lydia Taylor? She can't half knock them back....* There would be yet more gossip if the tears were noticed too.

Lydia got to her feet. 'I ... er ... there's someone I need a word with, in the ... in the public bar.'

She blundered through the doors into the public bar, taking the opportunity to dry her eyes, using the sleeve of her coat as she'd forgotten to bring a handkerchief. The public bar was empty: there was no one to have a word with except the barmaid polishing glasses. The landlady, of course, had known this; hence the sly look as Lydia left the lounge – as if the two of them were involved in some sort of secret conspiracy. The landlady liked to be involved in things.

'Gin and tonic, please.'

The barmaid put her cloth aside. 'Ice and lemon?'

'Of course.' Rather a pretty girl, thought Lydia: sandy hair, a small nose, a sprinkle of freckles. She had something about her: a mind of her own perhaps. Girls with minds of their own were a rare species these days. (*I must stop being so cynical.*) 'You are new here, aren't you?'

'I'm Sandra. I'm supposed to tell you, introduce myself. That's what the landlady said. "Hello, my name is Sandra, how may I help you today?"' Sandra raised an eloquent eyebrow, smiling as she used tongs to put ice in a glass, adding a half-moon of lemon too. 'The landlady is rather bossy,' Sandra confided, pouring gin from an optic. 'Everything I do is wrong. She spent fifteen minutes showing me the right way to cut up a lemon.'

'She knows everything about everything.' Lydia handed over a ten pound note. 'She's known as the Stasi around these parts.'

'As in the East German secret police?' Sandra gave change and laughed. 'It does seem to fit.' She picked up the cloth. 'I'd better get back to the glasses. I'm supposed to look busy at all times.'

'You seem remarkably unperturbed by the Stasi's strictures.'

'I'm immune.' Sandra leant on the bar, wrapping the towel round her neat hands. 'You see, I've met this boy – well, man, really: he's older than me. I met him at a party. It's early days, I know, but....' Her eyes grew wide and happy, she was smiling all over her face. It warmed the heart, thought Lydia, just as the fire warmed one's toes; but as she sat down she could not help feeling sorry for the girl, too. At that age, one was so unaware of the risks.

But perhaps there were no risks where this boy (or man) was concerned. Not all men were like Nigel.

Were they?

Swirling the slice of lemon with her finger, Lydia admitted that there was no escaping the risks even if one avoided men. She had thought she would be safe, falling in love with a dog. She had been wrong. But at least in the empty public bar she could let her tears fall with impunity.

She looked out at the December night through a window daubed with aerosol snow, her vision blurred, and wondered how long she could put off going home – going back to her empty cottage where Prize would not be waiting.

GWEN COLLIER, HOOVERING the hallway, was tormented by thoughts of spiders, earwigs and moths.

It is December, she said to herself sensibly. *They have all been killed by the frost, or else they are in hibernation – or whatever it is that creepy-crawlies do. (What do they do?) There are none in my nice, clean house. My house is creepy-crawly free.*

She told herself this, but she did not believe it. For one thing, there was never any frost inside a centrally heated house (Basil: 'Have you seen the size of this gas bill? Is it absolutely necessary to heat the place to the temperature of a sauna?'). And even if, by some miracle, the creepy-crawlies were all dead, that did not mean they had gone away. What about their corpses? What about their eggs? (Did creepy-crawlies lay eggs? Dean would know, she must ask him.) Aside from that – if one ignored the creepy-crawlies (one could try) – there were a thousand and one other manifestations of dirt to torment one. Human skin, for instance. Human skin was for ever flaking off, drifting across the carpets, accumulating in the corners, filling in cracks, settling under the settee.

It was never ending. One struggled to keep one's head above water.

The hoover hummed and whined on a rising note, matching Gwen's increasing frenzy.

I must calm down, she told herself. *I am becoming over-wrought. It is not good for me.*

With a sigh, she switched off the hoover and propped the attachment against the wall. It was all very well *telling* oneself not to get worked up, but it was almost impossible at this time of year, with Christmas stalking her and the calendar down to its last page. It was a race against time: so much to be done and the days running out.

She grabbed polish and a cloth, attacked the frosted panels in the front door (look at those greasy fingerprints). If only her family weren't so untidy, so messy. Basil, for instance: she spent half her life trailing after Basil, picking up books, newspapers, the remote, his brief case; closing doors and drawers; putting the toilet seat down; folding and arranging hand and bath towels. Amanda, it was true, was not quite so bad, liked her things in their proper places, was punctilious over her personal hygiene; but every inch of her bedroom walls was plastered with huge posters. Gwen could not look at them without imagining the swarms of creepy-crawlies massing behind them, breeding, gestating, hatching, multiplying. Did Amanda need *quite* so many posters? Who were the people in them? Many were scantily clad, looked faintly menacing, disreputable; nothing like Bucks Fizz or Shakin Stevens. But if Gwen ventured a remark on those lines, Amanda would roll her eyes and say, 'Oh my God, Mum, you're so out of touch.' It was the note of sympathy which Gwen took exception to.

As for Dean's room, it was a sink of iniquity. One could not see the floor for books, clothes, CDs, trainers. Alien moulds grew and evolved in long-forgotten mugs and beakers and cola cans. The curtains were permanently closed ('I need my privacy!'), the place was never aired ('You can't open the window, it's *freezing* out there, are you trying to give me *hypothermia*!'). There was a certain smell one could never quite put one's finger on; and the stains! Terrible, insanitary stains on the carpet, the duvet, the mattress....

Gwen looked through the frosted glass at a distorted view of the grey December afternoon. Her arm fell loosely to her side, the duster hung limp. It would be getting dark soon and she'd done nothing. Nothing. There were simply not enough hours in the day – even fewer this time of year, the weeks telescoping towards Christmas, daylight at a premium. No matter how much she cleaned, scrubbed, dusted, hoovered, polished, the house would never be completely free of dirt. It was a hopeless task. A losing battle. She was like that man, the one who'd tried to stop the tide (What was his name? She must ask Dean.).

She put her polish and duster aside. As she did so, her eyes alighted on the cupboard under the stairs. Oh Lord! Had she not promised that woman Lydia Taylor that she would look out some of her old paintings? That had been *days* ago. She had all but forgotten. People would talk. 'What's got into Gwen Collier? She is usually so reliable, so helpful.' Oh, but what was the use? People would talk in any case. 'There she goes, Gwen Collier, the woman who couldn't keep hold of her husband. Let's hope it's second time lucky, but I'm not holding my breath. She does try, bless her, but some women just can't cut it....'

Taking a deep breath, keeping the voices at bay, Gwen concentrated on the task in hand, ferreting out her paintings from under the stairs. They were not quite as awful as she'd remembered. Not good by any means, but neat, ordered, efficient. The thought of putting them on public display was just about bearable – if that was really what Lydia Taylor wanted. Of course, Lydia might simply reject them out of hand. And now that Gwen came to look at them more closely....

She frowned, inspecting one still life after another. It was rather a limited repertoire. Had she really painted nothing else?

Crawling on her hands and knees, Gwen poked around at the back of the cupboard. There were no more paintings, just her brushes and paints, and the old second-hand easel she had used. She heaved it all out into the wintry daylight in the hall. An idea began to take hold. One more painting. Something a bit different. She didn't want people to think that there was nothing to her, that her mind ran on fruit bowls and vases of flowers. She touched the tubes of paint, experienced a frisson of excitement. And here was an unused canvas....

She set up the easel in the kitchen as she had done in the past. The light was good. There were plenty of objects available to paint. But this time she would eschew still lives. This time she would paint from her imagination!

The thought excited her, and she looked around guiltily, as if about to engage in something indecent. She stood with her brush poised, waiting for inspiration. But, really: who was she fooling? She had no imagination – did she?

Only one way to find out.

She took a deep breath, dipped her brush in paint, reached out, drew back, reached out again, made a tentative mark on the canvas. She stepped away, experienced a sinking feeling as she looked at the mark. It was nothing. A black smudge, that was all.

But wait. What if…?

She added some spindly legs, two long feelers, red eyes. Yes! Yes! It was a creepy-crawly! Of course it was! But one was not enough. They never came alone. She would add a second … *there* … and some more … *here* … and *here*….

Engrossed in her work, the invading hoards took her unawares. She glanced at the kitchen clock, was horrified when she saw what the time was. So late, and she hadn't given a thought to dinner!

'For God's sake, Gwen, what's all this rubbish on the kitchen table?'

'It's not rubbish, Basil, it's my painting equipment.'

Basil sighed. 'You haven't started with that again, have you?'

He regarded her with a pained expression, holding his brief case up as if he was tempted to use it to sweep the table clear. As Gwen hastened to tidy up, trying to bring her thoughts round to dinner, it suddenly occurred to her that she'd spent the last hour in a state of transcendent calm. Time had passed in the blink of an eye, and yet she had not felt anxious about it. It was as if she'd stepped momentarily into another world: a world where there was no rush to get things done, where one could find time to take pleasure in things. She was amazed at how much of the canvas she had covered.

But now she was back in the real world. She could hear Dean and Amanda bickering in the hallway, no doubt kicking off their shoes and leaving them to trip the unwary; throwing coats and scarves towards the coat rack, missing; dumping bags and satchels willy-nilly. And all the time Gwen was aware of Basil's eyes roaming round the kitchen, noting that the oven wasn't on, that the saucepans were still hanging up, that the chopping board looked suspiciously clean.

'I am going up to change,' he said at length, in what she thought of as his council chamber voice: the real meaning was in the tone rather than the words. In the doorway he paused, looked back. 'I do wish you wouldn't wear that apron-thing, Gwen. It makes you look like Mrs Mop.'

Gwen regarded her husband with disfavour. He was such a hulking brute of a man. Look at those large clumsy hands: nothing artistic or sensitive about them at all. His craggy face was like the crumbling wall of a forsaken castle, his grey, straggly beard like moss rooted in the stones. His beard was only the half of it, too. There was hair all over his bulky, rather flabby, body – hair in which all manner of microscopic organisms might be proliferating. It made one's flesh crawl, thinking about it. Why was smooth, scraped skin not more fashionable? Those ancient people in Mesopotamia had more sense, they'd had no truck with body hair: she could not think of their name just now, but they'd built lots of cities and made triangular marks on clay tablets. Dean would know who she meant. Dean was clever like that.

Basil gave a little tut and a last censorious stare, then left the room. Gwen speedily tidied away the last of what Basil had termed her *rubbish*, seizing as she did so on the fact that it was Tuesday, running down her mental list of Tuesday meals: roast chicken, Irish stew, lasagne. No time for any of those. She needed something quick and easy. She had to produce a meal by sleight of hand.

Oh Lord! Think, woman, think!

She glanced out of the window seeking inspiration, straightening her apron as she did so, retying the tapes (*Mrs Mop, indeed*), only to see Richard pulling up in his grotty car – inviting himself to dinner, no doubt, as he sometimes did. Another mouth to feed. (But she must remember to call dinner *supper*: Basil preferred *supper*.)

Beginning to panic, Gwen saw in her mind's eye her family as a nest of hatchlings, beaks open, red gullets gaping, squawking, demanding food. She was the hard-pressed mother bird, flying hither and thither in search of something – anything – to give them. But there was nothing: no insects, no seeds or berries, no juicy worms—

Worms! Of course, that was it! She would do sausages! Sausages and mash! Oh, the relief!

As she set about peeling potatoes, her panic subsided, was

tamped down to manageable proportions. Sausages, mash, peas, onion gravy. That would do nicely; that would keep the greedy hatchlings quiet. With unwonted vindictiveness – startling herself as she chopped up the potatoes – she imagined stuffing mash into the gaping gullets and topping it with a sausage apiece. She smiled without realizing as she slid the potatoes off the chopping board and into boiling water, picturing the baby birds' eyes bulging with surprise and fear as they choked on the smooth, creamy, buttery mash.

What a wonderful painting that would make, she thought as she turned on the grill and opened the fridge to get out the sausages. Stabbing each sausage with the point of a knife, she made up her mind to buy some new canvases next time she was in town. It would give her an incentive to paint. With any luck, she might even recapture that brief moment of calm she had experienced that afternoon.

She needn't mention it to Basil. What Basil didn't know wouldn't hurt him.

Richard, with his mouth full, said to Dean, 'Crashed your car again, have you, you plonker?'

Having performed miracles in getting the meal onto the table, Gwen found her appetite had deserted her. She picked at her food, waiting for the inevitable squabbling to begin. They couldn't sit to a meal together without squabbling of some sort.

'What do you mean by *again*?' Dean was morose.

'I mean exactly what people usually mean when they say *again*. Or have you forgotten your little aquaplaning stunt?'

'I suppose you've never had an accident in your life?'

'Course not. I'm perfect. Didn't you know?' Richard bit into a sausage, grinning.

Dean muttered something that might have been *smart arse*, but it was drowned out by Amanda asking Richard to pass over the tomato sauce.

'For you, darling, anything.'

Amanda got on well with Richard. Dean did not. But did Dean get on well with anybody? One could pass it off as the awkward age, but up to now every age had been awkward where Dean was concerned.

Basil was watching through narrowed eyes as Amanda squeezed tomato sauce onto her plate. 'Is it really necessary, Amanda, to put so much ketchup on your plate when you know you won't eat it?'

'Sorry, Mr Collier!' Pert. Tantalizing. (Where did she get it from?)

'I don't mean to sound petty, but we have to watch the pennies in the current climate. You never know what emergencies might crop up. Garage bills, for instance.' Basil cocked an eye at his stepson.

'You should count yourself lucky,' mumbled Dean. 'If I'd croaked it, you'd have had a funeral to pay for. But I suppose you'd have preferred that.'

And so it went on. Gwen stifled a sigh (no point in drawing attention to oneself) and pushed her mash from one side of the plate to the other. Those people who claimed that sitting down to a family meal was one of the pleasures in life obviously did not have a family like hers. Anyway, what was so pleasurable about eating? It was rather nauseating, when one stopped to think about it, Richard talking with his mouth full, Dean shovelling his food down like there was no tomorrow, Basil chomping, Amanda mixing everything up on her plate so that it looked like slop. Eating, thought Gwen, ought to be done in private in a locked room – the same way that one used the lavatory. The very thought of all that chewing and slavering – all that saliva – was enough to put one off for life. And all the gobbets of masticated food sliding stickily down the throat to swill around in the stomach like bobbing effluent in a sea of gastric juices—

'Not hungry, darling?' Basil's eagle eyes had focused on her plate.

'No, Basil. Not very.'

'I'll have your spare sausage, then, if I may.' He reached over and stabbed it with his fork.

Gwen collected the plates, feeling worn down by the trauma of a family dinner (sorry, *supper*). Amanda's plate, she noted, was daubed with uneaten tomato sauce. Gwen could not decide which was more irritating: Amanda's profligacy or Basil's parsimony.

Why, in any case, did Amanda have to have tomato sauce with everything? One expected her to have grown out of it by now. Tomato sauce was so ... so ... Gwen struggled to find the right word. So *red*. That was it. Tomato sauce was so brutally red. It had quite spoilt the harmonious arrangement on her plate: the ivory mash, the rich brown gravy, the green shock of peas, not to mention the earthy-coloured sausages flecked with charcoal black. It had looked rather nice. A shame to eat it, really....

Gwen became aware of eight expectant eyes watching her.

'Banana splits for everyone?' she said brightly, as if she had been planning banana splits for a fortnight at least.

'Not for me,' Dean grunted. 'I've got practice.'

'Hey ho, hey ho, it's off to prancing practice we go,' mocked Richard.

Amanda laughed, playing up to Richard. (*My word, I'm going to have to watch her....*)

'Morris dancing,' sniffed Basil as Dean exited the room. His tone implied that Morris dancing might be considered somewhat sissified.

Taking the plates through to the kitchen, Gwen told herself that Morris dancing was not sissified, that it was very original of Dean to have taken it up. Morris dancing was traditional, was cultural. Basil did not have time for such things, often complained that listed buildings and conservation areas got in the way of progress. Rinsing tomato sauce off Amanda's plate, Gwen felt resentful of the way Basil cast aspersions where Dean was concerned without ever bringing his accusations into the open. She knew for a fact that Dean was not that way inclined (those dreadful magazines, hidden under the lining paper of his T-shirt drawer), but it was not a subject one felt comfortable bringing up in conversation. Not that she would have minded if Dean *had* been homosexual: at least then his bedroom would have been tidy. They were tidy people, homosexuals. They dressed well, too.

In any case, she said to herself as she stacked plates in the dishwasher, it was not just Dean. Basil cast aspersions about everyone. He simply couldn't help it; it was the way he was made. One could blame God or fate or the stars, or whoever it was that arranged such things. (Nobody, perhaps? But that seemed to Gwen unlikely. There was probably a cosmic version of Basil: a chief executive of the universe.)

Making the banana splits, Gwen found herself distracted by the different colours and textures of the bananas and the ice cream – although different *shades* would be a better description than different colours, ivory and pearl compared to the improbable white of the aerosol cream. Could one produce a painting of banana splits – or sausage and mash for that matter? Would it be considered frivolous – making fun of the serious business of art? One hesitated to venture into hallowed territory; but if it was merely for one's own satisfaction – and surely one would never have the courage to show them to anyone – where was the harm?

She shook the canister of hundreds-and-thousands, watched as the coloured strands rained down on the banana splits: so small and yet so vivid, so many bright colours, astonishingly different to the white of the cream. And the way they started to blur and smudge, seeping into the whipped cream as it began to sag and deflate: it was extraordinary! Why had she never noticed—

'Are those banana splits ready yet, darling?' Basil's rumbling voice came floating through from the dining room.

'On my way, darling!'

Gwen fixed a bright smile on her face as she picked up the banana splits.

Trekking round a packed Waitrose, shying away from admonishing reminders of Christmas, Gwen put her state of mind to the test by walking down the aisle where the cleaning products were stacked. She reached the far end with her trolley still empty. Did this mean that her obsessive urge to clean – which lately had threatened to take over – was now under control? One could only hope....

She paused, tempted to grab hold of one of the shelves to stop herself being swept away by the hustle and bustle, the headlong stampede towards Christmas. Like a mirage, a golden haven of calm, she thought of the peace she had felt when starting her new picture the other day. If only she could reach that place again.

She was nursing a wild idea in her head, a hare-brained scheme: she would ditch all her old paintings and produce a new series of canvases for Lydia Taylor's Exhibition. The thought made her tingle all over; but would she dare to do it? Would she *dare*? And even if she dared, how would she find the time?

There was one way of buying time which, wicked woman that she was, she had decided to investigate here and now, in the chaos of pre-Christmas Waitrose when she might bump into someone she knew at any moment. Her heart in her mouth, she scuttled sideways like a crab, dragging her trolley with her. She managed to reach the freezer section undetected.

Taking pot luck, she reached into a freezer and pulled out – what? Frozen chips. She hesitated, the frozen packet making her fingers numb. Did she have the nerve? Basil refused to eat anything but 'real' chips. He liked food cooked 'properly'. But Gwen had heard that frozen chips were so advanced these days that one could hardly tell the difference. And look! Not just frozen chips! Frozen roast potatoes, frozen Yorkshire puddings, frozen veg – whole meals, too. All she needed was to pluck up courage, take advantage of these conjuring tricks, and then—

'Frozen pizzas, Gwen? Not quite in your line, I would have thought.'

The imperious voice made Gwen jump. The box she'd been inspecting – reading the instructions – dropped out of her hands to land face-up on top of the bag of frozen chips in her trolley: damning evidence of her intended deception. Guilt-ridden, she looked round and found herself face to face with Imelda, otherwise known as Lady Darkley of Overbourne Hall. Tall and imposing, with improbably black hair (she must, after all, be well into her sixties), Imelda Darkley looked strikingly shabby in her tweeds and flat shoes. It was a shabbiness few people could aspire to: it did not come cheap. Some people referred to Lady Darkley as a village 'character'. Others used less flattering descriptions.

'I'm glad I've bumped into you, Gwen. I wanted a quick word. We were considering – I have decided, that is – to co-opt you onto the parish council. When old Smithson retires in May we shall have a spare seat. I know he's cried wolf before over this retirement business, but I've run out of patience with him this time: he has to go.'

Gwen sought protection, placing the ramparts of her trolley between herself and Imelda Darkley. 'I don't think I could ... I mean, I don't know anything about ... and I'm ... I'm far too busy.'

'Nonsense! It's not as if you've got anything else to do. You don't go out to work, do you? And your children are almost ready to fly the nest. You're just the ticket, Gwen.'

Gwen quailed. What exactly was the parish council? It sounded official, important: just the type of thing she steered clear of. What if people got the impression it had been her idea to put herself forward? They'd think she was getting above herself, a newcomer (anyone who hadn't lived in the village half a century at least was a *newcomer*), a woman who'd been married twice (this was bound to be alluded to).

Gwen said, 'I'm not really very well known in the village.' She fervently hoped this was true. She wanted nothing more than to be overlooked. 'Nobody would vote for me.' She clung to this certainty.

'My dear woman, we don't bother with elections! Oh no, no, no! Far too much fuss and palaver. We just co-opt you. It's quite simple. I will pop round sometime soon and tell you what's what. I can't stop now. I'm parked on a double yellow, and I don't think that new traffic warden is aware of quite who I am.'

Lady Darkley swept on her way, leaving Gwen quaking and starting to panic. The problem was, once Lady Darkley had set her mind on something it took an upheaval the magnitude of a tsunami – or a medium-to-large-sized meteorite – to deflect her from her purpose.

With a sinking feeling, Gwen scooped up the contents of her trolley and tipped them back into the freezers. What was the use of short cuts if all the precious time she saved was to be used up on Lady Darkley's schemes? It was enough to make one wail and beat one's breast – and with the Christmas epidemic in full spate, probably no one would have given her a second glance if she had.

But she didn't have the energy to wail, let alone beat her breast.

It was all she could do to push her trolley around to the (time-consuming) fresh veg: everything was such an effort.

Picking over the loose carrots, she let the Christmas chaos engulf her.

SIX

'I HATE BOXING DAY.'

Lydia was speaking to her microwave as it warmed up leftovers from yesterday's dinner. She looked through the little window as the plate of food slowly revolved.

'Boxing Day is even worse than Christmas Day. It's so much more pointless.'

The microwave hummed. A spoon in an empty mug rattled in sympathy.

'I'm not the sort of person who feels sorry for herself.' Lydia propped her head in her hands, resting her elbows on the work surface, contemplative. 'I don't mind being on my own. In fact, I prefer it— Sorry, what was that?'

Her eyes narrowed, regarding the microwave with suspicion. Its hum seemed to have changed in tone, risen an octave. Or was it her imagination?

'Of course it's my imagination. You are not the type to answer back, are you?' The microwave droned on, indifferent. Reassured, Lydia continued. 'I don't mind being on my own. It has its advantages. But once upon a time I had friends. I don't mean a microwave (no offence) or even a dog. I mean proper, human friends. Where are they now? What happened?'

She knew the answer. Nigel had happened, that was what. Nigel had skilfully pried her away from her friends, whom he disapproved of. He had isolated her.

'But,' she said to the microwave, 'I do not want to think about Nigel. Nigel is persona non grata.'

The microwave agreed, beeping forcefully. Lydia took out the plate using a tea towel, peeled off the cling film, set it on a tray where she had already arranged a knife and fork, a napkin, salt and pepper, and a jar of cranberry sauce. Carrying the tray through to the main room, she sat down on the sofa. There was a repeat of *The Two Ronnies* on TV to keep her company.

She poked at her meal with the fork. The turkey was cardboard-dry, the roast potatoes soggy. She munched on them, looking round the room. In one corner, Prize's basket sat empty, his blanket on top. The fact that the blanket was neatly folded seemed to indicate a dreadful finality.

'Four candles. Handles for forks,' Lydia murmured, listening to the TV but not watching it, her eyes glued instead to the basket. Poor Prize. He was missing his favourite. He had liked *The Two Ronnies*. The theme music had made him bark. But he would bark no more. He had expired in her own arms with barely a whimper. Remembering that moment, she saw in her mind's eye the topsy-turvy-faced vet. The hypodermic needle he had been holding had grown in her imagination to vast proportions, big enough to blot out the world.

Lydia shivered. What a way to go. What a horrid man that vet had been.

'And to think I usually like bearded men,' she said, cutting a slice of turkey, lifting it on her fork. She paused, looked at the desiccated meat with aversion, lowered it back to her plate. Scraping it off her fork with the knife, she speared a Brussels sprout instead, reflecting as she did so that Nigel might be persona non grata but there was no getting away from the fact that he was the one who had given her the dog, her consolation prize – and a constant reminder of all she had lost. Was that what Nigel had intended when he left?

'If I had been thinking clearly,' she said as she chewed the Brussels sprout, 'I would have got rid of Prize at the outset.'

But she had not been thinking clearly, reeling after Nigel's bomb-shell. He had left her to move in with a girl called Polly or Molly: the name hardly mattered now but had seemed important at the time, which only went to show what a state she had been in.

'Catatonic,' she murmured, stirring with her knife the cranberry sauce in its jar.

It had been Prize who finally roused her, licking her hand and whining, looking at her with those trusting eyes. He had been hungry.

'Prize was an innocent party,' she said, looking at the blade of her knife smeared with cranberry sauce. 'He couldn't help that he was being used.'

She licked the knife speculatively, pulled a face, screwed the lid firmly on the jar of cranberry sauce. Why had she even bought it? Habit, presumably. Nigel had liked to—

'But I am *not* going to think about Nigel.' She sighed, eyeing her microwaved meal with distaste. 'Why am I eating my dinner at eleven o'clock in the morning? This is ludicrous! It's not as if I am desperate for something to do. There are lots of things to keep me busy. I could finish my portrait of Prize for a start.'

She put the tray aside, stood up, turned off the TV (she'd lost the remote again: it was probably under that jumble on top of the cabinet). The half-finished portrait of Prize languished to one side of the sofa, leaning against the arm rest. There was a superficial resemblance to the deceased dog, but it was not really the Prize she had known. There was nothing of his mischief, his jealousy, his devotion. What she had produced, she decided, was comparable to those ghastly collectors' plates advertised in the Sunday supplements: the ones with titles such as *Faithful Friend* and *His Master's Voice*. The dog in her picture was a collectors' plate dog. The real Prize eluded her.

Her pictures were worthless. Inspiration was at a low ebb. Trying to paint in this mood would only demoralize her still further. But she couldn't simply sit around moping. She had to *do* something.

For a start, she could tackle the mess in here. Not just in this room, either: her whole cottage was becoming far too cluttered. She would change that right now.

Taking her tray through to the kitchen, she scraped the remains of her unappetizing dinner into the bin then dumped the plate and cutlery into the sink where there was already a pile of dirty crockery. It was a disheartening sight. Nearby on the work surface was something rather more alluring: a bottle of gin. She could almost see it winking at her.

No. She was not going down that path today. She would stand firm. Gin could wait. Her sights were set on the unnecessary clutter in her cottage. De-cluttering was the order of the day.

Buoyed up by the strength of her resolve, she set to work. There was a big cardboard box mouldering away in the back porch. She dragged it through to the main room. This, she said, would be the disposal chute.

'Everything must go,' she muttered. She liked the idea. It sounded good. It could be her mantra. She chanted it. 'Everything must go, everything must go!'

She forged ahead, cutting a swathe through the cottage, casting all and sundry into the disposal chute: gaggles of spoons inherited from her mother (wooden, not silver); redundant tins of dog food (never again, no more pets); piles of plastic containers waiting for the day when they would come in useful, a day that never came; paperbacks with bent spines that dribbled sand from distant holiday beaches; chipped statuettes, threadbare cushions, a broken table lamp, all the detritus from the top of the cabinet (there was no remote under the mess: it must be down the back of the sofa). Reaching a pitch of ruthlessness (easier than expected, but then it *was* Boxing Day), Lydia seized Prize's basket and the neatly folded blanket and balanced them on top of the crammed cardboard box.

'Everything must go! This will be a fresh start, a blank canvas!'

Staggering under the weight of the box, she kicked open the front door and wobbled across to the wheelie bin. She dumped the disposal chute next to the bin then took a step back, glowing with a sense of achievement. Now perhaps she could draw a line under—

'Yoo-hoo! Lydia! Hello! Merry Christmas!'

Startled, Lydia turned to look up her drive. There in the street, waving, was Gwen Collier. Her family was gathered round her as in a photo album snap: the tall, heavy-set, bearded husband; the stepson Richard (purveyor of vodka jellies, Lydia remembered with a spark of curiosity); the impish daughter; and, lurking in the background, shifty and sulky-faced, the boy Dean: her nemesis.

'We're just going for a quick drink before lunch,' Gwen trilled.

'It's tradition.' Lanky Richard raised an ironic eyebrow, mocking tradition.

'It'll only be the one,' Gwen continued. 'Why don't you join us?'

'Oh, no, I couldn't possibly, I—' Lydia's instincts, as she stood there being gawped at by the family group, told her to run into the cottage and slam the door; and she felt she must steer clear of Dean at all costs. But then she glanced at the disposal chute and the sense of achievement stirred in her again, giving her courage. What about the fresh start, the blank canvas? And wasn't it lily-livered to flinch from Dean, to run away? Their paths were bound to cross; she couldn't avoid him for ever. This anxiety she felt – this incipient panic – needed to be nipped in the bud.

On top of all this there was something else: a half-heard inflection in Gwen's voice, a sort of false brightness. Was it imagination, or did Gwen look rather ragged round the edges? Was there more to her casual invitation – *why don't you join us?* – than mere politeness: a sort of desperate hopefulness, in fact?

I have never been very good, thought Lydia as she loitered by the wheelie bin, at all that female solidarity stuff. But one did, in a roundabout way, feel that one was in debt to Gwen: Dean was her son, after all. In addition – this happy thought came to her in a flash – there was the exhibition to consider. That albatross was still hanging round her neck. Now might be the perfect opportunity to scupper the idea once and for all.

'Of course I'll come – why not, it sounds like fun!' Lydia managed a dazzling smile. 'I'll just get my coat.'

The pub was packed. She was not the only one, Lydia surmised, searching for ways to escape the Boxing Day blues. The landlady – the Stasi – was having to work behind the bar for a change. Her strident, rather resentful tones rose above the hubbub. 'No, you weren't next, wait your turn … I've only got one pair of hands, in case you hadn't noticed … must you take all my change, haven't you got anything smaller than a twenty … no, no, you definitely said medium white, you'll have to take it now, I've poured it….' The new barmaid was conspicuous by her absence.

There was one free table in the lounge bar, up a corner by the window. Richard nabbed some extra stools. As she squeezed into her place and slipped off her coat, Lydia kept a wary eye on Dean.

He seemed more or less oblivious of her presence, but that might be an act. Some of the students at the college were cunning as well as precocious, went out of their way to get one over on you. Was Dean of this ilk? The problem was, she simply did not know. He wasn't in any of the classes she taught. She had a vague idea that he was more science-oriented; but that didn't help her in her present predicament.

Drinks were being discussed. It was Basil's round. What could he get her?

'Gin and tonic, please,' she said automatically before remembering her vow to avoid gin today. 'Actually, I'll—'

It was too late. Basil had gone, elbowing his way through the crowd.

They sat in a bubble of silence amidst the crush and the jabber, Lydia facing Gwen and Amanda across the table, Richard squashed between them, framed by cold grey daylight. It was Richard who broke the silence.

'Well, this is cosy.'

Facetious, thought Lydia, who did not like the way Richard was looking at her – the way he was grinning.

Gwen stirred. 'Oh, by the way, Lydia, I haven't forgotten that I promised you my paintings. It's just that with Christmas and so on....'

'That's quite all right. There's no hurry.' Lydia tried to be as offhand as possible. Would Gwen get the message?

'I had hoped,' said Gwen tentatively, 'to paint something new, but ... well....'

'Dad disapproves,' said Richard.

'Oh?' Lydia's hackles rose, resenting Richard's smirking expression and remembering that Nigel too had also disapproved of her painting. (*You'll never make anything of it, so why bother? Your stuff is old hat. It's your Tracey Emins, your Damien Hirsts: that's where the money lies these days.*) Was Gwen squashed by Basil the way she had been squashed by Nigel? Did Gwen realize this, or would she too only see it in hindsight? Lydia was tempted to make her feelings known but reined herself in. It was none of her business. She didn't know Gwen that well, knew Basil even less. In any case, it was best not to speak out of turn, best not to draw attention to herself, until she knew how the land lay vis-à-vis Dean.

She glanced at Dean, who refused to meet her eye. His silence, his air of sullen embarrassment, gave her confidence – almost as if his attitude was a tacit acceptance of complicity. It allowed Lydia to shift the blame in her mind and assume a studied air of innocence.

Emboldened, she looked round nonchalantly: a woman with nothing to hide. She took in the glowing fire, the dancing bear, the multitude of faces with expressions both replete and subtly dissatisfied: Christmas had failed to live up to expectations yet again. Muzak was dribbling from speakers bracketed to the walls. Snatches of conversation reached her. '… yet more points on my licence, an absolute joke, it's not as if I was going all that fast, barely a hundred … oh, but don't you use goose fat for your roast potatoes, I always use goose fat, I wouldn't use anything else … marvellous sermon yesterday, don't you think, old Dick Emery was on top form….' And then the landlady's fractious voice rose above all else: 'Does it look like I've got time to change the barrel? There are two other real ales – why can't you have one of them?'

Basil reappeared, ferrying drinks. 'That bloody woman,' he muttered darkly, before going off to fetch the rest of the round.

Dean and Amanda snatched up their colas and edged towards the pool room. Making way for them, Lydia – bolstered by her new-found innocence – tried to catch Dean's eye, but he hung his head, cheeks glowing, and shuffled off as quick as he could. For some reason, Lydia felt vindicated. She sat back contentedly, pouring tonic into her gin.

Basil eased himself into his chair. 'The service in here is appalling. That woman hasn't a clue.'

'She's doing her best, Basil,' said Gwen.

'Her best isn't good enough. There aren't enough staff on. It's no way to run a business.'

'Perhaps they didn't expect to be this busy.'

'They should have been prepared. A little market research goes a long way.'

'I hardly think—'

'I beg your pardon, Gwen, but what experience have you had in running a business?'

'None, Basil.' Meekly.

'I rest my case.' Basil, with an insufferable air of self-importance, applied himself to his pint.

Lydia poked the slice of lemon in her drink with one finger, uneasy. It was like watching one of those wildlife programmes, she thought: the ones in which a big brutal lion pulls down a doe-eyed gazelle and proceeds to suffocate it. When this happened in the Serengeti there was nothing you could do about it; when it was happening right in front of you....

'What's this I hear about you forbidding Gwen to paint?'

'*Forbidding?* ' Basil stuck his bottom lip out. 'Nobody does any *forbidding* in our house.'

'Then you've no objection if Gwen dashes off a few canvases? We are in desperate need of them for the exhibition.' (*Curses! Why bring up the exhibition? I am meant to be nipping it in the bud, not encouraging it to flourish. On the other hand, if it gets up Basil's nose....*)

Basil groaned. 'You're not another of these would-be artists, are you?'

'Lydia's not a would-be anything, Basil,' said Gwen. 'She *is* an artist.'

Richard piped up. 'Dad's worried about getting his meals on time. He's a stickler for routine, is Dad.'

Basil gave his son a withering look, but Lydia felt a stab of irritation, sensing that her attack on Basil had been undermined by Richard's interruption. She turned her attention on this younger version of Basil – although, actually, he didn't look much like his father at all. Lydia had long known – or guessed – what Basil was like, but Richard had been something of a mystery. Now a picture was emerging. Had he not ruined Dean's party, stolen Dean's girl? (*Why am I feeling protective of Dean? This is preposterous.*)

What was the best way to wipe the smirk off Richard's face? 'It's no laughing matter. Art is a serious business.'

'I'm not laughing,' said Richard, who was. 'Women should be able to paint if they want to. I'm all for women's rights.'

'It's very revealing,' said Lydia caustically, 'the way men pay lip service to women's rights while somehow implying that it's all some sort of joke.'

Richard's grin remained. Lydia gathered her forces for another assault, but before she could begin, Gwen stepped in as peacemaker.

'You've booked the village hall, I suppose, Lydia?'

'Village hall?' Lydia blinked, at a loss. 'Why should I want to book the village hall?'

'For the exhibition, of course. I don't mean to interfere, but it does tend to get fully booked months in advance.'

'Oh yes, I see, the exhibition.' *Noodles to the exhibition.*

'I could,' said Gwen tentatively, 'if you liked, book it myself. I wouldn't want to tread on anyone's toes, but I'm expecting a visit from Imelda Darkley, and as she is on the village hall committee....'

'Ah, yes, of course, that would be ... that would be a great help.'

'Why,' said Richard, looking at Gwen curiously, 'is Lady Darkness coming to see you? Are you being banished from the village, or what?'

'I'm ... she's....' Gwen shot a look at her husband. 'She wants me to stand for the parish council.'

Basil's nose went up. 'What nonsense is this? You know how I feel about parish councils, Gwen.'

'Talking of councils and committees,' said Lydia, coming to Gwen's rescue, heading Basil off, 'we ought to get a group together to organize the whole thing: the exhibition, I mean. It will be too much work for one or two people alone.' Her heart sank as she listened to herself. Why did the exhibition seem to be the only topic of conversation she could think of in a tight corner? There was no knowing what she might land herself in if she wasn't careful. 'There will be lots to do. Booking the village hall will be the least of it. Potential exhibitors will need to be contacted, exhibits collected and displayed. Flyers and catalogues will have to be designed and printed, a rota drawn up for selling tickets on the door....' Lydia spoke off the top of her head, laying it on thick, hoping to put Gwen off.

'Sounds right up your street, Mum,' said Richard to Gwen. 'You're a great one for organizing things.'

Lydia interpreted *Mum* as some sort of sly dig at Gwen and opened her mouth to slap Richard down, but Basil got in first. He was frowning at his wife in a most off-putting way.

'I do hope,' he said with emphasis, 'that all these extra-curricular activities are not going to take up too much of your time, Gwendolen.'

'Of course not, Basil. The exhibition will be run by a committee – I won't need to do much at all. As for painting, that can be squeezed in any time. Look at Lydia. She manages, and she has a full-time job.'

Lydia did not like the ominous way that Gwen spoke of the exhibition as if it was real, a fait accompli. There were also rumblings of discontent from Basil at her side.

Once again Gwen got in first, turning the conversation, speaking with a brittle sort of brightness. 'Are you painting anything yourself at the moment, Lydia?'

Caught off guard by the question, Lydia stumbled over her words. 'Well, I'm ... er....' *This is a ridiculous conversation. We are lurching from one quagmire to another.* 'I'm not having much success, to be honest. I'm trying my hand at ... at....'

'Yes, yes?' Gwen and Richard were looking at her expectantly; even Basil was showing signs of interest.

'At a portrait.' *Help! What can I say next? I mustn't mention Prize. Whatever happens, I mustn't mention Prize. I will only fall to pieces if I do, and that doesn't bear thinking about in the midst of this rabble.*

'A portrait of whom?'

'Well ... er ... that's just it. I don't have a suitable subject. I mean, I have no one ... no one to pose....'

'Oh.'

'Ah.'

'What about me? Would I make a suitable subject?' Richard grinned, flexing his biceps (such as they were). 'This face, these muscles: how could you resist? Twenty quid and I'm yours.'

Another quagmire opened up in front of her, and Lydia lurched helplessly into it.

She was not exactly sure how it had come about. How had she

gone from making arrangements for an exhibition she did not even want, to more or less agreeing to paint Richard's portrait for a fee of twenty pounds? (Wasn't it meant to be the other way round? Didn't the sitter usually pay the artist?)

Sinking fast, Lydia buried her head in her gin and tonic, making a mental note not to even bother getting out of bed next Boxing Day.

SEVEN

Parting from Lydia at the turning to her cottage, Gwen experienced a twist of envy as she continued up Well Lane with Basil plodding beside her. How wonderful to be able to go back to an empty house, to know that everything would still be exactly as one had left it (Dean and Amanda had gone ahead, were probably wrecking the place); to wallow in the silence; to have no one to think about but oneself....

Basil cleared his throat noisily. Gwen braced herself for the inevitable onslaught, feeling trapped, as if hostile forces were closing in on her from every side. One had grown used to it from Basil, but now there was Imelda Darkley to contend with, too, not to mention Lydia and the exhibition. Lydia was obviously very keen on the idea; mentioned it at every opportunity. If one was honest, one felt a little tremor of excitement at the prospect: something to look forward to, something unusual – unlike the parish council, which was a different kettle of fish. Was there any chance of ducking out of that? Had anyone ever had the temerity to say 'no' to Lady Darkley? Had anyone ever said it and lived to tell the tale?

But what was the use of thinking about the parish council or the exhibition? Basil would never let her get away with either. He liked her to be at his beck and call. ('There's a button missing on this shirt ... I can't find my calculator ... what have you done with the newspaper ... why don't you come and sit down, I can't relax with you buzzing about the place ... what on earth are you doing *now*...?') Perhaps, said Gwen to herself, puffing a little as she reached the top of Well Lane, her thoughts darting here, there, seeking a way of escape, perhaps she could try the frozen food and microwave meals after all. Pizzas, pies, pasta: she could dress them up, disguise them, pass them off as her own. If anyone noticed – expressed doubt – she could say that she was experimenting: *I have been watching Jamie and Nigella. If they can experiment, then so can I.*

There was a rumble deep in Basil's throat as they turned into the top road on the last lap home. It was like an early warning of an eruption (oh, wouldn't that be marvellous, a volcano in Well Lane, an explosion of molten rock blotting everything out: the exhibition, the parish council, housework, lunch— oh Lord, lunch!).

The rumble sounded again. 'That boy ...' Basil began.

So it was to be Richard. Richard was *that boy*. Dean was *your son*. Richard, of course, was not here to listen to his father's strictures. He had taken himself off, would be safely back in his flat by now.

'Why must he make a show of himself all the time? As if that woman would really want to paint a slob like him. Absurd.'

'Yes, Basil ...' (Now would be a good time for that volcano.)

'And he calls you *Mum*. I don't know why you stand for it. It's not as if you even like him.'

'No, Basil.' (Well, what he didn't know wouldn't harm him.)

'*Mum*, indeed. If his mother really was here to see him....'

Gwen shivered. This was dangerous territory, skirting round the subject of Richard's mother, Basil's first wife. There had been an awful, unforgettable scene early in their marriage. Basil had got drunk. He had tiraded about his first wife, calling her a selfish bitch, claiming that she had only died in order to spite him – everything she had done in her entire life had been done to spite him. Even now the memory of that scene made Gwen go cold all over. At the time it had nearly finished her off. One had slowly and surreptitiously weaned Basil off heavy drinking after that.

Trying to steer the conversation into calmer waters, Gwen said, 'I thought we might have some of the turkey for lunch, darling. Cold turkey, pickles, nice crusty bread—'

'Yes, yes.' Basil wasn't listening; waved her words aside as if swatting a fly. 'What was all that talk about the parish council, Gwen?'

'Imelda Darkley has decided that—'

'Contrary to popular opinion, Imelda Darkley does not rule over this village like a feudal baroness. We are not her serfs to be ordered about. As for parish councils, they are amateurish, inefficient, a waste of public money.'

'Yes, Basil.'

'I am serious, Gwen. You can't imagine how many times we have to pick up the pieces after parish councils have meddled in things that don't concern them.'

'Yes, Basil.'

'And another thing.'

'Yes, Basil?'

'This nonsense about an art exhibition.'

'It's not—'

'No one is interested in amateurs of any sort in this day and age, Gwendolen. It's a well-known fact. Leave things to the professionals: that's my motto.'

'But—'

'Parish councillors would do well to heed that message – all councillors for that matter. It's the council *officers* who do the work, who know what they're talking about, not these fly-by-night, ten-a-penny meddlers, making life intolerable.'

Whose life? Your life?

'People must learn to trust to experts. Only experts know what's good for them.'

You mean, only you know what's good for them.

'It's their job, after all, for goodness' sake. They get paid to— Are you listening to me, Gwendolen?'

'Yes, Basil.'

'Good, good.' He cleared his throat again as they walked up the drive, a sound that turned Gwen's stomach (as indeed did the very phrase *clear one's throat*). 'I do hope,' he said, waiting for Gwen to get out her key, 'that we are not going to be treated to more turkey today.'

'Of course not, Basil,' said Gwen, opening the door. 'The thought never even crossed my mind.'

EIGHT

'WHAT,' LYDIA ASKED as she lay in her bed in the little bedroom with the sloping roof, 'have I let myself in for now?'

Her mother's ghost, lurking somewhere in mid air, maintained a significant silence. Lydia groaned as she went back over the events of yesterday, pulled the duvet over her head but felt it necessary to give the alarm clock at least a cursory glance. Nearly ten.

'I must get up,' she told herself, but felt no inclination to move. Last night had not been good. She had been unable to sleep.

She yawned.

Ever since Prize's death, she had got into the habit of swilling back gin in the evenings and falling comatose into bed, to wake up eight hours later with a thumping headache but having traversed many long and depressing hours of darkness. Last night the formula hadn't worked. She had tossed and turned as the night stretched into infinity. Unsettling thoughts had run amok in her head: *nearly forty, you're getting old ... what have you got to show for it ... you wasted your youth, wasted it on Nigel; your youth is gone now, you don't get a second chance ... why haven't you got further in your career, you should be head of department at least by now, your income is paltry for a woman of your ability; it will take years to pay the mortgage at this rate ... why did you buy this cottage, anyway: it's just a millstone round your neck....* She had tried to get away from all these thoughts, but all escape routes had failed her: there had been blind alleys at every turn, not a single safe haven left in her head. And so, aeons later, here she was at ten o'clock in the morning lying like a fish washed up on a beach, more tired than if she hadn't gone to bed at all.

Perhaps the answer was even *more* gin.

She lay still, listening. Her mother remained incommunicado. No malicious remarks about alcoholism, no snide asides about the menopause. She was refusing to speak. Lydia recognized these signs only too well. They had been accompanied in life by a closed-up expression, lips pursed, eyes fixed on the horizon; but her mother had never been able to keep that up for long. You had waited, guts clenched, for the inevitable explosion. 'Oh, get away from me, go on, go! I can't bear to look at you! You're such a naughty, wicked, shameful little girl!' Lydia had often been confused as to the precise nature of her naughtiness. She had racked her brains, trying to work out what she had done.

'It never occurred to me at that age,' she murmured, staring up at the ceiling and picturing herself at eight, nine, ten, 'that it might be my mother who was in the wrong and not me.'

She glanced at the clock again. Ten past ten. Time was galloping. She must get up. The last thing she needed was for Richard to come along and find her in her nightie.

Richard. Oh Lord.

'Perhaps he won't come.' With a gargantuan effort, she heaved herself out of bed. 'Now there's a thought.' Yawning copiously, she staggered to the bathroom. 'I could well be worrying over nothing. No proper arrangements were made. It was all a bit of a joke, really.'

Sitting on the toilet, she did her best to rationalize Richard out of existence.

He refused to go.

'I would pay twice twenty pounds just to keep him away.' She got up, pulled her nightie back into place, flushed the toilet, rinsed her hands, splashed her face, dabbed with a towel ('Lord, this is absolutely filthy: do I never change my towels?').

'Perhaps I am being unfair to him.' She addressed her reflection in the bathroom mirror. 'He is no worse than most other young men of his age. They are all irresponsible, insensitive, irritating. Why should he be different?'

She sighed, looking at her reflected self with a critical eye. Her heart sank. Baggy eyes, slack chin, lines all over her face like the cracks in drying mud. And grey hairs, too, no doubt. Her fingers probed, searching. 'Come out, grey hairs, come out, wherever you are....'

Why did one always have this picture in one's head of a self that was ten years younger? Disappointment was inevitable. The mirror always told the truth.

In her bedroom once more, she searched through her wardrobe, opened drawers, tried to make up her mind what to wear. She fingered the femme fatale clothes, asking herself once more why she had chosen to wear them on that terrible night just before Christmas. A deep-seated masochistic streak, perhaps? Could that be the reason she had stayed with Nigel all those years? She shivered, wondering if she might still have been with Nigel now if he had not walked out on her.

It was Nigel who had bought the femme fatale skirt. ('I like you to show off your legs.' 'I hate my legs, they are like sticks.' 'You must make the best of what you have, darling.') The low-cut blouse had been a blunder of her own. She had expected it to work miracles, to make her look glamorous – sexy, even. ('That's a nice blouse, Lyddie, pity about your....' 'My what?' 'Have you ever considered implants, darling? It might be worth the investment.')

She had assumed Nigel had put his finger on the truth. She had admired his honesty. She had congratulated herself on bagging a straight-talking man instead of one who gave her a load of old flannel.

She cringed, recalling the night she met Dean by the roadside, the way she'd walked towards him trying to emulate a model on a catwalk but instead wobbling around on unaccustomed heels, nearly turning her ankle. Cold air on her exposed skin had raised goose pimples. She had felt scrawny and saggy: *mutton dressed as lamb*, as her mother would have put it. And instead of dazzling some beefcake or a debonair man of means, all she'd ensnared was a spotty, clueless teenager.

She flung the femme fatale clothes aside, opted for plain, simple, functional. As she dressed, she prepared herself mentally at the same time, summoning up all the meagre details she could remember about Richard Collier. If he did happen to show up, she had to be ready for him.

Dean had called Richard a *bastard*. Mr Wetherby had been known to refer to him as a *yobbo*. Basil had once been overheard saying, 'That boy is twenty-three, it's time he grew up, pulled himself together, got to grips with life.' (In what way did Basil believe one ought to *grip* life?) The Stasi, of course, knew more than anyone. Lydia recalled her saying that Richard worked in a warehouse in town (she probably also knew what his hourly rate was and how much tax he paid); that he lived in a council flat on one of the estates (name? number?); and that – though as a responsible landlady she never listened to malicious gossip – she had been reliably informed that he had once or did still dabble in Drugs (the Stasi always spoke of Drugs with a capital D).

Shimmying into her jeans, Lydia heard a snippet of pub talk replaying in her head. She was not sure now who had been speaking. The subject had been Richard's flat.

'There's meant to be a waiting list.'

'Ah, but his old man is a big cheese up at the council.'

'There you go. Proves my point. Nepotism.'

'I don't think Basil Collier is the type. A stickler for the rules, I've heard.'

'When it suits him, yes. But ...'

'Oh?'

'It's a case of do as I say and not as I do.'

'Ah.'

'Power corrupts. They're all the same. Out for what they can get. And look at the mess he's made in town, all the old buildings demolished, all the character gone: it could be any one of half the towns in the country, bland and featureless.'

'Hmm, you may have a point. But when you think about the lad's car—'

'What about his car? Skoda, isn't it?'

'It may well have been, at one time. But that's just what I'm saying. If Collier won't even buy the lad a decent car, he's hardly likely to pull strings over a flat.'

Searching for socks, Lydia wrenched open a reluctant drawer and found herself face to face with the Christmas present she had bought for Prize over a month ago. It was all wrapped and ready but had – until now – been forgotten. The unexpected reminder took her unawares, slipping under her defences. Tears sprang into her eyes; her heart lurched.

At the same moment, the doorbell rang.

She slammed the drawer shut, pulled on her jumper, took a deep breath. She was ready.

Richard was on the doorstep, grinning. 'Am I early?'

'No. Not at all. You're exactly on time.' What was so funny? Why was he smirking like that? 'Come in, do.'

'Thanks.' Richard stepped past her. 'You might want to do your flies up.'

Lydia ground her teeth, tugged at the zip of her jeans. It always got stuck. She had to yank it inelegantly. Following Richard into the main room, she found him looking round as if he was a builder or decorator who had been called out to a job. He was scruffy enough to be a builder in his saggy combats, filthy trainers and shapeless hooded top. She felt quite smart in comparison, undone flies notwithstanding.

'Nice place you've got here.'

Nice? Her eyes roamed the room, trying to see it from Richard's perspective. Reasonably tidy. Newly de-cluttered. But she could not stop her gaze straying to the place where Prize's basket had always been. She felt tears prick once more.

I mustn't think of Prize. I mustn't cry. Whatever happens, I mustn't cry.

'Oh, Prize ...' she whispered.

He turned round, looked at her quizzically. 'Did you say something? I didn't quite catch ...'

'No. Nothing. I didn't say a word.' *I have to stop talking to myself. It's becoming a bad habit.*

'Where's your Christmas tree? Decorations?'

'I don't bother with all that. I'm far too busy. But you didn't come here to make small talk.'

'Right. Got you. I'm here to pose. So, where do you want me?'

They were getting off on the wrong foot. He was mocking her, taunting her, throwing her off balance. She needed to pull herself together. Was she, or was she not, a teacher, used to dealing with whole classrooms full of obnoxious, refractory teenagers? One Skoda-driving, warehouse-working, drug-dealing disappointment should not present too much of a challenge. Even Nigel, at times, had been known to wither before her wit and wisdom. That had been in the early days, before she knew any better. Nigel had not forgotten. What was it he had called her on the day he dumped her, just before presenting her with Prize? *Iconoclastic.* That was the word. She had not been sure what he meant by it but had gathered from his denunciation of her that it had something to do with the way she had once poked fun when he was drunk and incapable; the way she had occasionally scoffed at his inability to navigate when driving; the way she had, when he'd been wearing shorts on one of their first holidays together, teased him about his bow legs. Those were just a few items in the catalogue of her sins (he had used that word, too, *sins*: she had known what that word meant).

She shook her head, trying to clear it of unwelcome memories of Nigel, but the pouting expression and accusing voice lingered like the Cheshire cat's smile. 'You are a cold woman, a cruel woman. You have never taken me *seriously.*' That had been the worst sin of all, not taking him seriously. He had taken himself very seriously indeed.

She found herself trembling as Nigel's voice faded away. It irked her. There was no excuse in this antiseptic age for letting wounds fester. Why then could she not be rid of Nigel, be cured of him?

'Are you OK?' Richard was staring. 'You look rather pale.'

'Of course I am OK.' She spoke sharply, uncomfortably aware that Richard was a man, the same species as Nigel. 'Stand over there.' She pointed to a spot on the far side of the room. 'Strike a heroic pose.' She took refuge behind the sofa, picked up her sketch book, licked the end of a pencil.

'What sort of hero am I?'

Lydia quickly improvized. 'St George.'

'As in St George and the dragon?'

'So you have heard of him.' She used the tone of voice that she had perfected for putting smart-alec students in their places.

Richard grin widened.

He's grinning. I must try harder, pull the rug out, let him see who's boss....

'Who will be posing as the dragon?' Richard asked.

'Who do you suggest?' *Good: a question countered by a question – excellent ploy.*

'How about Lady Darkness? She's an old dragon.'

Lydia smothered a smile. This was bad. She must stay in control, laugh *at* Richard, not *with* him.

'Stop talking. Take off your hoody.' She used the Voice of Authority to wrest control of the situation.

Richard obeyed. Pupils always obeyed the Voice of Authority. He slid his top over his head, let it fall to the floor. He was not wearing anything underneath.

Lydia had not expected this and debated whether to tell him to put it back on again, or if it would unsettle him more to leave it off. Slowly she became aware that her prevarication could possibly be interpreted as staring – ogling, even. This thought had obviously also occurred to Richard. The way he was grinning at her made her uneasy.

She tore her eyes away; made some rapid pencil marks on her sketch pad.

'I see that you are impressed by my toned and muscular physique.'

'Silence! I'm working!'

Muscular? Who did he think he was kidding? He was all flesh and bone, had spindly arms, a narrow chest, no hips to speak of. His trousers sagged round his thighs, she could see the waistband of his underwear.

Finding that her eyes had strayed back to the disturbing sight of his naked torso, Lydia forced herself to concentrate on the sketch pad; drew some swift lines and curves, the outline of an emaciated body. How soon could she tell him to leave? He'd only been here five minutes; it would look foolish dismissing him so quickly. Give it a quarter of an hour, then she could pretend that she had got everything she needed, show him the door, inform him his services were no longer required. But she could not let the time pass in silence. Nigel's silences had always intimidated her. She was determined not to be intimidated by Richard. She needed to think of a way of taking him down a peg or two.

Drawing jutting ribs and a shrunken belly, she seized on the first thought that came into her head. 'Why did you gatecrash your brother's party the week before Christmas?'

'I didn't gatecrash.'

'You weren't invited.'

'I'm family. I didn't need to be invited.'

'You also,' Lydia continued, drawing a straggly few hairs on a concave chest, 'stole Dean's girlfriend.'

'His *what*?' Richard chortled. 'Dean hasn't got a girlfriend. I mean, come on, you've seen him. He's a geek. No girl in their right mind would go near him.'

No girl in their right mind.... Lydia's hand gave an involuntary jerk. The point of her pencil snapped. But Richard was right. She hadn't been in her right mind that night, meeting Dean on the side of the road. She'd been in shock, grieving. (*Don't think about Prize....*)

Reaching for another pencil, she looked down at her sketch pad, and was disconcerted to find that, instead of producing an unflattering caricature of Richard, she'd drawn a passable likeness by mistake – slim rather than skinny, no superfluous fat, a flat stomach, young and athletic, not a wrinkle, not a grey hair, no spots either, and that disquieting sparkle in his eye. Venting her spleen, she defaced her drawing, adding acne, crossed eyes, a squint, obliterating the cheeky-boy grin which she had captured with worrying accuracy.

Keeping the threatening silence at bay, she said, 'Tell me about the vodka jelly.' (*Why do I keep harping on about that party? I am not interested, it means nothing to me.*)

'The vodka jelly was a bit of fun, to liven things up.'

'You think it's clever, I suppose, to gatecrash other people's parties, to make vodka jellies, to dance on tables and perform a striptease?' *Oops, why mention the dancing and stripping? It's a detail, unimportant: I don't know why I even remember it. I wish he'd put his top back on.*

'You know about that, do you? Wow. That's top-level snooping. You'll be out-Stasi-ing the Stasi next.'

'You think it's funny, do you?' Exasperating students – invariably male – usually quailed when this question was flung at them, but Richard seemed immune. His grin got wider.

'Yeah, I do think it's funny. My dancing usually is.' (Impudent.)

'I can well believe it.' (Crushing.)

'Would you like to see?' (Audacious.)

This is getting out of hand. 'There's no table in here for you to dance on.' Lydia hedged.

'True.' Richard gave ground.

Encouraged by this retreat, Lydia gambled with, 'But I've got music. I dare you.'

She caught her breath. The femme fatale was speaking, surely? Where had she suddenly sprung from? Anything might happen now. She must tread carefully.

'I only dance when I'm pissed.' Richard backtracked still further.

Sensing victory, Lydia advanced from behind the sofa – only to be met by a late and unexpected counter-attack.

'I'll take my kecks off, though, if you want. Seeing as you're so interested in seeing me strip.'

'It's your dancing we are talking about.'

'But you are more interested in the stripping, I can tell.'

Not me, it's the femme fatale. She's shameless....

Lydia clutched her sketch book to her chest, watching Richard warily. The femme fatale had led her to this point and now left her high and dry. But there was no need to be alarmed. Richard wouldn't go through with it. Of course he wouldn't. He didn't have the nerve.

Richard slowly squatted, undid his laces, looking up at her all the while in a way that made her shiver, afraid: the polar opposite of how the femme fatale would have felt. He straightened up, kicked off his trainers and unfastened his combats, which needed no further help in cascading down his legs. He stepped out of them to stand there in stripy boxer shorts and white trainer socks.

Lydia felt dangerously exposed, as if she was the one standing in her underwear rather than Richard.

She held up her sketch pad as if to examine what she'd drawn, shielding herself. There was nowhere to run. She was trapped. If

Prize had still been around, this wouldn't have been happening. Her life had been safe, sensible, with Prize at its centre. Now everything was sliding out of control and she was terrified.

'Who is that meant to be?'

The voice in her ear made her jump. Richard had crossed the room without her noticing. He was standing behind her, looking over her shoulder at the sketch pad. He sounded miffed – and no wonder, given the acne and crossed eyes. She quailed, knowing what Nigel's reaction would have been in these circumstances, knowing what he would have said, what he would have done.

'I don't really look like that, do I?'

'Artistic licence.' *Help! Emergency! Do something!* 'W-what are you doing?' She shied away as he leaned against her. 'No. Don't.'

'Come off it.' He talked softly, lips against her ear. 'We both know what's going on here.'

This was not what she wanted. It was not what she wanted at all. It was far, far too dangerous.

'That blouse you were wearing in the pub yesterday....' His breath tickled her ear. 'It was driving me crazy. I couldn't take my eyes off you. You must have noticed.'

She let go of her sketch pad, raised her arms to push him away – but found instead that she was pulling him closer, wrapping her arms around him.

She closed her eyes, surrendering. His lips melded with hers.

She could feel him fumbling with her jeans, trying to undo the zip. Opening her eyes, she slapped his hand away, felt a surge of relief: this was it, the moment when she would give him his marching orders. She opened her mouth to speak – but the words that came out were, 'The zip sticks. Let me.'

No, no, no! This was all wrong! She shouldn't be helping him to seduce her. She should be—

Her eyes widened. Was he actually nibbling her ear? What on earth would her mother say? And yet, contrary to expectations, it felt almost … almost … *hmmm … ahhh….*

He had one sinewy arm round her shoulders, was stroking her hair; with his other hand he tugged down her jeans, slid his fingers inside her knickers. Her head swam as she tried to keep abreast of the situation. It was all so unexpected, so spontaneous. She was getting carried away.

It had never been like this with Nigel.

Thoughts of Nigel spurred her to one last effort. 'We shouldn't....' (*Oh yes we should!*) 'This is ridiculous....'

'That's what makes it so much fun.' He kissed her again, putting a stop to further conversation.

She ran her hands up and down his back (his skin ... so smooth ... so warm ... so exciting ...), paid no attention to the sketch pad trampled underfoot, raised her arms obediently as he pulled her jumper over her head. He was caressing the back of her neck, kissing her lips, her throat, her breasts, her stomach....

'Oh goodness! Oh my!' Where had he learned to do *that*! Nigel would never have dared, he would never have lowered himself: he'd have thought it unhygienic.

Unforeseen laughter bubbled up, exploded out of her. It had been so long ... so long.... With a shiver of anticipation, she realized that she had quite forgotten how much fun it was possible to have without recourse to gin.

NINE

'HEY, MORLEY! DO you realize what an absolute fanny you look in that get-up?'

Dean, shivering with cold but resplendent in his Morris kit, was dismayed to see Charley and Ashraf thrusting their way to the front of the crowd. Charley and Ashraf were the biggest piss-takers on earth. It was just Dean's luck that they should attend the same college as him.

'What are you two doing here?' he muttered. As if having his mother gawping at him wasn't embarrassing enough.

'That's a nice way to greet us,' said Charley. 'I'm wounded, Morley. Wounded.' (Charley was too thick-skinned to be wounded by anything.)

'We've come to see you, innit.' Ash grinned, looking Dean up and down. 'Man, I wish I had a camera. No one will believe this.'

'You have got a camera, dumb-ass,' said Charley. 'There's one on your phone.'

'You're right, Charley, man!'

Ash fished out his phone from his pocket, lined up his first shot. 'So what's with the fancy dress and stuff, Morley?'

Dean was full of anguish. There was absolutely nowhere to hide. He was standing in the middle of the pub car park with half the village staring at him. He might have wished for the ground to swallow him up, except that he knew very well that the ground never did things like that. It went against the laws of physics. Only brainless fools who had no understanding of science would hope for something like that. He could make a break for it, of course, but the squire would collar him before he'd even made it off the car park, and that would be even more humiliating. There was nothing for it but to grit his teeth and get on with it. It was not as if there was anyone else he could blame for this. He was the one who'd chosen to do Morris dancing. Although, on second thoughts, didn't this situation show up one of the glaring faults of society? Why, when you decided to do something a bit different, did people jeer and make fun of you, instead of respecting you for being an individual? People like Charley and Ash, for instance.

'Come on, Morley. What's it all for?' Ash was busy taking Dean from yet another angle.

Dean kept quiet. He knew from bitter experience that anything he said would be taken down and used against him. That was the sort of piss-taking bastards they were, Charley and Ash.

Charley said, 'It's traditional British culture. Isn't that right, Morley?'

'It's English.' Dean spoke through his gritted teeth, unable to stop himself. 'The Morris is English.'

'English, British.' Charley shrugged. 'It's all the same thing.'

'No it isn't. You cannot use "England" and "Britain" interchangeably.' How many more times did he have to tell them? But he felt a little better for it. Charley and Ash might be the champion piss-takers of the universe, but they were also imbeciles. Why should he – or anyone else – take any notice of people who didn't even know the name of their own country?

'You're such a geek, Morley, innit.' Ash, trigger-happy, spoke from behind his camera phone. Dean could just imagine where the photos would end up. Everyone in college would have them by the end of next week. 'So what's with the freak over there?' Ash pointed. 'Is he on day release from the nut-house, or what?'

'That's George,' said Dean. 'He's the fool.'

Ash hooted. 'Man, you is all fools, innit!'

Charley changed the subject. 'So where's your brother, Morley? Has he made any more vodka jellies lately?'

'Richard is not my brother.'

'Yeah, yeah. So you keep saying. He's a top bloke. Made your party go with a right bang. Is he knobbing Sandra Hays now, the lucky bastard?'

'I don't know. I don't care. It'll serve her right if he is.'

'What do you mean?'

'He's got diseases. Herpes. Crabs. Gonorrhoea.' Dean heaped it on, finding vindictive satisfaction in being economical with the truth – although Richard probably had caught something, the way he carried on. What was the point of having the most sophisticated brain in the animal kingdom if you just let your base instincts take over?

The names of a wide selection of venereal diseases tripped off Dean's tongue but made him feel uneasy, reminding him of the panther. Up to now, he'd noticed no ominous symptoms in himself despite careful monitoring, but even if he was lucky enough not to have caught anything, it would be no thanks to *her*.

Just then the music began. The squire was calling them to order. Dean was glad to get moving, and not just because it gave him an excuse to get away from Charley and Ash. Standing round like a spare part, he'd begun to freeze to death. People laughed when you said it – *I'm freezing to death* – but it was no joke. He could actually feel the circulation slowing in his extremities and he could have sworn that his skin looked whiter than usual. Also, his hands were burning. That was a dangerous sign. Before long, they'd turn red, swell up, and there'd be permanent nerve damage due to oxygen deprivation. These things happened; he hadn't made it up, it was scientifically proven. And it would be just his luck to get hypothermia on a bank holiday when it wasn't even midday and he should still have been in bed.

It was the Stasi's fault. This was all her idea. Some traditional entertainment for New Year's Day, she'd said: putting on something the whole village could enjoy. Ha! Lining her own pockets, more like. Drumming up trade. The squire had been only too pleased to go along with it – which was not really surprising as the squire was also her husband, the landlord of the pub. He was all right, the squire (that was what you called him when you were with the Morris men), but there had to be a screw loose somewhere, getting himself hitched to a woman like the Stasi.

As he concentrated on the patterns of the dance, Dean was glad to find that this left his overactive imagination with less scope to torment him. He even found it possible to ignore Charley and Ash. What he couldn't help noticing, however, was that his mother was standing right next to the panther – that they were talking together, *smiling*, as if they were old friends.

Talking about what? It made his blood run cold (colder) to think about it.

Skipping across the car park, he shook his leg with an angry jangle as the music wheezed and bubbled in the icy air. He told himself to be realistic. Whatever it was they were discussing, it wouldn't be anything to do with his sex life. The panther, of course, was more than capable of bringing the subject up: she was plainly a sex maniac as well as a lunatic. But his mother wouldn't have been smiling like that if she'd been talking about sex. She would be more likely to die of embarrassment. His mother was the biggest prude in the entire universe.

All the same, Dean wasn't entirely reassured. Sex might be out of the window, but they could still be talking about him, discussing him. It wasn't that he was big-headed or anything: people really did seem to take an unreasonable amount of interest in him, usually to find fault and pin labels such as *untidy, difficult,* and – most often – *odd*. OK, so he *could* be a bit odd at times: he admitted it. But that was just a cunning disguise. He pretended to be a bit of a freak to cover up the fact that he was actually the biggest freak in existence. He was pretending to be pretending that he was a freak: a double bluff. It kept people off the scent.

He hoped.

Turning on one foot, waving his handkerchief in the air, Dean found time to regret once more that he'd ever let the panther anywhere near him. He hadn't had much choice, of course, seeing as she more or less *raped* him; but he realized with hindsight that he might have put up more of a struggle if he'd known who she was. He'd thought she was a complete stranger but it turned out that *everyone* knew her: even his sister.

'Lydia Taylor? Of course I know Lydia Taylor. She works at the college and she lives in that little cottage down Well Lane. She hasn't got a boyfriend, lives on her own. She used to take her dog for walks, a golden retriever, fat and smelly. It licked my hand once. Ugh! But it's dead now.' Amanda was a know-all. He detested her. She would be a positive menace when she grew up.

The dance ended on a loud, rusty note from the harmonium. There was a smattering of polite, if bemused, applause. Dean bowed low. As he held this position, counting to ten, he saw the brown fetlocks of a horse come clip-clopping into his restricted field of vision. The horse came to a stop, scraping the tarmac with a casual sweep of its hoof.

Slowly Dean straightened up. The rest of the horse came into view: vast flanks the colour and texture of sandpaper; large brown eyes regarding him; rubbery lips curled back over chunky teeth in what looked suspiciously like a sneer. Perched on top of this great brute, silhouetted against the dead grey sky, was a girl in black jodhpurs and a cream polo-neck sweater. Her curly blonde hair had been partly stuffed into a hard hat.

'Hello, Dean. Still doing your Morris dancing, then?'

Dean grunted. Why did people persist in stating the obvious? Although in Cally's case, the obvious was about her limit. She had never been, as his mother might have put it, the sharpest knife in the drawer. Talking to Cally had always given him a rich feeling of superiority. Today, though, as he peered up at her, he found he was overcome by a quite different sensation – a sensation he did not care for one little bit. It caused his cheeks to burn and prickly sweat to break out down his back. He felt suffocated by his collar. When had Cally got so grown up? Was it really that long since he'd seen her?

'Ding-dong! Who's the hottie?'

Dean looked round. Charley was there, Ash trailing behind him.

'Aren't you going to introduce us to your friend, Morley?' Ash's eyes were popping out of his head.

Dean muttered, 'She's not my— ' but the girl interrupted.

'I'm Cally.'

She dazzled them with her smile. Even her smile was different to how Dean remembered it, not a sickly, girly smile any longer. He tried to muster a sneer, but his face seemed paralyzed: he couldn't even manage to close his mouth.

'Hello, Cally. It's very, *very* nice to meet you. My name's Charley. Oh, and this joker is Ash.'

'Oi, joker yourself, Charles, you fat bastard, innit.'

The way that Charley and Ash were ogling Cally was getting on his nerves. Dean roused himself from his torpor to inform them that Cally went to an all-girls school, a private school: just to underline that their chances were zero.

Cally laughed. 'I don't go to that school any more. I decided to leave and—'

'*You* decided?' said Charley.

'I persuaded Grandma to let me start at the sixth-form college in town.'

'But that's where we ...' Ash's eyes grew even bigger and rounder, if that was possible.

'We'll be happy to show you about the place,' said Charley eagerly. 'We know everybody who's anybody. We can introduce you.'

Dean was disgusted, watching the pair of them, falling over themselves, tongues hanging out. It was pathetic. If they'd shut their mouths, it would at least stop them drooling. (He should shut his own mouth, come to that. He must look like the village idiot, gaping.)

'I'm sure Dean will take me under his wing,' said Cally.

'Do you know Morley?'

'I've known him for years. We used to play together.'

'Whey-hey, I bet you did!' Ash jabbed his bony elbow into Dean's side, his eyebrows jerking up and down.

'What did you play?' asked Charley, his eyebrows also waggling. 'Kiss chase?'

'No. Mummies and daddies. Me and Dean and all the other village kids.'

They were all grinning like idiots, Dean noticed: all except him. Even the horse appeared to be smiling, its lips working back and forth across its teeth in an unpleasant, mocking sort of way.

It had always been easy to make fun of Cally because she was so thick, so ditzy; because she went to a posh school; because Lady Darkness was her grandmother. But today Dean did not seem to be able to get past the way her jodhpurs clung to her legs, the way her breasts made a bump in her sweater like a shelf (she had not had breasts in the old days). He thought it was unfair of her. She was playing dirty. Not that she was actually *doing* anything, just sitting there; but it made him feel hot and sticky and breathless.

He realized that his mouth had dropped open again. He closed it with a snap.

'You don't want to hang around with Morley,' Ash was saying. 'He's a nerd, innit. He's got no mates and he's still a virgin.'

'I am not a virgin!' Dean hissed.

'So you say.' Charley grinned up at Cally. 'Morley claims to have done it, but he won't tell us who he's done it with.'

'It don't count if you do it with yourself!' Ash guffawed, but suddenly his expression changed as his eyes veered towards the back end of the horse. His lips twisted in revulsion. 'Ugh! Your horse, man! It just shitted all over the road! That's so gross!'

'Shut up, Ash, don't be such an idiot,' said Charley. 'It's what horses do, you moron.'

Charley was full of himself, as if he was an expert in the defecation habits of horses, as if he was doing horse shit at A level – when really he was so dumb he didn't even know the difference between England and Britain. Dean ground his teeth, wished he could show Charley up for what he was, wished he could hate Cally, slap her like in the old days when they'd played mummies and daddies. ('You've been a very naughty girl – Daddy is going to smack your bottom.') But you weren't meant to hit girls, not when you were grown up and civilized. All the same, he would have liked to do *something* to her, to push her off her pedestal. The only problem was, you couldn't do anything – slapping or otherwise – with that great beast watching you. Dean did not trust the horse one little bit.

Ash nudged him in the ribs again. 'Morley. That weirdo over there is waving to you.'

It was the squire, gathering them all together for the final dance. Dean knew that their performance was supposed to finish on the dot of twelve, when the Stasi would throw open the pub doors with a flourish. Woe betide her husband if he messed up her big moment.

The music began wheezing and swirling round the car park. Dean took his place in the group. On balance, it seemed the safest place to be. Danger beset him on all sides: his mother, the panther, Charley and Ash, Cally, not to mention that perfidious horse. What was the point of horses anyway? (He began slowly circling round, his handkerchief at the ready.) Horses were surplus to requirements in this day and age; they ought to be abolished.

All the same, he was surprised to feel a pang of disappointment when, halfway through the dance, he saw Cally jab her heel into the horse's sandpaper flank to clip-clop away up the High Street.

As Cally rode off, a tiny figure came darting between the onlookers, clutching a bucket and a spade. It was Mrs Pole, who lived opposite the pub: a bird-like, twittery widow of indeterminate age. Dean watched in amazement out of the corner of his eye as she began shovelling horse dung into her bucket.

He rolled his eyes as he turned a circle on the car park. He was surrounded by lunatics. And people had the nerve to call *him* odd!

TEN

GWEN HESITATED OUTSIDE the pub door, her hand almost but not quite touching the handle. She could never quite rid herself of the idea that it was somehow improper for a respectable woman to go into a pub on her own. Basil disapproved of pubs altogether. Town pubs, he said, ought to be transformed into bars on the continental style, with waiter service and no riff-raff. Village pubs, on the other hand – unless they could be put on a sound financial footing – should be shut down and redeveloped. Their own village pub, he opined, could be bulldozed (there was, after all, very little left of the original seventeenth-century building, it was hardly worth bothering English Heritage about) and three or four new houses (or *desirable residences*, as he called them) could be built on the same plot. Villages, he perorated, must move with the times.

Gwen shook her head to clear it. It was high time, she told herself, that she stopped taking so much notice of what Basil thought. She was quite entitled to go into a pub if she wanted to, even if that pub was not on a sound financial footing. It was a free country. ('Nothing in this life is free, Gwen, not even fresh air. Don't you think there is a price to be paid for keeping all those millions of acres of unproductive rain forest?') *One day soon*, she said to herself, *I shall put my foot down, give Basil a piece of my mind.*

It was just a question of finding the right moment.

She pulled the handle down firmly and opened the door.

Lydia seemed very pleased to see her; but then any interruption would be welcome, Gwen reflected as she took off her coat and unwound her scarf, if one was trapped alone in a room with the landlady, as Lydia was. The landlady was in full flow, standing in front of the fire, shifting her weight from one leg to the other then back again.

'I was just saying, Gwen, that Lydia would look quite pretty if she had her hair done properly. She's got a very noticeable face. Don't you think she's got a noticeable face?'

'Oh?' Gwen was never quite sure what to say to the landlady who carried on as if she was one's closest friend when one actually knew very little about her.

'Now then, Gwen,' the landlady continued, 'what's this I hear about you joining the parish council?'

'Oh, I—' Gwen, caught off guard, quickly gathered her thoughts. 'Nothing's actually been decided—'

'That's not what I heard. It's all settled, I heard. You'll be taking Mr Smithson's place.'

Gwen was reminded of a rumour she had heard that people sometimes referred to the landlady as *the Stasi* behind her back. One might have been forgiven for thinking it rather an apt nickname. The landlady *did* appear to know everyone's business. She could also be tactless at times, even a little crass, but she was only young when all was said and done (mid twenties?) and she was doing her best to keep the pub afloat in difficult times. One had to make allowances.

Even so, Gwen thought with a sigh, one wished that Imelda Darkley had picked on someone else for the parish council. One really did prefer to keep one's head down, not to be thrust into the public eye.

Gwen took a seat and the barmaid brought the drinks over ('It's not as if she's got anything else to do, ha ha ha!'). Quite a pretty girl, the barmaid, thought Gwen: sandy haired, freckled, open faced. One could get away with calling the barmaid *pretty*, but the landlady had used the word just now of Lydia – *she would look quite pretty if she had her hair done* – and it didn't seem to fit. *Pretty* was such a *pliant* word. Lydia was not a pliant person. *Striking* would be nearer the mark, Gwen decided, stealing a glance at the younger woman. Yes, *striking* was much more like it, with those high cheekbones and a pale face framed by wavy black hair (a little tousled, one must admit).

Sipping her tonic water, Gwen glanced at Lydia again. Was it merely imagination, or was there something different about her today? More animation in the face, more of a sparkle in the eyes, perhaps? She had nice eyes – *striking* eyes. But her hair.... The landlady was right about her hair. And not just her hair. The way she dressed might have been described as somewhat quirky. That high-collared, cream-coloured blouse was not too bad, but worn with a man's patterned waistcoat: what was she thinking? One had heard it said that Lydia had been seen in charity shops in town – buying, not donating. One might venture to say that Lydia was *bohemian*, but one was never sure if that was an entirely nice thing to say about someone one liked.

And I do – Gwen admitted, surprising herself – *rather like her. It's not often I feel so at ease in the company of another woman.*

Gwen blinked; realized that she had not been paying attention. She was getting into bad habits, allowing her mind to wander. The problem was, Basil did tend to go on a bit and one did tend to lose the thread. If one was not careful, one would find that one had stopped listening altogether: to anyone, ever.

Trying to get the gist of the conversation, Gwen realized that Lydia was explaining in a rather apologetic way that the landlady had offered to join their committee and that they couldn't very well – with volunteers being so thin on the ground – refuse. Nobody else was going to show up for the meeting, it seemed.

'Why don't we have Sandra on the committee too?' the landlady suggested. 'She's quite clever. You're quite clever, aren't you, Sandra? She's doing art at college.'

'I'm doing English literature and—'

'Art, literature: same thing,' said the landlady. 'At least, literature is arty even if it's not art. I'll just go and call my husband down. He can watch the bar and Sandra can join our meeting.'

She moseyed towards the inner door.

'Clever,' murmured Lydia as the landlady disappeared. 'That'll save on an evening's wages.'

'Oh. Do you really think that is what she...?'

Lydia smiled.

Does she think me naïve, or is she making a joke? Gwen felt it best to change the subject. 'How is your painting coming along, Lydia?'

'I've rediscovered my muse.' The puzzling smile continued to play on Lydia's lips. 'Richard has been a help.'

'Oh?' (In what way could Richard help in the matter of art? Surely as a life model he just, well, *stood* there?)

'I thought the Morris men might make a good subject for my next piece,' Lydia continued. 'Their performance on New Year's Day was rather enthralling.'

'Yes. Yes, I suppose it was.' (Dean, enthralling?)

'What about you, Gwen? Anything in the offing?'

'Well....' Gwen hesitated to say that just recently Basil had been more amenable about the matter of painting. It would make her sound rather feeble, as if she needed Basil's permission, as if Basil pushed her around. Basil didn't push. He was more like a sheep dog, steering one in the direction he wanted. 'Ever since you spoke to Basil on Boxing Day—'

'Yes?'

'He has raised no objection if I....' ('Since when have I forbidden you to do anything, Gwen? Where do people get such ideas?' 'I really couldn't say, Basil. It's only a turn of phrase, I expect. I shouldn't worry about it.' 'But I do worry. A man in my position has to consider his public image. I never *forbid* anyone from doing anything. I *discuss*, I *argue*, I *reason*. Of course you must paint if you want to. It is what you want, I suppose?' 'Well....')

'That's good, isn't it?' said Lydia.

'Of course, yes, but ...'

The conversation lapsed. Gwen glanced at the clock. They had been sitting here for – what? twenty minutes? – and nothing had been accomplished. She hated wasting time. And there were dishes in the kitchen at home, dishes from dinner (supper) that she had neglected in order to come to this meeting. Would Basil notice?

The landlady reappeared, her husband in tow. He looked less than delighted to have been summoned downstairs but it seemed as if it was more than his life was worth to disobey. One would not dare to treat Basil like that, of course, but would it perhaps be possible (Gwen mused) to *manage* him a little better?

'Come and join us, Sandra,' said the landlady as she settled herself into a chair by the fire.

Lydia greeted the girl with a smile. 'How is that boyfriend of yours?'

'He's....' Sandra hesitated.

'Trouble in paradise?' Lydia suggested.

'It's been two days. He hasn't called, he hasn't texted.'

'Ah.' Lydia nodded wisely, as if she wasn't surprised.

'But he does have to work.' Sandra rallied, putting on a brave face. 'He works shifts. It's not always convenient. I can't expect him to be at my beck and call.'

What a sensible girl, thought Gwen. *Dare one hope that Amanda...?*

The meeting got underway at last. Gwen found it a frustrating experience. Making any headway was next to impossible. Sandra, it was true, had some useful ideas, but most of these were squashed by the landlady who disparaged Sandra's youth and inexperience. The landlady herself kept going off at a tangent, bursting with village gossip, while Lydia seemed oddly detached and ambivalent, as if she didn't care one way or the other. Had she grown bored of the exhibition already? Or did she have something else on her mind?

Becoming agitated (profligate misuse of her time had been known to keep her awake at nights), Gwen realized that the onus was on her to force through a few decisions. Easter was fixed as a date. Nobody objected to the village hall as a venue. But what if they could not muster enough exhibits to fill the hall? In which case, Sandra suggested, why not open it up to handicrafts as well as art? The landlady, for once, did not pooh-pooh the idea. She knew 'for a fact' that several people in the village had interests in that line, including Old George who carved wood. Old George would be in the public bar by now. Why didn't they all go round and ask him if he'd be interested in their exhibition?

Gwen felt like tearing her hair out. They'd drifted from the point again and the dirty dishes at home were beginning to prey on her mind. If only she'd had time to put them in the machine! But she'd been in a hurry and of course supper could not be rushed. Basil had regular habits, got dyspeptic if his routine was upset.

Old George also had regular habits and was sitting in his accustomed place in the window seat with his first light and bitter. He looked at them one by one, a deadpan expression on his face, then denied that he'd ever carved wood in his life.

'Oh, George, you're such a fibber!' shrieked the landlady. 'I sat here and listened to you! You make egg cups and toast racks and things like that, and you sell them at car boot sales!'

'No. That weren't me. No. Never been to a car boot sale in me life. Never.' He took a sip of beer, smacked his lips, set his glass back on the beer mat. 'So what is this *art show*? We've not had one of them in these parts before. Never needed one. It's you incomers, that's what it is. All you incomers, spoiling the village.'

Toying with her coat, Gwen decided that the meeting could now legitimately be said to be over. She had no desire to listen to the protracted wrangling over wood carving and car boot sales that Old George and the landlady were engaged in, and the way George smacked his lips made her feel bilious. She wished he'd put his teeth in of an evening.

Walking with Lydia up Well Lane, Gwen found the conversation somewhat stilted. Lydia seemed preoccupied. Perhaps she really had lost interest in the exhibition? But no, that was a silly idea. It had been Lydia's suggestion in the first place. Of course she was all for it. It had to be that dog of hers which was preying on her mind. She was pining for that dog.

I must, said Gwen as she took her leave of Lydia and continued up the hill on her own, *I must do more to help, be more wholehearted, move things along. This exhibition will be just what Lydia needs to take her mind off things.*

Gwen's steps slowed as the house loomed ahead. She felt a great reluctance to go inside. It was the dirty dishes, it had to be. She was worried that Basil might have seen them.

She told herself not to be so silly. There was no reason for Basil to have gone anywhere near the kitchen. All the same, she felt very weary as she searched in her bag for her keys: and was it any wonder she felt weary, when it took all one's courage merely to open one's own front door?

ELEVEN

LYDIA SAT IN her car, looking out at the wet, dark January evening. WET and DARK ought to be in capital letters, she felt. It was only just gone five and already it seemed as if it had been dark for ever. The rain didn't help, nor the gusting wind. It was utterly depressing.

And now, just to top things off, her car wouldn't start.

Her car was conspiring against her, had to be. Of all the days to stop working – of all the horrible, miserable evenings after a horrible, miserable day teaching horrible, miserable kids.

But it was no good dwelling on it. That would be playing into her car's hands. Tempting as it was to leap out and do a Basil Fawlty on the malignant machine, she knew that was just the reaction her car wanted and she was not going to give it the satisfaction. She would sit here, pay no heed, twiddle her thumbs for ten minutes (well, perhaps five: it was very cold) and then, having lulled the contrary contraption into a false sense of security, she would lean forward in an offhand way and casually turn the key in the ignition. With any luck, the car would be taken by surprise. It would forget that it was meant to be playing hard to get, start up by mistake, and once it realized that it had been outwitted by a mere human, it would be far too embarrassed to conk out again.

A sardonic voice in her head cut across her thoughts: not the voice of her mother. The femme fatale, perhaps? 'You do realize, I suppose, that people who imagine their cars are out to get them are generally classed as psychologically disturbed?'

'Can you think of a better plan?' Lydia said sharply. 'Then shut up.'

The voice seemed suitably cowed. Nodding her head in satisfaction, Lydia searched around in her mind for something to occupy her time while she waited. There was little enough to inspire her. The car park was all but empty; acres of tarmac glistening in the sordid yellow light of the sodium lamps. Spots of rain were being dashed against her windscreen. Wind hissed and moaned, whipping through the damp darkness, setting the car rocking.

Lydia pulled her scarf closer round her neck; sat on her frozen hands to warm them.

What could she think about?

Richard?

No. Not Richard.

Prize, then?

Oh, all right, Richard.

She felt a twinge which she imagined someone younger and less experienced might have mistaken for their heart skipping a beat. It was more likely to be angina at her age. After all, she was hardly likely to get all goo-eyed over someone like Richard: the very idea was laughable. He wasn't even her type (what was her type?). He was coarse, crude, brash; puerile too. All that jack-the-lad, devil-may-care nonsense got on your nerves after a time. And he wasn't exactly an Adonis. So just what was it about him? She couldn't put her finger on it, but whatever it was, he had it in bucket loads. Perhaps it was nothing more that the attractiveness of youth. (Oh to be young: no snipping out grey hairs, no bulging in inconvenient places, no feeling shattered at the end of a working day.)

'I hope,' Richard had said last night as he pulled on his hoody, 'that you're not getting the wrong idea about all this. I'm not your boyfriend or anything like that.' Anxiety had been evident in the jack-the-lad, devil-may-care facade.

Lydia remembered that she had not deigned to reply, looking up at him from the sofa, a blanket artfully arranged over her, covering much, revealing just enough. *I must have looked*, she thought, *every inch the femme fatale....*

'Ridiculous is the word, my girl. You looked ridiculous.' Her mother's ghost was there, the disembodied voice hovering somewhere over the passenger seat.

'Oh, shut up, go away. I'm not listening.'

She returned to the scene in her cottage, pictured herself lying there like the Venus de Milo, an arch smile playing on her lips. Richard had lingered, unable to tear himself away. Who could have?

'As long as we're both clear on this,' he'd reiterated. 'It's a casual thing, a bit of fun—'

A snort of derision from the passenger seat. 'Fun? Huh! *Cavorting* is what I'd call it.'

'No one asked you.'

Had there been, perhaps, the merest whisper of regret at his words? Staring out at the bleak evening, Lydia felt it safe to admit to a dash of disappointment, but no more.

'Did you really expect anything else, my girl? You're old enough to be his mother.'

'Go away. Leave me alone.'

'Huh! *Obsessed*, that's what you are.'

'Why don't you just mind your own business? There's only room for two in this relationship—'

'Relationship! Ha! There's no relationship. You're just convenient, that's all. Available. Easy. We had names for girls like you in my day.'

'I am not a girl. I am a grown woman.'

'Woman? *Nymphomaniac* would be nearer the mark.'

'Nymphomaniac? Chance would be a fine thing!'

'It's obscene, that's what it is. And afterwards, all that guilt and shame: I don't know how you bear it.'

'There is no guilt. There is no shame.'

'Keep telling yourself that, my girl, and you might even come to believe it!'

'We are not living in Victorian times. I am free to do whatever I like. I can take responsibility for my own actions.'

'You? Take responsibility? That'll be the day!'

Lydia had heard enough. She flung open the door of the car, at the same moment reaching forward to pull that catch that opened the bonnet. She had better things to do than sit here and listen to her mother's ghost. She could poke about in the engine, might strike lucky. And if all else failed, there was always the Basil Fawlty routine.

She pulled her woolly hat down to cover her ears. Cold air was blasting across the wasteland of tarmac. Rain was swirling through the air. Her fingers as she fumbled with the bonnet were quickly frozen into sticks of ice. She looked down into the engine with a sense of despair. Where did one begin? Pull a few wires, see if that did the trick? Clean the spark plugs? But where, in the name of wonder, would one find the spark plugs?

'Hello there! Having a spot of bother?'

The sudden voice made her jump. She spun round, half expecting to meet the glinting eyes and sinister smile of a would-be rapist, but it was only one of the other lecturers, an entirely harmless-looking man in a baggy waterproof with the hood up. Hesitant eyes looked out at her from under the elasticated rim of the hood, tapes tied beneath his bearded chin.

She tried to place him. Wasn't he science? Surely he was science? He was not much by way of a white knight, but beggars....

'I wonder...? Could you...?' She even managed a smile. It seemed only fair, considering that he was about to rescue a damsel in distress. All men loved tinkering with engines. He'd have her malignant machine up and running in no time.

'No good asking me.' He held his hands up, a gesture of helplessness.

'*What?*'

'I haven't got a clue when it comes to cars.'

'Then why...?' She felt cheated. 'Aren't you science? I thought you were science.'

'Physics.'

'Isn't a car engine physics?'

'Theory and practice.' He held out one hand, *theory*, and then the other, *practice*. 'Two different things.' He smiled, diffident. (Diffident? He ought to be ashamed, not diffident!) 'Can I give you a lift anywhere?'

'What about my car?' She prevaricated. She knew she ought to be grateful – anything was better than being stranded on the tundra of the college car park – but quite honestly, what was the point of a man who couldn't fix a car engine? 'Will my car be safe here?'

'Quite safe, I should think.' (Blind faith. Not very scientific.) 'My vehicle is over there.' He pointed. 'If there's anywhere I can drop you ...'

It was better than nothing. Better than slowly freezing. Perhaps he was a white knight, of sorts, after all.

But what the hell was his name?

John? Was that it?

It had to be. He looked like a John. She was sure it was John.

'Thank you, John. A lift would be marvellous. I must warn you, though, that I live out in the sticks.'

'I know. It's OK.'

He smiled again, that diffident smile. An odd smile, thought Lydia. Somehow it seemed younger than his face – his beard, for instance, was going grey. But weren't all scientists still children at heart?

Installed in his battered old Renault, Lydia felt it beholden on her to make conversation – tit-for-tat, as it were: amusing chit-chat in return for a lift home. There was plenty of material to draw on. Picking holes in the college principal was always a favourite staff-room pastime, as was grousing about the students. 'You know what he's like, John ... I'm sure I don't need to tell you, John ... so I said to him, John ... and then I just sent her out of the room, John: I'd had enough....'

He seemed a lot less chatty in the car than he had out in the car park. Maybe he needed to concentrate on driving. Men couldn't do two things at once, it was a well-known fact. Or perhaps the offer of a lift had been out of politeness only; perhaps he hadn't expected her to accept. Well, tough luck.

She paused, watching the windscreen wipers, gathering her thoughts for another measured critique of the students (lazy, idle, ignorant). In the little silence he suddenly spoke.

'Terry,' he said quietly. 'My name is Terry.'

'Terry?' Terry! Not John. *Terry!* 'Of course it is! Of course. Ha ha! I must be going senile in my old age. Ha ha!' *Oh Lord, why do I always do this? Why don't I learn to look before I leap? Why must I keep putting my foot in it?*

Her embarrassment seemed out of all proportion. *Anyone can make a mistake*, she insisted as she flushed hot then cold, her cheeks burning. It was John's – Terry's – fault if the mistake had been magnified into cringe-worthy proportions. Why hadn't he put her right at once, instead of letting her call him John over and over? Why should she be expected to know his name? It wasn't as if she knew him. They must have exchanged half a dozen words at most in as many terms. Who did he think he was, anyway? He looked ridiculous in that shapeless waterproof with the hood still up. And what sort of stupid name was Terry for a science teacher? All science teachers ought to be called John. It was obvious, it was patently—

'You've had your roads resurfaced.'

'I beg your pardon?' Lydia blinked, interrupted mid-flow. (Flow? Torrent, more like.)

'Your roads. They are all smooth. No bumps. You should see some of the streets in town. Pot holes the size of the Grand Canyon. I am for ever getting complaints.'

'Oh?' Complaints? What complaints? Why should people make complaints to John – Terry – about their street surfaces?

'And look,' he went on, 'a brand new bus shelter. Wooden, too. Not cheap plastic.'

There was a strident tone to his voice now. Was he like this when he was lecturing?

'It's always the same with this bloody council. Half the revenue is from the town, but most is siphoned off by Tory councillors to lavish on their villages.'

Lydia said, 'I'm not a proper villager. They call me an incomer.' *Why am I defending myself? I have no control over how the council spends its money. And I never use the bloody bus shelter.*

Terry ignored her, carried on. 'But if you try to find out where the money is going – if you want to know how much they are actually spending – you never get anywhere. They bamboozle and stonewall and lead you up the garden path....'

Oh my word! I really shouldn't have called him John. It has obviously opened up deep wells of bitterness. 'You can drop me here.' False brightness. *Help! Let me out!*

Terry pulled up. His brakes squealed. Lydia scrambled out. It was raining heavier now, the icy wind gusting, but she was simply thankful to get away.

Or nearly away. Terry wound down his window.

'Will you be OK?'

'Yes, fine. Thanks so much for the lift, Joh— Terry. It was so kind of you.' She was much less daunted now that she was out of his car, felt she ought to offer him some sort of reward for saving her. Encouragement, perhaps? She leant towards the window. 'If you really feel so strongly about what the council gets up to, you should try and get yourself elected. I'm sure you would stand a good chance, being so eloquent on the subject.'

'I have been elected. I'm a district councillor.' A quiet, weary tone. 'But you've no idea how difficult it is to get things done when there are only six councillors from the town and twenty from the villages.'

He wound up his window and drove off, tyres swishing along the wet road, leaving Lydia standing in the rain. For some reason that she could not fathom, she felt more than usually crushed.

TWELVE

HEARING THE DOORBELL, Dean decided that the safest course of action was to beat a quick retreat, even though he was halfway through a very instructive TV programme about the Large Hadron Collider. There was probably some old dear at the door come to have a gossip with his mother. They would sit in the front room and he wouldn't be able to hear the TV above the chatter. He could, of course, try to interest them in the Large Hadron Collider but he was painfully aware that, past a certain age, women (his mother) developed a condition that might be described as *myopia of the intellect*. The conversation would be a long litany of 'Have you heard … what do you think … and I said … then she said … can you believe it?' They talked such drivel that you began to wonder if humans might actually be evolving *backwards*: back towards our ape-like ancestors, and further back, towards an ultimate form that would be something like a puddle of apathetic slime. Many people, Dean theorized, had already gone so far on this road as to have brains that had dissolved into slime.

Switching off the TV, Dean slipped out into the hallway, but then disaster struck. He was nowhere near the stairs when his mother popped her head round the kitchen door.

'Oh, Dean, just answer the door, would you?'

'Mum! I'm busy!'

'For goodness' sake, Dean! It won't take a moment. It'll only be Imelda Darkley, come to have a word.'

Her head withdrew, giving him no time to argue. He shuffled towards the door. Having to open it – even if Lady Darkley was on the other side – was definitely the lesser of two evils. The alternative was to risk one of his mother's *moods*: the sighs, the shaking of the head, the glances of disillusion and despair: it was more than he could bear. Why couldn't she just lose her temper and yell, like any normal parent?

He opened the door. Lady Darkley swooped in without waiting to be asked. She thrust her umbrella at him as she passed.

'Dreadful weather! Absolutely filthy! Put this somewhere for me, would you? I've come to see your mother. Let her know I'm here.'

Dean muttered, 'If you'd like to wait in the …' but she swept past him and sailed into the front room, her coat tails flying. Her head was wrapped in a paisley scarf.

He stuffed the umbrella up a corner, conscious that she'd taken no more notice of him than if he'd been a slave, but on the whole he thought he'd got off lightly. He prepared once more to retreat to his room.

Once more he was thwarted. His mother emerged from the kitchen, straightening her skirt, patting her hair, a flustered look on her face.

'Dean. There's a tray with tea and biscuits. Will you bring it through to the living room?'

'Do I have to?'

'Yes please.'

'I'm not … not a *slave*!'

'I know, dear. I don't need a slave. I've got you.'

Ha-bloody-ha. Did she think she was funny or something? He went through to the kitchen, grumbling to himself, feeling hard done by; but he also made a note not to use in future the phrase *do I have to?* That sort of thing – whining and moaning – was all very well when you were a kid, but he was eighteen now and it was beneath his dignity.

The cups rattled in their saucers as he carried the tray across the hallway. It was the best china, he noticed. Why was his mother using the best china? In honour of Lady Darkley? It was about time his mother realized that she was living in the modern world – the twenty-first century. All this bowing and scraping was an anachronism. There was no need to treat Lady Darkley differently just because she was a *lady*. It was nonsense, in this day and age. The

French had the right idea: they'd chopped the heads off all their lords and ladies, leaving no one to bow and scrape to, no one to treat you like a slave. They probably used their best china all the time in France.

He kicked open the front room door, flinched at the sight of Lady Darkley ensconced in Basil's easy chair, tried to blot out all thoughts of guillotines and the like, hoped that she couldn't read his mind (he wouldn't put it past her, the old witch). He had to kneel so that he could slide the tray onto the low table.

Lady Darkley was in full flow. '... and so I've made it *absolutely* clear to Smithson: we've accepted his resignation this time and there's no going back. He retires in May and there's an end to it. Not a moment too soon, if you ask me. Man's going senile.'

In the hair's-breadth pause which occurred here, Mrs Collier said quickly (but firmly), 'Will you pour, please, Dean.'

'Do I have—' Dean gulped back the words, remembering his dignity just in time.

'No sugar, plenty of milk,' Lady Darkley barked in an aside before launching on another monologue. 'What happens, Gwen, is this. We co-opt you, put a notice to that effect in the parish magazine, and then it's all done and dusted. There's only one meeting a month – I won't tolerate any more that that – so it won't take up much of your time. But I do think it's important to have the *right* people for the job. When I came to consider the alternatives – such as they are – I realized that we can't *possibly* do without you.'

Dean poured tea, surly, feeling demeaned. It was a mercy Ash was not around with his phone/camera. This was far more degrading than being caught in his Morris kit. Pouring tea! From a *teapot*! Into *cups and saucers! ON HIS KNEES!*

He ground his teeth, wishing he had some arsenic at hand with which to lace Lady Darkley's sugarless, milky tea.

As he passed Lady Darkley her tea, he stole a glance at her, looming over him like an Amazon. Except he'd always imagined Amazons to be beautiful, whereas Lady Darkley looked like a cross between a walnut and a horse: a long, tanned, wrinkled face, great sturdy legs, big feet. She was not looking at him, which was something of a relief, but she didn't say *thank you* either as she accepted her tea. Perhaps such a word did not exist in her plummy dialect. Or were slaves undeserving of such notice?

He handed a cup and saucer to his mother, realizing by the look on her face that she was not sold on this idea of the parish council. Why didn't she say so? Why act like a doormat?

He shuffled backwards on his knees, made ready to stand up, but at that moment Lady Darkley's eyes swept over him briefly before returning to fix his mother with a terrifying penetrative stare. One glance was enough. Dean found he dared not move again, in case he attracted her attention. And that was not all. A new and insidious fear gripped him: what if she really *could* read his mind?

The idea was irrational. Idiotic. Human beings did not have the ability to read minds. It was scientifically impossible.

But what if it *was* possible? What if it was a secret known only to a select few, kept hidden from science – kept hidden from him?

You're being a moron, he told himself: *there are no secret mind-readers, just as there are no panthers roaming the countryside.*

He couldn't quite convince himself. There was a million-to-one chance that mind-readers *did* exist – and it would be just his luck if Lady Darkley was one of them. What if she could see right through him? His blood ran cold, thinking of all the things she would see: guillotines, arsenic, walnuts, horses, sex, sex, sex—

Oh shit! Why did he have to think about sex at a time like this? As if Lady Darkley wasn't enough to put you off for life!

Except that nothing put you off, not if your name was Dean Morley and you were burdened with a runaway libido – even more of a slave to it than you were to Lady Darkley. It was all down to his genes. They were tyrants. He could almost hear them at times. 'Now look, sunshine: we only built this body of yours so that we could replicate ourselves. When are you going to get on with it? Because if you don't.... Well, let's just say we have our ways and means. We can ensure that your instincts drive you round the bend, don't think we can't.'

Agh! This was worse than a nightmare! He was trapped here on his knees with his brain going into meltdown, and there was nothing he could do about it! Or was there? Perhaps if he listened in to the conversation, it might anaesthetize the worst of the pain.

After all, that was the effect his mother's conversations usually had on him.

Lady Darkley had been going on and on non-stop for about an hour, raising her cup towards her mouth, lowering it, never letting it actually touch her lips. Finally his mother got a word in edgeways (no mean feat). She was asking about the village hall, seemed to want to book a slot for some reason – some exhibition or other.

Lady Darkley's cup hovered near her lips. 'Hmm ... I'm not sure. Is it really the sort of thing we want to encourage in the village? And Easter is our busiest time.'

'I *was* rather worried about that. But you see, if I could just get it settled – get somewhere booked – I would then have more time for other things ... the parish council, for instance.'

'There is that, I suppose.'

'And we were hoping ... I mean, naturally we thought ... if you would do us the honour ... a small opening ceremony...?'

Dean looked at his mother in some wonder. Had he actually just witnessed her being devious? Had she really just bribed the old battleaxe with the offer of opening the exhibition whilst simultaneously dangling a carrot in the form of the parish council? That was clever. Too clever. It couldn't possibly be intentional. It must be serendipity.

The alternative – that she was actually capable of manipulating people like that – was rather too worrying to contemplate.

'Well, of course, I would be quite willing to play any little part that was required, as it were.' Lady Darkley put her cup and saucer on the table. Peering into it, Dean was astonished to find the cup was empty. How on earth...?

'We would only require a week at most. The exhibition would not go on beyond that.'

'I see.' Lady Darkley selected a biscuit, bit into it with implausibly white teeth (fangs), and chewed thoughtfully. 'Now that I think of it, I may be able to fit you in after all. There is a sixtieth birthday booked for Easter Saturday – the Morrells – but I will tell them to rearrange....'

'Perhaps you yourself would like to contribute to the show, Imelda?'

'Well, let me see. There is a Stubbs you could borrow.'

'Oh, no, you misunderstand: it has to be your own work.'

'My dear woman, I hope you're not under the impression that I'm in any way artistic. I don't go in for that sort of thing, goodness me, no! One needs to be soft in the head to be an artist.' She selected another biscuit, forged on. 'I trust that this exhibition is not going to be *modern* art, Gwen. I can't be doing with all that rubbish – pickled sharks and so on. Modern it may be, but art it is not. In my book, pickling is something you do in the kitchen, not for display in a gallery. Why they wasted all that money on the Tate Modern is beyond me. Tate tripe would be nearer the mark.'

Dean's knees were killing him. He would be crippled for life, he could just see it. At the very least he'd get housemaid's knee. (What were the symptoms of housemaids' knee? He must look it up on the internet.) He was just plucking up courage to move – to ease his aching knees – when, without warning, Lady Darkley's eyes swivelled round to fix him with her piercing stare. Dean cowered. Being looked at by Lady Darkley was akin to being physically assaulted. There ought to have been a law against it.

He would never recover from this ordeal. He would need therapy.

'I believe,' said Lady Darkley thoughtfully (he knew she was still looking at him, even though he had his eyes firmly fixed on the carpet), 'that your son attends the college in town?'

'Yes, he does, he's—'

'My silly granddaughter has got it into her head that she wants to go there, too. Don't ask me why. I gave up trying to understand her long ago.'

'Teenagers can be—'

'I can't see what's wrong with the school she attends at the moment. It costs enough. But this college, now: is it quite *comme il faut*, as it were?'

'It's a very good college, from what one hears. Dean is doing very—'

'Yes, yes. But it was always my impression that such places were for children whose parents could not afford anything better.'

'Oh, I don't think ... at least, I'm sure....'

Dean stole a glance at his mother, wondering how she liked being lumped in with *parents who could not afford any better*. She looked demure – humble almost – sitting there with her hands folded in her lap like some old granny.

His eyes darted recklessly across the room to Lady Darkley. Was she going to say any more about her granddaughter? But for the moment she was quiescent, like a sleeping dragon. Her keen gaze had receded; she looked thoughtful.

He took the opportunity to shift his position so that his weight was not falling so directly on his knee caps. At a pinch he felt he could have crawled out of the room (like a worm), but, on balance, he decided to hang around, just in case Cally cropped up in conversation again.

He was in luck. Lady Darkley stirred, spoke in a distracted way, almost as if talking to herself. 'I shall have to keep a close eye on that gal. I don't want her going down the same road as her mother. *She* was impossible. Always smoking dope. She was a dope, in fact. There was something not quite right. But that's the way it is. One gets these anomalies, even in families with the most impeccable pedigrees. I suppose you know, Gwen, that my daughter ran away to Italy with some feckless hippy. They lived in a campervan. Cally was born there: in a campervan, in Italy, if you can believe it. In Calabria, to be exact. That's how she got her name. *Calabria!* Typical hippy name. They weren't married, of course.' Lady Darkley snorted with contempt.

Calabria, thought Dean. *Her name is Calabria.*

'Of course, as soon as I heard about the child I went straight out there, I flew to Italy. I told my daughter in no uncertain terms that she was free to waste her own life – I'd washed my hands of her by then – but that no grandchild of mine was going to be brought up in a *campervan* by a man with *dreadlocks*. "You're not fit to be that gal's mother," I told her. "I'm taking her with me." And I did.'

'Oh. I see.'

'She's illegitimate, of course, but that can't be helped. We all have our crosses to bear.'

Illegitimate, thought Dean reverently. Born in a campervan, in Italy. It couldn't get any better, any further from the boring norm.

Why had he never heard about it before? How come he'd never *known*? No wonder Cally was so fascinating!

'I'm afraid, Gwen, that one simply can't let one's feelings get in the way,' said Lady Darkley. 'One has to be firm with one's children – and one has to learn when to cut one's losses.' Dean could not be sure, but he thought she might have glanced at him as she said this. 'I do hope,' she added, menacingly, 'that there are no *hippies* at this so-called college?'

'Oh, no, Imelda … I mean, I don't … I'm sure….'

'Anyway, Gwen, I can't stay chatting.' Lady Darkley got to her feet, knotting her scarf, retrieving her handbag. 'I have to call in on the vicar. He does rather rely on my vetting his Sunday sermon. Now. My umbrella … my umbrella.' She patted her pockets as if her umbrella might have fallen in one of them unnoticed, then swung round to face Dean, clicking her fingers. 'You! My umbrella!'

Dean scrambled, half-crawling, into the hall, scooped the umbrella out of its corner, and handed it over meekly with bowed head as Lady Darkley swept past and out into the squally afternoon.

Gwen shut the front door. 'Well,' she said, letting out a breath, 'so that's over. And now, Dean, if you'd just help me tidy up a bit.'

'Do I have—' Dean bit his tongue, remembering not to use such a childish phrase, and, resigned, followed his mother back into the front room.

THIRTEEN

LYDIA HURRIED DOWN the smooth, newly resurfaced street past the smart wooden bus shelter, late for the meeting. But so what? It was their own fault, the rest of the committee. Saturday afternoon was a ridiculous time for a meeting. Saturday afternoon was when she did her shopping. Waitrose was less crowded on a Saturday afternoon, she could whip round in a flash so that Prize would not get impatient waiting in the car, looking forward to his run round the Country Park—

She tripped over a pot hole, nearly fell, managed to keep her balance (so much for the resurfaced roads). Coming to a halt, she found anger was bubbling up inside her. She wanted to scream. She couldn't go into the pub in this state. She needed a moment to herself, to gather her thoughts.

She went back to the bus shelter, sat down (might as well use it, no one else would). Why could she not get it into her thick head that Prize was dead? He was gone. Finished. Incinerated. Forget him. Stop harping on. Move forward.

But it was not her slip over Prize that was making her angry. It was something else entirely.

It was Richard.

Deep breaths ... count to ten ... eight, nine, ten ... and relax....

She looked out from the bus shelter at the damp, grey day: a dead sort of day at the fag-end of January, not a breath of wind to liven it up. But the smell of new wood was delicious. It was a very well-built shelter, very sturdy – even if had been constructed at the expense of the poor, downtrodden townspeople. (Was that what Terry had said? Something along those lines. But best not to bring Terry into it. She had enough on her plate as it was.)

She sighed. It was no good. However hard she tried to stay calm, her thoughts kept spiralling back to Richard. He'd turned up out of the blue earlier whilst she was unpacking her shopping. (Waitrose had been heaving, she hated shopping on Saturday morning, and all because of this bloody meeting. But what did it matter now how long it took to get the shopping done? It was not as if Prize would ever again be waiting in the car.) Richard had turned up. They were still using the excuse that Richard was coming to model for her and that the … other stuff … happened each time by accident. To be fair, it wasn't entirely an excuse. Although she never actually got any painting done when Richard was around, St George was none the less slowly taking shape and Richard had a starring role. The picture had become something of an allegory on the struggle of youth to escape the tyranny of the old. St George – Richard – represented heroic youth turning the tables on the aged dragon. The dragon looked suspiciously like Lady Darkley, but that was purely coincidental (wasn't it?).

Today, for the first time, Richard had begun to irritate her, swanning in like he owned the place, expecting her to drop everything (including her knickers), when all she had really wanted was to finish putting her shopping away. (Had she really bought tins of dog food? Surely she wouldn't have been so stupid.)

They had got down to it – not the posing and the painting, the other stuff – and her irritation had prompted her to take more of the initiative. She was, after all, a femme fatale (ho, ho). He was supposed to be putty in her hands, not vice versa.

Her attempts to spice things up had not been appreciated.

'What are you doing? Get off me! Leave my boxers alone! Stop it!' He had been gruff – rude – had pulled away, glowering like a scolded child.

'I don't see what your problem is. What have you got against being naked? I am naked, look!'

'It's cold in here, freezing,' he had grumbled. 'You should get central heating.'

'I don't need central heating. I have a nice cool fire. And if that isn't enough for you, then let me warm you—' She had climbed on top of him, let her hands wander as she imagined a femme fatale's would, but he had pushed her roughly away, had sat up on the sofa hunched over his knees.

'I told you not to touch me.'

'Excuse me?'

'Down there: don't touch me down there.'

As she pulled the blanket up to cover herself, she had begun to resent the fact that he had her at a disadvantage – that she was expected to strip off completely whereas he kept his underwear on, sometimes his T-shirt too, as if he'd popped into a knocking shop for a quickie and it wasn't worth his while taking his clothes off. She'd begun to point this out to him, keeping it nice and simple so that he would comprehend, but without warning he'd flared up, told her that she was making a fuss over nothing, demanded to know why she had to spoil things when they'd been quite happy going on as they were.

She didn't understand men. They obviously saw the world in a different way, lived in a parallel universe. Nigel was the only man she had ever got to know in detail, but was Nigel representative? Were other men *really* like Nigel? Nigel, like Richard, had been liable to flare up without warning. Like Richard and his underwear, Nigel too had had his little foibles.

Sitting in one corner of the bus shelter, Lydia wrapped her scarf closer, shivering as she thought of Nigel and his nipples. She knew she ought to be laughing about it but was wary of doing so – even here in the safety of the new bus shelter with Nigel hundreds of miles away, perhaps thousands (he'd always wanted a holiday home in the Med for when the English winter got too much, and now that he'd married into Polly or Molly's money...).

She reasoned with herself. Laugh, she said: laugh. Because it had been ludicrous, Nigel and his nipples. 'These are my control buttons, darling.' Said with a straight face, as if he'd meant it seriously. Perhaps he had. She wouldn't have put it past him. 'These are my control buttons. This one turns me on, and this one sends me into overdrive!'

But it was no good, she couldn't find it funny. She remembered only too well the consequences of laughing at Nigel out of turn. ('Oh darling, darling Lyddie, I'm so sorry, I wouldn't hurt you for the world, please say you'll forgive me. You don't know what it's like, the effect you have on me, the extremes you drive me to....') She shrank into the corner, shivering violently, his voice loud in her head, almost real. And was that his aftershave she could smell?

She sniffed apprehensively – but then breathed deeply, relieved, because all she could smell was new wood: new wood and nothing else. This bus shelter had yet to acquire a tinge of urine or a whiff of vomit. She hugged herself, feeling the cold as she tried to rationalize Nigel out of existence. It was Richard's unexpected anger that had caused all this, stirring up memories of Nigel. But Richard was completely different to Nigel, much younger, without the build of a rugby player. He smelt differently too, no expensive aftershave like Nigel (no cheap body spray like Dean, either); Richard had a clean and subtle smell, a hint of soap and shampoo, a touch of deodorant, a whisper of sweat, a lingering layer of washing powder (he obviously put far too much powder in his machine, someone should tell him).

But that someone will not be me, she said, getting up to stamp her feet. Why should she worry about Richard? Why should she think of him at all? She would wash her hands of him. *Don't touch me*, indeed!

'Do you think your body is a temple? Do you think I might defile it if I touch it with my unworthy hands?'

To be fair, he had been apologetic, the flash of anger swiftly fading. 'I'm sorry, all right? I shouldn't have shouted.' (But Nigel too had sounded plausible when he apologized.) 'Let me make it up to you,' Richard had continued. 'Think of *your* body as a temple. Let me worship it. Lie back and enjoy.'

Stamping her feet in the bus shelter, Lydia realized that if she truly wanted to be rid of Richard then she should have sent him packing at that point instead of letting him talk her round. Had she always been so compliant and forbearing, or was that Nigel's doing? She felt a pang at the thought, lamenting the Lydia who might have been, the Lydia who had never met Nigel.

Stamping her feet harder to get the circulation going, she also stamped out thoughts of Richard, memories of Nigel. If she didn't get a move on, the meeting would be over before she got there. Not that she was keen to be there: it was just that she needed to keep an eye on things. If wrecking the entire project was out of the question, then she could at least keep it under control, make sure it impinged on her time as little as possible.

She set off down the hill.

In the pub, the lunchtime rush was over, the lounge bar all but empty. Gwen was buying drinks, the landlord serving. At a table near the fire sat Sandra, the Stasi and Dick Emery. Lydia joined Gwen at the bar and asked for a gin and tonic.

Waggling her eyebrows in the direction of the vicar, she said in an undertone, 'What is Dick Emery doing here?'

'We really shouldn't call him that,' murmured Gwen, handing the landlord a twenty pound note. 'His name is Reverend Harker.'

'But what's he doing here?'

'He's joined the committee. Imelda Darkley rang me—'

'Lady Darkley? What's it to do with her?'

Gwen looked shifty as she accepted her change. 'Imelda felt that as the exhibition is a village event, one of the village movers and shakers should be on the committee. She is far too busy herself—'

'And so she nominated Dick Emery?'

'I really couldn't put her off.' Gwen was apologetic.

Lydia felt a sense of despair as she took her place at the table. The exhibition was beginning to take on a life of its own.

'Well, ladies.' Dick Emery smiled, displaying his prominent teeth. 'Shall we call the meeting to order?'

To call them *ladies* was somehow faintly disparaging, Lydia felt – especially as the vicar was the most feminine one amongst them (with the possible exception of Gwen). She took a sip of her gin and tonic and watched the Stasi take an unladylike swig of her pint of lager.

The meeting got under way. Nothing was decided. No one could guess how many (or how few) exhibits they would have. Lydia tentatively promised St George. Gwen ventured to say that she might have one or two pieces. The landlady chipped in with morsels of gossip.

Proceedings were drawing to a close when, unexpectedly, Richard walked in. He didn't look round, went straight to the bar, began to laugh and joke with the landlord. Lydia felt herself bristling all over like a cat. She reached for the last of her gin and tonic as Sandra got to her feet, pulling on her coat.

'Well, there's my boyfriend come to pick me up.'

Lydia, caught in the process of swallowing her final mouthful, spluttered, choked, sprayed gin and tonic across the table. Dick Emery recoiled, his lips drawing back over his big teeth like a horse's in his surprise.

'Miss Taylor! I say! Are you quite all right?'

The Stasi, unfazed, laughed her nasal laugh. 'Choke up chicken, ha ha ha! I'll get a cloth, shall I?'

'So sorry … went down the wrong way … so very sorry….' Out of the corner of her eye, Lydia saw Sandra greet Richard with a kiss on the cheek, put her arm round him. Richard put *his* arm round *her*, began to stroke her hair just as he'd stroked Lydia's the day after Boxing Day.

What had Sandra said? Her *boyfriend*!

There had to be some mistake. It couldn't be the real Richard. Did he have a doppelganger? But if so, then the doppelganger was wearing the same hoody, the same grubby jeans that Richard had been wearing at the cottage earlier. The same boxer shorts, too, presumably: the ones he'd refused to take off.

This was no doppelganger, Lydia told herself. There could only be one Richard. He must be the new boyfriend Sandra had been so excited about in the run-up to Christmas. And Sandra – the penny finally dropped – Sandra must be the Sandra Hays who had so disgusted Dean by being won over by Richard's vodka jelly at that unfortunate party.

A little group was now leaving the pub, chatting and laughing: Gwen, Dick Emery, Sandra, Richard. The last to leave, Richard glanced behind him. For a split second, Lydia met his eye. There was no jack-the-lad grin. He might have even looked a little sheepish, but before she could make up her mind about this, he was gone. The outside door banged shut.

The landlady had collected the empties, wiped the table and now paused, looking round speculatively.

'Well,' she said, as if unimpressed by what she saw, 'I might as well have another lager.'

'Let me....' Lydia jumped up, quite willing to buy the Stasi a lager if it gave her the opportunity to order a double gin at the same time. She needed it. Her head was spinning.

'Let's go through to the bar,' said the landlady. 'It's a bit quiet in here.'

Quiet was exactly what Lydia wanted, but she did not have the wherewithal to argue. The world had been knocked out of kilter; it was like standing on the deck of a ship in a gale. It was all she could do to keep her balance.

In the public bar only a few lunchtime stragglers remained at this time in the afternoon. Old George was prominent amongst them, holding court in his seat by the window, fulminating against the council (what had Basil done now?). The landlady perched herself on the edge of the skittles table, her feet dangling (she was short in stature as well as amply proportioned). Lydia took the seat set into the wall by the fireplace, out of the way.

She sipped her gin and tonic, unable to concentrate on what George was saying (even the Stasi found it difficult to get a word in when Old George had had a few). All she could think about was Richard and Sandra, Sandra and Richard, Richard, Richard, Richard. *How*, Lydia asked herself, *could I have been so stupid?*

Very easily, her mother would have said. (Where was the old bat today?)

Lydia rallied, the gin working its magic. *I am not in the wrong,* she told herself. *It is Richard who is at fault. I acted in good faith. All I am guilty of is getting carried away. Love, of course, doesn't enter into it, but I was beguiled by the idea that he liked me, wanted me. I should have known that he was just using me. How ironic that Dean, of all people, was right all along: Richard is a bastard.*

Feeling the cold and shivering as she had shivered in the bus shelter, Lydia stretched her booted feet towards the fire. Ice cubes rattled in her glass: her hand was shaking. What made it all so much worse was that she *liked* Sandra, she had wanted it to work out for the girl, this paragon of a boyfriend. *I might have known,* thought Lydia, *that it was too good to be true. Perhaps Nigel was not such an aberration after all.*

Would it be possible to warn Sandra in some way, drop a hint?

Not very well, Lydia admitted. Not without dropping herself in it at the same time.

The worst of it was, St George was ruined now. The painting would have to be scrapped. It had been produced under false pretences. How could one in all honesty depict the triumph of Youth over Age when Youth turned out to be a spineless, double-dealing, degenerate—

'Are you all right, missus?' Lydia surfaced from her thoughts to find George peering at her through his alcoholic haze. 'You're away with the fairies over there in the corner.'

All eyes turned to look at her. For a second she felt horribly exposed, as if the onlookers could see inside her – could see the patched-up, glued-together state of her, clinging on by her finger-tips. But then, thankfully, there came an interruption from outside: the clip-clop sound of a horse being ridden along the High Street. George turned in his seat to watch. Lydia from her place by the fire could not see out of the window.

'It's that girl from Overblown Manor,' said George. (It was a village joke to refer to Lady Darkley's home at Overbourne Hall as *Overblown Manor/Manner*.) 'Two farthings short of a penny, that one. Takes after her mother. Takes after her grandmother, too, for that matter. Look at her, nose in the air.'

'Her name is Cally. She goes to boarding school.' The Stasi, of course, knew all the details. 'Her mother was – let's say – somewhat eccentric. Oh, look! Her horse has just done its business all over the road, ha ha ha!'

'I'll have that for my garden!' cried George, getting unsteadily to his feet. 'Good bit of manure, that.'

He pulled a plastic bag from his pocket, grabbed the coal shovel from by the fire. There was a draught of cold air as he left the bar. Flames leapt up in the grate to die down again into an orange glow.

'He'll have to be quick.' The landlady was leaning across from her position on the skittles table to watch the goings-on outside. 'Mrs Pole has just turned up with a bucket and spade.'

Lydia was drawn from her seat by the fire to stand by the window. Out in the middle of the street, the horse's excrement was gently steaming on the newly surfaced road. Old George, wobbling slightly, was standing over it, his plastic bag in one hand, the coal shovel in the other. Facing him was the bird-like figure of Mrs Pole with a bucket and spade.

'A funny one, that Mrs Pole,' said the Stasi. 'Won't be seen dead in the pub, but she doesn't mind scraping horse's doings off the—'

Lydia interrupted, a spurt of laughter bursting out of her as if from nowhere. 'Drawn spades at twenty paces!'

As the stand-off continued outside, Lydia was astonished to find more and more laughter hiccoughing out of her. Soon she was hooting, tears running down her face. The landlady turned away from the window to watch her, a bemused expression on her face, as if she was missing out on something.

If only she knew, thought Lydia: and the thought made her laugh all the more.

FOURTEEN

SLUMPED IN A low chair in the common room, beset by drizzling music and mindless chatter, grey light seeping through wide rather grimy windows, Dean watched as Sandra came in through the open doorway to stand poised, looking round.

It was funny how you could go off people, he thought, as Sandra caught sight of him (and Charley and Ash) and began making her way across the room. Once upon a time – as much as a month ago – he had thought Sandra the epitome of beauty. But now: now you could almost see Richard's grubby paw-prints all over her. And what about those freckles? How had he ever convinced himself that he *liked* freckles? (Cally didn't have freckles.)

His former feelings for Sandra had been very primitive, Dean reasoned. He had idolized her the way pagans idolize a totem pole or ... or the sun. They are ignorant of the true nature of their gods. The sun, for instance, is not a divine being. It is a fiery ball of hydrogen with a surface temperature of five thousand degrees. Dean knew this. He also now knew about girls – what girls were really like, their surface temperature and everything. They were no longer a mystery to him, since the panther had ... had....

Whatever.

He was not sure how he felt about Sandra now. He felt sorry for her, he supposed, having Richard as a boyfriend. She ought to have known better than to get entangled with someone like Richard, but perhaps she couldn't help herself. Girls were like that, running after the meatheads, not sophisticated enough to appreciate more refined attributes such as a superior brain, a wealth of knowledge, *intelligence*. Poor Sandra. She had no idea that Richard was a sort of reverse King Midas: everything he touched turned to shit.

'Hello, boys.' Sandra looked down at them. 'Budge up, Ash. Let me sit down.'

'How do, Sandra.' Charley had his cool-as-fuck face on. 'Haven't seen you around much lately.'

'I've been too busy.'

'Busy doing what?'

'This and that.' She smiled: a dreamy smile.

Busy with Richard was what she meant, thought Dean. How deluded could you get?

'I'm helping to organize an exhibition,' she added.

Charley raised a cool-as-fuck eyebrow. 'Oh yeah?'

'It's an art exhibition but for ordinary people. Anyone can have a go. I might enter a couple of my collages.'

'Art is a pile of pants,' said Charley. 'Isn't that right, Ash?'

He waited for Ash to concur, but Ash had fallen into a trance, mesmerized by Sandra's proximity and the fact that she was rocking back and forth and wiggling about so that her knee kept brushing against his thigh. You could almost see the sparks coming off him.

'That's just the sort of comment I'd expect from you, Charley,' said Sandra.

'That's a slur on my character, that is.'

'What character is that, then, Charley?' said Sandra pertly before turning towards Dean, her knee scraping all along Ash's thigh as she did so. Ash's eyes bulged. He looked like he was about to pass out.

'Are you entering anything in the exhibition, Dean?'

'Dunno.' Dean gave her a superior look. He wasn't gullible like Ash: she couldn't cast a spell over him any longer.

'You should give it a go. It'll be fun.'

'Morley's not an artist. He's a geek.'

'Don't be so horrible, Charley. He's not a geek, are you, Dean?'

The way she looked at him, like he was deserving of charity or something, made him want to yell out, *Why are you lying, Sandra? You know I'm the biggest geek that ever lived!* But he didn't say anything. Merely shrugged.

From his side-on perspective, Dean could see that Charley's eyes kept sliding down, distending as they took in the sight of Sandra's blouse stretched tight across her breasts. Charley could get away with doing things like that because girls mistook his cool-as-fuck face for butter-wouldn't-melt. He had a sort of angelic, unblemished look about him. Nobody would ever guess what a pervert he was; whereas with Ash it was written all over him. Ash, in fact, was a borderline freak. Dean might have even felt a certain comradeship with him – had Ash not bluetoothed photos all round the college of Dean in his Morris gear.

Sandra was waving at someone. 'Look! There's Cally!'

Indeed it was. Cally with her straight hair (it had been curly when she was younger), a red polo-neck jumper, blue skirt, pale green tights, flat prosaic black shoes.

'Cally! Over here!'

'The new girl,' said Charley. 'Stuck up.'

'No she's not,' said Sandra. 'You have to make an effort, that's all. She's shy.'

'Inbred. The upper classes are always inbred.'

'She's not upper class.'

'She's up herself.'

'Shut up, Charley. She'll hear you.'

Cally's arrival caused an upheaval in the seating arrangements. Ash was sent over to perch on the edge of Charley's chair. Cally squeezed in next to Sandra. Dean gazed at Cally. *Calabria*, he thought. *Her name is Calabria*. It said it all.

Cally and Sandra were talking, but Dean could only hear Cally's voice. '... what exhibition ... oh, I see: I'm not really into painting and all that ... well, riding mainly: horse riding ... he's called Phlogiston, he's not mine really, he belongs to Grandma ... I live with Grandma, my mother's not, er, not around....' What a voice. Sublime.

It was Charley's unaccustomed silence which roused Dean out of his stupor. It was most unlike Charley not to have elbowed his way into the conversation. Dean tore his eyes away from Cally, looked over at Charley, who had slid right down in his chair so that his bum was hanging over the edge. He had his head on one side, too – trying, Dean realized, to see up Cally's skirt.

Dean was aware of his fists clenching; he experienced an incomprehensible desire to punch Charley in the face.

What was going on? Charley pissed him off a lot of the time, but Dean had never felt the need to punch him before – not even when Charley had made sarky comments about Dean's spots clearing up 'at long last'. (Charley never had spots, never exhibited any outward sign of his utter depravity. There had to be a picture of Charley in an attic somewhere that you'd need health-and-safety goggles to look at.)

If I wasn't such a freak, thought Dean, *I'd be able to think up a really clever remark to put Charley in his place.* But it was no use. He wasn't a smart alec like that. It was difficult enough to talk at all, hidebound by his inhibitions as he was. Sometimes it felt like he was trapped inside his own body, would never get out. What was shyness *for*, anyway? Why had it evolved in the first place? (Cally was shy: Sandra had said so.)

'There's Miss Taylor!' said Sandra suddenly. 'She's helping with the exhibition too.'

Dean didn't dare look, felt his cheeks begin to glow.

'Miss Taylor!' Charley was disparaging. 'She's whacko.'

'Menopausal,' said Ash knowledgeably.

'Her clothes!' Cally giggled.

'I like the way she dresses.' Sandra stuck her nose in the air. 'She's an individual.'

'Charity shop chic,' mocked Charley. 'And she's old. Past it.'

'She's not that old, Charley.' Sandra knew best. 'She's only about forty.'

'Forty's, like, *ancient*.'

'Grandma says she's a misfit,' Cally put in.

'Miss Fit.' Ash guffawed. 'Fit Miss Fit.'

'Destined to remain a miss for ever,' said Charley. 'Though Ash would still do her. Ash would do anything with a pulse.'

'Shut up, Charley man, innit! Nobody would do an old bird like what she is!'

Dean sank down in his chair, wondering if his cheeks were as red as they felt. He wished the panther would go away, wished they'd shut up about her. Why had she come in here anyway? Who was she talking to? Dying of embarrassment, he couldn't bring himself to look at Cally anymore. Perhaps it was for the best. He didn't want people to get the wrong idea, to think he was interested in her or something. He didn't *fancy* her. He had a perfectly understandable scientific curiosity about her, that was all.

But the others wouldn't see it that way.

Oh God, why didn't the bell go? *Anything* to put him out of his misery!

FIFTEEN

LEAVING HER CAR in the car park where the open-air swimming pool used to be, Lydia walked past Basil's latest monstrosity – an arcade of empty shops to join all the other empty shops ornamenting the town – and then, dodging marauding packs of half-term kids, she slipped into Boots to buy a pregnancy test kit.

'It's not for me,' she told the girl on the till, whom she remembered teaching a year or so back. 'It's for a friend.'

'Would you like any stamps or top-ups?'

'No thanks.'

'Have you got a Boots card?'

'No.'

Would you like a Boots card?'

'No.'

'Pease check the amount and enter your PIN number.'

'You don't need to say "number".' Lydia did her best to be enlightening, continuing where she'd left off in college. 'The N in PIN stands for number, so you don't need to say it again.'

The girl's smile didn't falter. 'Thank you. Next, please.'

Nice to know, thought Lydia as she exited Boots, hurried past Waitrose, that some things never change. There had always been something impenetrable about that girl. You might as well have banged your head against a brick wall.

Popping into Wetherspoons, she climbed the stairs to make use of their prize-winning toilets, too impatient to wait until she got home before using the test kit.

Sitting on the toilet lid, she awaited the verdict.

It can't be the menopause, she told herself: I'm not nearly old enough. But wouldn't the menopause be preferable? Or maybe it was simply down to stress: Prize, Richard, that sort of thing.

She was most definitely not pregnant.

She looked down, removed her hand that had been shielding the indicator.

She was pregnant. Pregnant.

Stuffing the test kit paraphernalia into her bag, she flushed the toilet, let herself out of the cubicle, washed her hands, looked at herself in the mirror. Blooming? Glowing? Pasty would be nearer the mark. Gaunt. Bags under her eyes. Those pernicious grey hairs.

Going down to the bar, she ordered a gin and tonic.

'Would you like to double up for an extra pound?' asked the girl behind the bar.

'Yes. Why not. A double. No, on second thoughts, make that a double double.'

'A double double?'

'A double double. Two doubles. Two times two.'

'In the same glass?'

'That's right, you've got it.'

'With ice and lemon?'

'Spot on.'

'And tonic?'

'And tonic.'

'One bottle of tonic or two?'

Oh Lord, this could go on for ever. Didn't I teach her, too, at one time? Didn't do her much good. But this girl here, and the one in Boots, they hadn't got themselves pregnant: they had more sense, so the last laugh was theirs.

Finally in possession of her drink, Lydia threaded her way between tables to a sofa in one corner, sank down feeling suddenly weary, as if hours and hours had passed since she'd been sitting in the toilet with the test kit.

They weren't very reliable, anyway, those kits.

It was probably a false alarm. A mistake.

A mistake? You bet it was a mistake!

She turned to look out of the window. The pavement was glistening in the February dusk (it had started drizzling), reflecting the bright lights of Waitrose opposite. People passed in and out of the super-market, pushing trolleys and baby buggies, laden down with shopping bags, juggling car keys and purses, perusing shopping lists. A fat woman eating a Mars bar turned to yell and scream at a reluctant toddler who was grizzling and rubbing its eyes. (*That will be me in a couple of years' time.*) An elderly lady with a walking stick stopped to talk to the Big Issue man. The Big Issue man's dog looked miserable, rain dripping off its nose. (*He's still got his dog; it's not fair.*)

'You shouldn't be drinking in your condition.'

The sudden voice made her jump, choking on her gin. It took her a moment or two to realize that there was no one there – no one near enough to have spoken directly into her ear, anyway. The voice was a disembodied one. Her mother's ghost.

That was all she needed.

'Why don't you just mind your own business,' she hissed.

'This is what happens, my girl, when you carry on like a trollop.'

'Do you think, just this once, you could be supportive in my hour of need?'

'Supportive? Ha! That's a laugh. Why should I support you? When have you ever supported me? What did you ever do for me when I was alive? What do you do for me *now*? You don't put flowers on my grave, you never visit. You're an ungrateful, unnatural child.'

'Why would you want flowers? You always hated flowers.'

'Oh-ho! Trying to be clever now, are we? Well, you'll see. You'll understand what I mean when your child grows up and abandons you, leaves you high and dry, *neglects* you!'

'I'm not having a child. I'm going to abort it.' Lydia spoke without thinking, as she so often had when speaking to her mother. Her mother knew (had known) just how to tip her off balance.

But an abortion: she hadn't thought of that until now. It would solve everything.

Her mother's ghost's voice was cold. 'Well! That's you all over! Selfish.'

'Oh, go away. You're dead. I can't hear you.'

'I don't know what I did to deserve a daughter like you.'

'La-la-lah. La-la-lah.'

'In fact, I don't believe you are my daughter. You're a changeling.'

'LA-LA-LAH. LA-LA-LAH.'

'I wash my hands of you.'

'Good.' Lydia scrambled to her feet, felt a bit wobbly, leaned on the low table for support. The gin had gone straight to her head. That was what came of forgetting lunch. But she couldn't be expected to remember everything. Her head was crammed full as it was.

Another double double. That was the solution. Blot out her mother's ghost. Blot out everything, if she was lucky.

She managed to negotiate her way to the bar and back, sank thankfully onto the sofa, listened suspiciously but – heaven be praised – there was no further sound from the ghost.

She looked out of the window again. It was raining heavily now; the street was empty, litter the only evidence that people had ever been there. The *Big Issue* man had gone, along with his poor dog.

Prize had hated getting wet.

'Hello.'

Another unexpected voice. This one, however, was a masculine voice – diffident, quietly spoken – and belonged to a real, live body, not a ghost.

'Mind if I...?'

He sat in the big comfy chair opposite, placed his pint of real ale on the low table. It would be real ale, of course.

Terry, she said to herself: *his name is Terry.*

'I don't like to impose, but there's nowhere else to sit.'

Was this true? She glanced around, found that the pub was crowded, noisy, the bar busy with queuing customers. When had all that happened?

Focusing her eyes on Terry, she racked her brains for something to say, but found her gaze drawn to his beard. It reminded her of the vet ('It's only an animal, Mrs Taylor...'). But Terry was nothing like the vet. He was not bald, he had a thick thatch of hair on his head. She could see raindrops in it, glistening silver. His face, she thought, looked rather square, ruled off by the margins of his beard and the hair falling across his forehead.

Oh, Lord, this was ridiculous. She must say something.

'Have you had any luck getting the roads resurfaced?' (That would do.)

'Don't get me started. They're more slippery than snakes down at that council. The Tories are bad enough, but the officers....'

He was off. Her opening gambit had been successful. Not that she was the least interested in roads or the council, but Terry was quite loquacious on the subject, which meant she wouldn't need to think of anything else to say. Her brain was in no state for thinking.

His voice – rumbling, growling, grumbling – was strangely comforting after the shrill and piercing tones of her mother.

'... roads are down to the county council, of course, but council officers are the same everywhere, they have their own agenda....'

'Oh? Really? Hmm.'

'... bamboozle and stall you ...'

'Ah.'

'... planning policy is conjured from thin air, developers ride roughshod ...'

'I see, yes.'

'... mistakes costing millions are quietly swept under the carpet—' He stopped, peered at her. 'Sorry, but are you all right? You've gone a most peculiar colour.'

'I'm pregnant.'

For a split second she did not realize that she'd said it aloud. It had been reverberating inside her head ever since she'd done the test – *pregnant, pregnant, pregnant*. Now it had slipped out by mistake, stopping Terry in his tracks.

The gravity of her words slowly sank in. She hadn't got to grips with it herself yet, and already she was announcing it to all and sundry. She might as well tell the whole pub while she was at it, why not? Did all women get like this as they drew near to forty, lurching from one crisis to another? This, though, was the last straw.

She picked up her glass, gulped gin and tonic, looking at the blank expression on Terry's square, bearded face. 'Well?' she said. 'Aren't you going to say anything?'

'I ... er ... that is ... I mean, should you be drinking, in your ... condition?'

Anger surged. 'That is none of your business. Who do you think you are, my mother?'

'Sorry. I didn't mean to ... I'm ... sorry.' He looked like he meant it too.

Anger drained away as quickly as it had come. She said in a flat voice, 'It is me who should be sorry, I shouldn't have told you, it has nothing to do with you.' Words kept coming. She couldn't stop them. 'I don't know why I mentioned it, why I blurted it out. I am going mad, that's the problem. It's no laughing matter. You don't realize. I have conversations with my microwave, I imagine I can hear my mother's ghost, I do the most ridiculous things, I had sex with an eighteen-year-old boy by the side of the road. Why am I telling you all this? You are a total stranger, a—'

'Not quite a stranger,' said Terry quietly.

'Not quite? Well, we are colleagues, I suppose. I wouldn't want you to think I am like this all the time. I'm not. Usually I have more control. It's because my dog died. My dog died. And then I threw his basket away. Why did I do that? Why? I have nothing to remember him by. I tried to paint a picture but it came out all wrong. But what use is a picture? It's *him* I want, *him*, Prize, my darling— Oh, goodness, I seem to be crying. Oh, how silly, all these tears. And I don't appear to have a tissue. Fancy coming out without a tissue. I really am going ... going—'

She was scrabbling in her bag as tears slid down her cheeks, leaked into her mouth, dripped off her chin. Whatever would Terry think? Oh, but he wasn't there, he had gone, and no wonder. No, wait a minute, he was back.

'Here.' He handed her half a dozen white napkins. 'They're quite clean. I fetched them from the bar.'

'Thank you, that's very kind, you really shouldn't have bothered, so very nice of you.' She dabbed her eyes, tried to smile, but she seemed to have forgotten how to, her mouth was all twisted. 'He was only ten, my dog. No age. It was cancer. There was nothing anyone could have done.' She dabbed again, thrust the sodden napkins into her bag, straightened her skirt. 'I'm so sorry. It's ridiculous to get like this over a dog.'

'A bereavement is a bereavement. It doesn't matter if it's animal or human. It hurts just the same.'

'Yes, you are right. How clever of you. How perceptive.' Could it really be true, a man who understood, who sympathized? But she had not really thought of him as a man until now. He seemed curiously sexless, an odd sort of creature, diffident one moment, bombastic the next, and yet there was a sort of gentleness about him that one didn't notice most of the time – perhaps because he was so maladroit. One didn't notice him much at all, come to think of it – not really. He looked so mundane.

But that was because he *was* mundane, she told herself, snapping her bag shut, pushing her drink away from her. All he'd done was fetch some napkins and she was making him into some sort of saint. She'd be falling into bed with him next, if she didn't watch it. She'd already made some deplorable errors of judgement – telling him about the baby, her mother's ghost, Prize. If she didn't leave immediately, there was no knowing what might happen.

She got up.

He half rose out of his chair. 'Are you sure you're...?'

'Yes, quite sure.'

'You don't want me to...?'

'No need. I am more than capable. I had a silly moment of weakness but it's passed, it's over. I shall be fine now. Thank you so much for the napkins. Goodbye!'

She flung the last words over her shoulder, couldn't get away quick enough, weaving through the crowds to the exit. Outside it was still raining. She hurried through the deserted streets to the car park where the open-air pool used to be, got in her car, slammed the door, pulled on the seat belt.

Now. All she had to do was pilot her way home and she'd be safe. She could go to ground in her little cottage, forget about Terry, forget about everything; shut the world out, cocoon herself in blankets.

But when she reached home, a nasty surprise awaited her. Richard's rusty car was parked on her drive. Richard himself was loitering by her door.

Her heart sank.

She pulled over, parked on the side of the road, squashed thoughts of escape: it was too late for that, he had seen her, she would have to face him now. If only she didn't feel so drained, so empty. But it shouldn't take too much of an effort to put Richard in his place.

Getting out of her car, locking the door, she saw out of the corner of her eye a flicker of movement in the lit window of the house next door: Mr or Mrs Wetherby – or both – watching through the net curtains. Lydia turned, waved. The curtains billowed, then were still. But she realized she would have to take Richard inside. The last thing she wanted was to air her dirty laundry with the Wetherbys spying on her.

'I thought you were at work at this time of day.' She pushed Richard aside, unlocked the door.

'I'm on earlies this week. I finished hours ago.'

'Oh.' She picked up the post. Bills and junk mail. Why did this make her feel under attack, as if someone was targeting her out of malice?

Richard followed her into the kitchen, watched her circumspectly as she tossed the post aside, put the kettle on.

'I sense hostility,' he said at last.

Oh good, not so thick-skinned after all. 'Shall we talk about Sandra?'

'Ah.' Hovering in the doorway, Richard looked like he might be making his mind up whether to make a break for it or not.

'Is that all you've got to say for yourself?'

He rubbed his jaw, fiddled with something in his pocket. 'You're jealous. Is that it?'

'You really are the most self-centred—'

'Yeah, yeah. I've heard it all before.'

'You'll hear it all again.'

'I tell you what, why don't we just leave it? I could do without the aggro.'

He was backing out of the door now, was definitely going to run. She lassoed him with, 'You should have thought of that before you started anything.'

'Me start it?' He stopped, held his ground. 'What about you, throwing yourself at me?'

A whisper, like the faintest of echoes: *trollop*. 'Stop avoiding the issue.'

'What is the issue? You knew it was just a laugh, a bit of fun. You knew that.'

Did I? 'Not much of a laugh for Sandra. Not much fun for her.'

'I can't help that. She knows what I'm like. She's got her eyes open. And I haven't exactly ...'

'What?'

'Encouraged her.'

'But you haven't exactly told her the truth, am I right?'

'Look—' He took a step towards her and she flinched, backed away. She felt the work surface behind her, knew she was trapped. He seemed to loom over her, casting a menacing shadow.

This was Richard, she told herself. She had nothing to fear from Richard. It was old habits dying hard that made her cringe and cower.

But weren't all men the same when it came down to it? Why should she let them get away with it?

'Your bit of fun,' she said, gripping the work surface behind her, steadying herself, 'might cost you more than you bargained for.'

'What do you mean?' he asked, suspicious.

'I'm pregnant. I'm going to have your baby.'

That shut him up. That made him go pale. Very pale, in fact. Like he was about to pass out.

It couldn't be as much of a shock as all that, surely?

'It's not mine,' he said at last, his voice rather unsteady. 'You can't pin that on me.'

'Oh, really?' A part of her was disappointed. He didn't even have the guts to own up to his mistakes. The last of her illusions vanished into the February dusk. What had she ever seen in him? 'I would have thought at your age you would know how babies are made.' She said venomously, 'They are not found under gooseberry bushes, you know.'

'You don't know what you're talking about. You haven't a clue.'

'Trying to wriggle out of your responsibilities?'

'I'm not ... you don't....' His voice rose, cracked. 'Just ... just fuck off! Fuck off!'

He turned on his heel and fled. She heard the front door slam, heard his car cough into life. She wanted to chase after him, to make him face up to things, to rub his nose in it, and to hell with the Wetherbys. But suddenly she felt terribly weak, as if the stuffing had been knocked out of her. She sank down towards the kitchen floor, her legs folding underneath her. As she listened to his car backing precipitously up the drive, she was just glad he'd gone when he did, that he hadn't been here to witness this collapse.

As she sat there with her back against a cupboard door, she heard in the silence a faint but distinct sound: a contemptuous noise made in the back of the throat.

'Humph!'

She curled up on the lino, trying to protect herself, but she had no defence when there weren't even any words to block out.

It had always been what her mother *didn't* say that had hurt the most.

SIXTEEN

GWEN LET HERSELF out of the house with a sinking feeling. It was no good saying that she was just popping out for a breath of fresh air. She knew very well what she was up to, and she just couldn't help herself.

It was not as if she cared about the exhibition one way or the other, she said, checking in her bag to make sure she had her keys before pulling the door to. She had not wanted anything to do with it, had been more or less bamboozled into getting involved. But now that she was involved, she could not just let it lie. She wanted things to happen, she needed progress to be made. After all, time was getting on, February was almost over, Easter would be upon them before they knew it. She could simply not bear to think of the rush and mess and confusion that would ensue if everything was left to the last minute. She hated the way some people bumbled along, not planning ahead. It brought her out in a cold sweat even to think about it. Organization was the key. Why didn't people realize?

This was why she was going to visit Lydia Taylor. It had nothing to do with fresh air – although the air this morning was wonderfully fresh and had, if she was not mistaken, a hint of spring about it. Well, perhaps not spring as such, but on a day like today one really believed that spring would come again, that it wasn't just a myth. The sun was shining, the thin clouds high and white, the patches of blue deep and vivid, and a blackbird was trilling, perched on a garden wall, watching her with a black beady eye as she turned right into Well Lane.

As Gwen reached the top of Lydia's drive, the Wetherbys were just getting into their car.

'Good morning, Mrs Collier.'

'Hello. Lovely morning. Are you off somewhere nice?' *Why must I make small talk when I am busy, on a mission? A simple 'good morning' would have sufficed.*

'Going into town. Lunch,' said Mr Wetherby. 'Calling on *her*, are you?' He nodded towards Lydia's cottage. 'You'll find she's already got a visitor.'

'Oh?'

'We always notice when people go up her drive.'

'Yes, I suppose one would.'

'Not that we snoop.'

'No, of course, one wouldn't—'

'There's a man in there.' He leaned forward, confidential. 'A man with a beard. She gets a lot of men visiting her just lately. Your son, for one, Richard—'

'Stepson.' Gwen bit her lip, annoyed. *I am starting to sound like Basil, pedantic; or, worse, like Dean, disassociating myself. Let them call him my son if they want, it's not as if I mind.* 'Richard has been helping with a painting, doing some modelling.'

'Ah. Yes. She's an *artist*, isn't she?' Mr Wetherby smiled, or grimaced (one could never tell which) and got into his car, slamming the door.

Gwen watched as the car stuttered into life before shooting out into the road (*There's going to be an accident one day if he doesn't start looking where he's going*). She felt rather soiled, not uncommon after an encounter with Mr Wetherby. It was not that he actually said anything one could put one's finger on; it was more his manner of speech, *artist* pronounced as if it was synonymous with *strumpet; man with a beard* suggesting that a beard was the mark of Cain. He was harmless to look at, Mr Wetherby, all bone and wrinkles: he must be eighty at least; but one could not help recoiling a little, as if he had bad breath. Which he didn't, to be fair: he was far too fastidious for that.

It was her own fault, Gwen reminded herself as she walked up Lydia's drive. One needn't do more than pass the time of day, one needn't start a conversation. The problem was that *good morning* on its own was so cold: anyone could say *good morning* and not even mean it, whereas Gwen did mean it and wanted people to know that she meant it. It led her to overcompensate, rather. Basil derided this habit. It was wasting one's time, he said. One should only ever do the absolute minimum or one squandered one's resources (making it sound as if there were only a finite number of times one could say *good morning*, as if the well would run dry). It was patently impossible, Basil insisted, to get on with *everyone*.

But if one didn't try, if one didn't even make the *effort*.... And whatever one thought of Donald Wetherby, he had not actually mentioned strumpets, the words *mark of Cain* had not passed his lips. Nor was it fair to tar his wife with the same brush, but if one didn't say 'good morning' to Mr Wetherby, one was somehow slighting Mrs Wetherby too. And the poor woman always looked so distracted. She hardly ever got a word in edgeways, either. Imagine being trapped in a marriage like that.

In the silence that followed this thought, a small voice spoke up at the back of Gwen's mind: 'Well, actually, if you think about it—'

Gwen pressed Lydia's front door bell firmly. The small voice was extinguished.

Mr Wetherby had been right about the bearded visitor. Gwen gave him a little smile, didn't squander her resources by actually greeting him, sat down on the edge of the chair nearest the door. The bearded man was sitting on the sofa, sharing it with a spread-out newspaper. He was perhaps in his mid-forties, Gwen guessed. Slightly shabby: from which one deduced that he had no wife to check him over before allowing him out. He looked, she thought, like a teacher. Perhaps a colleague of Lydia's from the college?

Gwen averted her eyes, not wanting to be caught staring. She looked round the room, waiting for Lydia to come back (she had gone to make tea). It was a pleasant room, Gwen decided. Could even be called cosy. And yet ... and yet ...

She wrinkled her nose, trying to put her finger on it. The room was clean enough, if not exactly tidy, but there was something ad hoc about it, as if Lydia's personality had not been stamped on it, as if it was a work in progress. There were rugs on the floor, no carpet. The walls were bare. Lydia's canvases were stacked backs outward under the side window. The sofa was higgledy-piggledy in the middle of the room, not squared neatly against a wall. And that cabinet: rather chipped, rather worn. One had heard it said that Lydia bought her clothes from charity shops. Might her furniture be second hand too?

Lydia came in with a tray.

'Lydia, I ...' Gwen half got up. 'I didn't realize you had visitors. I don't want to interrupt. I could always come back later.'

'It's only Terry. He won't mind. And I've made the tea now.'

'Well, if you're sure ...' Gwen sat back down. (*Only Terry?* Who was Terry, exactly, and what was he doing here? Gwen had a vague idea that she'd seen him somewhere before.)

Lydia put the tray on the floor. (No useful little side tables, thought Gwen: one noticed these things.) Kneeling, Lydia began to pour tea.

'What was it you wanted, Gwen?' Lydia hauled herself up, handed a mug to Gwen. (No cups and saucers. Just mugs. One would never dream ... with visitors ... but each to their own.) 'Help yourself to sugar.'

'It's nothing really, just the exhibition.' Gwen decided against sugar. The sugar basin was down on the tray and one could hardly go crawling on the rug with one's bottom in the air – not in front of Terry, anyway.

'We're organizing an exhibition of village art.' Lydia annotated for Terry's benefit as she handed him his tea.

'Ah.'

Gwen experienced a flicker of irritation as she blew surreptitiously on her tea (there was not nearly enough milk in it, but one didn't like to fuss). Why did men do that? Why, when one informed them of some interesting fact – for instance, that one was organizing an art exhibition: why could they not simply say 'Are you really?' or 'That's nice'. Why did they have to say 'Ah' in that slightly condescending way, as if to suggest that one didn't know what one was talking about? Basil did it all the time. One sometimes wished that one had the nerve to point it out to him.

'I've been thinking about the exhibition,' said Lydia as she took her place on the sofa, sitting on top of the newspaper, cradling her mug. (Why not move the newspaper first, before one sat down?) 'I wondered if it should have a theme.'

'Do we really need a theme?' Gwen was anxious. She had come here to get things clear in her head, to organize a timetable and get the ball rolling, not to add further layers of complication.

'A theme could be useful,' Lydia insisted. 'It would give structure to the exhibition.'

'Always good to have structure.' Terry nodded wisely.

Gwen glanced at him irritably; was taken aback to see him recoil from her look.

He added hurriedly, 'Of course, I don't know anything about art. I'm more on the science side of things.'

Well, really, thought Gwen, *what sort of man is he if he is intimidated by me?* She looked down at her mug, balanced on the arm of the chair, wondered if it was making a mark. But did that matter, if the chair was second hand?

She took a deep breath, getting her mind back on track. 'We have the dates now,' she summarized. 'Easter week, starting on Good Friday. Imelda Darkley telephoned to confirm. And she will be delighted to attend the opening ceremony.'

'It's a great honour,' Lydia explained to Terry, 'being permitted to use the village hall. One has to go cap in hand to the local aristocracy.'

'That's not quite true,' said Gwen.

'I'm speaking metaphorically.'

'At least you still have somewhere to mount an exhibition of that type,' said Terry. 'Our exhibition rooms were part of the museum.'

'Didn't I hear that the museum is closed now?' said Lydia.

'Demolished,' said Terry.

'Oh, of course, it was where the new shopping arcade now is – the one with all the empty shops.'

'Wanton vandalism,' said Terry. 'Typical of the district council.'

Gwen winced as she listened to Terry itemizing the Council's crimes from demolishing the museum to bulldozing the outdoor pool – the pool which (Terry informed them) had been one of a dwindling number of lidos left in the entire country, of historical interest in addition to being locally popular, but which had now vanished without trace thanks to another act of wanton vandalism motivated by developer-led greed. Terry was not mumbling now, Gwen noted, but what he didn't understand was that Basil liked things neat and tidy. Demolishing old buildings was his way of making the town look spic and span. In some ways, Gwen admitted, they were quite alike, her and Basil. After all, she had been known to throw away perfectly good kitchen utensils and quite decent crockery, merely because they didn't fit into her neat system of hooks and racks and shelves and cupboards.

Gwen finished her tea, put the mug on the floor (one wouldn't normally be so untidy, but in this room it didn't seem to matter). She was itching to get on, to get the details of the exhibition settled; it would have been easier if it had been just the two of them. But Lydia seemed in no hurry to interrupt Terry's monologue, as if she was actually interested in all that council business. Perhaps she was. One had grown in recent weeks to think of Lydia as a friend, but what did one really know about her? *I am apt*, said Gwen, *to misjudge my friendships.* She remembered uncomfortably a survey she had done once, a survey in a magazine where one had to rank one's acquaintances on a scale of one to ten depending on how close a friend they were. *Too often I work on the assumption that I'm at the eight or nine out of ten stage, when really we would only scrape to four or five.* Was there anyone in the village, she wondered, with whom she had risen above five? Possibly – quite probably – not.

But all this had nothing to do with anything. It was what happened when one sat idle for too long: one began to feel sorry for oneself.

She was about to make her excuses and go when Terry got up and said it was about time he went. Gwen got to her feet too, smiled, said it was nice to have met him; she hung around in the main room while Lydia saw him out. If she could just get a few things settled with Lydia, then she wouldn't feel that her visit had been a complete waste of time. A sense of urgency wouldn't come amiss (February all but over, Easter drawing ever closer). If one could just impress on Lydia the need to get organized.

But would that prove to be as easy as it sounded? Was there not something a little odd about Lydia today, something different? She seemed distant, distracted, out of sorts.

Gwen, lost in her thoughts, suddenly realized that she had begun tidying up by instinct, collecting the mugs and putting them on the tray, straightening the rug, folding up the newspaper. Now she had got hold of Lydia's canvases, was squaring them, stacking them neatly. She took a step back. She had one of the paintings in her hand. She turned it round to look at it.

Richard as St George. It was rather good. Lydia had got Richard to a T – although he looked rather more heroic in the picture than he ever did in real life (Basil would have been astonished). If one wanted to pick holes one could have queried whether, in all honesty, St George would really have gone out to fight a dangerous-looking dragon without his shirt on, but with a painting one could do as one liked: that was the beauty of it.

She looked at another canvas. My word, how odd. That boy in the middle looked almost like Dean, but why was he surrounded by all those cats – or lions, were they? What did it mean?

She replaced the canvases with a feeling of dissatisfaction. Her own productions rather paled in comparison. She must remember when painting in future not to be too clinical, too symmetrical. She must learn to cut loose. But, really, how could one, with the exhibition weighing one down and not a stroke of work done today. Nothing prepared for dinner, the house getting shabbier and shabbier by the second, dirt accumulating, dust multiplying—

'I do apologize, Gwen.' Lydia came back into the room. 'Terry has taken to visiting. I think he feels sorry for me.' She laughed, but her laughter had none of that staccato, almost subversive quality that it usually had.

'Who is Terry?' Gwen asked, not really interested but needing time to gather her thoughts.

'He's from college. A colleague. Science. He's also a local councillor, I believe.'

'Oh, *that* Terry.' Buffoon, Basil called him. A demagogue. A pain in the – *ahem* – bottom.

'Terry thinks I need looking after. Rather tiresome in a way, but it's my own fault. I daresay I gave him the wrong impression, crying on his shoulder.'

Gwen watched Lydia moving around the room, restless, picking things up, putting them down (*no wonder the place is so untidy*), unable to recognize in her the sort of woman who would cry on Terry's shoulder (*why, for goodness' sake?*).

It's happened again, thought Gwen. *I thought that we had reached seven at least, but we are virtual strangers, we are only four on the scale.*

'I wondered, Gwen,' Lydia began hesitantly, 'if I might ask you something? It's advice I want, really. I want to … to put my mind at rest. I feel I can talk to you. I....'

'Well, of course, it's....'

'One knows about these things in theory. One has read about cravings....'

'Cravings?'

'But I have this urge to eat....'

'To eat?'

'Coal.'

'Coal?'

'You see! You're shocked! It can't be right, can it? There must be something amiss. But I just sit at night watching the fire, and the coal bucket's there, and I get this overwhelming urge to....'

'But surely one only gets those sorts of cravings if one is.... Oh. Oh, I see.'

'Do you?'

'Well, yes, I suppose so, if...?'

'You disapprove. An unmarried woman – a *single* woman....'

'No, no, not at all, I'm not that old-fashioned!' (Such fibs!)

'It's come as a bit of a shock.'

'Ah.'

'It wasn't planned.'

'No.'

'I don't quite know what to …'

'That's understandable, perfectly natural. It does tend to throw one off balance.'

'I'm not at all sure I can ... and when I think about ... and, oh Gwen, I don't know what to do! Richard is—'

'Richard?'

'—no help, he—'

'What has Richard—?'

'—refuses to talk and—'

'*Richard!*'

'Yes, Richard! Oh, I know, I know, I'm shameless. A trollop: that's what my mother says—would have said. I've never, ever done anything like it before, but Prize, you see ... and then Richard ... and so I ... and he ... and then we ...'

'But, Lydia, it's not possible!'

'The age gap, you mean? But it isn't anything serious. Just a bit of fun, he says. And I—'

'No, you misunderstand. It's not *possible*. Richard can't—'

'Can't?'

I mustn't tell her, it's not my place, it's confidential; even if we'd made it to eight or nine, I still couldn't tell her.

'I don't know what you mean, Gwen! Of course it's possible! It's happening. I am having Richard's baby!'

'No, Lydia, you aren't. Whoever the father is, it can't be Richard.' *I shall have to tell her. I have no choice. There's no knowing what might happen if I don't. And, really, all this secrecy: it's not as if it's something to be* ashamed *of.* 'Richard had cancer, testicular cancer. He can't have children. The cancer – the treatment ...'

Lydia fell back onto the sofa. Gwen sank down into the chair. *We are like puppets*, she thought, *puppets whose strings have been cut.* Then: *What have I done? Never mind puppets – why did I open my big mouth? It was not my secret to tell.*

Although she was sprawled in the chair – undignified, gulping for air – she had the illusion that she was still falling, that she had yet to hit the ground, that she was speeding up as she fell, that her landing would be hard and painful.

This is not over yet, she thought. *Not by a long chalk.*

SEVENTEEN

DEAN LAY ON his bed, listening. The house was quiet. He knew that
Basil was out, that Amanda was out too, but where was his mother?
She was a tricky customer. She *lurked*. You thought the coast was
clear, that you were safe, and then – BAM! – she came barging
straight into your room *without even knocking*! It was out of order.
An infringement of your human rights. Everyone was entitled to
their privacy. It was the law. But no matter how many times you
explained it to her, she never changed. She carried on blundering in,
not giving a thought to the fact that you might not want to be
disturbed, that you might be trying to concentrate, that you might
be doing something private and confidential – that you might be
doing *anything*. (You wouldn't, of course, be doing *anything* –
you'd learnt to be extra-super-careful before doing *anything* – but
the principle was the same.)

Once upon a time, when he was young and naive, he had thought
his room was a place of safety. He knew better now. Nowhere was
safe. He was constantly under siege. The world intruded even in
here. (He thought of the intruding world as a cold draught seeping
under the door. The thought made him shiver. He turned the radiator up full.)

And people (Basil) had the cheek to call him lazy! It wasn't lazi-
ness. It was exhaustion. How else were you meant to feel when you
had to be on your guard *the whole time*? You couldn't even relax
in *your own room*! The world (Basil, Charley, the panther) was
always on the lookout, trying to get at you, to trip you up, to make
you look stupid. You had to be ready every minute of every day.
You had to be poised for action, your defences had to be up, you
had to be prepared for fight or flight (the latter, of course, was the

sensible option, but when did anyone ever get the credit for showing sense?).

How did other people manage? Did they have more courage than him? Or were they just too stupid to care what happened to them? In some ways, Dean ruminated as he stretched out on his bed, the world was civilized; in other ways it was a cruel and brutal place. If, for instance, he'd been born as a gannet (he'd been watching David Attenborough on TV, always edifying), you could bet your life he'd have been eaten by seals when he was still a baby. If he'd been a turtle hatchling, digging himself out of the sand, tottering full pelt towards the safety of the sea, it would have been just his luck to be gobbled up on the way by some prowling predator. It was only because humans were top dogs on earth that he'd survived this long. By rights he should have disappeared into some beast's ravenous belly years ago (at least it would have been quick).

He gave a heartfelt sigh, turned onto his stomach, propped his head in his hands, worn out by the struggle to survive. And as if that wasn't enough to deal with, there was now something else weighing on his mind: girls. For ages and ages, he'd been able to keep girls at arm's length, treat them as if they didn't really exist (and, you had to face it, the boundary between what was real and what was not was somewhat blurred: even science admitted as much). Girls had been like tempting mirages, or like myths and legends told at night round a camp fire (Dean quite liked the idea of a camp fire, but it wasn't very practicable in his bedroom). He'd liked to think about girls, lying in bed until late on a Saturday or a Sunday morning, the real world a vague and misty place somewhere in the remote distance, his duvet like armour, stronger than steel. But now—

Well, look at it. He grabbed a handful of his duvet in his fist. Flimsy. Pliant. It wouldn't protect you from a fly. And it was all the fault of the panther: he couldn't put it plainer than that. She'd let the world in, she'd made girls real – and it was torture.

He rolled about on the bed, stuffing his fist into his mouth to stop himself from groaning aloud because you never knew who might be listening (his mother). Yes, it was torture, it was agony. Had he really struggled through eighteen and a half years for *this*?

He sighed and sat up, reached for one of the books on the floor where he liked to keep them: anything to take his mind off all the crap in his head. His atlas. That would do. He slid down the bed again, lying flat, opened the atlas, held it over his face like a roof. Europe. Italy. The toe of Italy. Calabria. A place he'd never been, remote, exotic – a land (surely) of marvels. He could understand why Cally's mother had been so keen to go there. Lucky Cally, having a mother who'd gone to Italy in a campervan! What had he got? A hopeless mother, a sheep, bleating and following the flock; a father who was an arch-traitor and scumbag, you didn't even name him; Basil; Amanda; the boys at college. All nobodies. None of them worth knowing. You'd be better off on your own.

Calabria. Calabria. A place. A girl. Both alluring and out-of-the-way. Both beyond his reach.

He laid the atlas over his face, hiding himself. He stood no chance with any girl, having a face like his. His spots might be clearing up (Charley was right, but that didn't justify broadcasting it all around college), but spots were the least of his worries. It wasn't as if he was even ugly. He had a face that was just dull and boring. Bland. Every day it grew less and less memorable. He could hardly bear to look in the mirror. And the worst of it was, his face didn't even *look* like him. It bore no relation to the boy – the man – inside. The real Dean Morley – dynamic, intelligent, sparkling – was hidden beneath some sort of monotonous own-brand packaging, his false face and weedy body. How could he ever talk to *her* looking like this? What could he say?

Oh, Calabria, Calabria! The toe of Italy. The girl from the campervan. The toes of Calabria. Even her toes would be perfect. Her lovely wonderful toes. He wanted to see them, touch them, stroke them, kiss them—

Kiss her feet? What was he saying! He was turning into a foot fetishist! (His genes, laughing at him.) Oh God. As if he didn't have enough to cope with.

He rolled back and forth on the bed. He couldn't suppress the groan any longer, couldn't hold it in, because it was not just her toes, it was all of her: all of her was perfect and he couldn't stand it.

The atlas dropped to the floor, the duvet rode up in big twisted creases. God, he wished he could do *anything* right now, right this minute. He was going crazy....

But the risk was too great (his mother lurking, Amanda might be back). All he could do was lie there as if he was stretched on a rack. All he could do was carry on being tortured, feeling helpless, hopeless.

And exhausted.

EIGHTEEN

In the staff room – a haven of relative peace in a building swarming with hormonal teenagers – Lydia sipped her coffee whilst flicking through the *Independent*, isolated up one corner. Her reputation as something of an eccentric had its advantages. Not only was it expected in an art teacher, it also tended to keep people at bay. They were wary of approaching her, which suited her just fine, allowed her peace and quiet when she needed it.

As she turned the pages of the paper, she kept half an ear on the conversations going on around her. The talk was about work. It always was. It was as if they couldn't find anything else to talk about.

She tossed the paper aside (boring, as usual) and straightened her skirt, taking a moment to admire it. At £10 from Help the Aged, it had been a real bargain. Ankle-length, voluminous, swirling, it made her feel rather prim. Probably made her look prim, too, but that was all to the good. No one would have expected her to wear a skirt like this and she enjoyed confounding expectations. In some convoluted way, she thought that wearing this skirt served people right for judging by appearances. It was a useful disguise, too. No one seeing a woman in a skirt like this would possibly imagine that she was carrying an illegitimate child whose father—

But anyway. She wasn't prim. Nor trim: not for much longer, anyway.

Her mood became dismal as she tried to guess how soon she would grow too big for her Help the Aged skirt. She would get fat, bulge, waddle. At long last, there would be something else for the staff room to talk about besides work.

It was unutterably depressing. She stared down at the dregs of her coffee, swirled them round at the bottom of her mug. Perhaps she ought to get rid of the baby, wipe the slate clean. But she couldn't wipe Richard – or Dean – away. And then there was poor Prize, the way it had ended: she couldn't bear to go through all that again, even if the victim this time would be an embryo with no personality. Personality might be lacking, but it was always there, always on her mind. It was taking over, and it hadn't even been born yet.

A pair of rather scuffed brown shoes came into her field of vision. Looking up, her eyes met Terry's. It was, she thought, rather bold of him to come over like this. One expected more caution.

'Erm, hello … er … hmmm …' He scratched his beard, looked round, found inspiration in the *Independent*, discarded on the floor.

'That paper,' he said, pointing, 'is a complacent, middle-class rag written by blinkered journalists sitting in their bourgeois ivory towers. It belongs in a BBC world where poverty is an Issue with a capital I, where the working class only exist as a conversation piece, where the disadvantaged are quarantined inside patronizing articles written by self-appointed experts, where racism and bigotry and prejudice are concepts that we've conveniently outgrown in this country, something only foreigners do….'

He paused for breath. The pause lengthened.

'Goodness,' said Lydia brightly. 'Have you finished?'

'Yes, I've finished.' He blinked, trying to hide behind his beard, if such a thing was possible. 'Was it a bit much?'

'Some people might find it a bit much.'

'But not you?' Hopeful.

'I'm not some people, I'm me. Politics have no power over me. I'm immune. Nigel used to go on. He was a great admirer of Mrs Thatcher.' (Though he had, she remembered, insisted that Mrs Thatcher must secretly be a man, finding it impossible to believe that a mere woman would have the capability to turn the country upside down in what Nigel had considered to be such a novel and interesting way.)

'Who is Nigel?' Terry was suspicious.

'No one,' said Lydia. 'No one important. You must remember,' she continued, swerving away from the subject of Nigel, thinking of

Gwen's recent visit instead, 'not everyone is as interested in politics as you are.'

'I do tend to put my ... er ... foot ...'

'Poor Gwen! She didn't know where to look.'

'Why *poor* Gwen?'

'Basil Collier is her husband.'

'Ah. Oh. I see. So she's Collier's wife. Poor Gwen, indeed.'

'And Dean Morley is her son,' said Lydia, sailing close to the wind, unable to stop herself. 'Do you know Dean?'

'Hmm. I believe I do. Quiet lad. Acne.' He was looking at her stomach. 'How's the, er, um, little one?'

'Hush! There's no need to tell everyone!' Social ineptness was not always amusing, she thought, as she glanced around the room, but the work talk continued unabated. Nobody paid much attention to Terry at the best of times. Terry was unimportant – which was why one could talk to him. One didn't have to make an effort; one could talk off the top of one's head, say anything—

Well, *almost* anything.

'It's all a bit of a mess,' she said, forcing a smile onto her face. *Much worse than I'd thought*, she added silently, because if the child wasn't Richard's then it had to be ... it must be.... Oh Lord, would the child get acne too? Would it turn out to be *odd*?

'Chin up,' said Terry. 'It can't be as bad as all that.'

When Nigel had said such things, it had set her teeth on edge, made her want to scream. But there was something soothing about Terry's banality – perhaps because he so obviously didn't realize he was being banal.

He frowned, said hesitantly, 'This Nigel person. Is he your ... husband?'

'No. We were never married – thank goodness.'

'But you were together...?'

'For ten years.' She blanched as she said it. It sounded such a huge span of time. She had spent a quarter of her life building castles in the sand; whereas Nigel had just been marking time until someone younger, prettier – richer – came along.

'I do ... do ... understand,' Terry bumbled.

'I doubt it.'

'I've got an ex-wife.'

Yes, he would have. 'I think we should leave both our exes in the past where they belong.'

'A good idea.' A smile broke out, faded; he scratched his beard. 'I don't suppose ... I mean we could ... if you liked ... go for a drink later?'

Was he asking her out? A date? Surely not! He was just being kind. If he'd been Prize he'd have been licking her hand.

'I'm sorry, Terry, I really can't tonight. I've got a meeting.' The Exhibition – which was now a fixture, referred to with a capital letter – provided a good excuse, but as she spoke she felt a pang of regret, which was silly. It must be Prize she was thinking about, not Terry.

'Are you sure ... sure you're up to going to a meeting ... in your condition?'

'I'm pregnant, not a cripple.' No wonder his wife was an ex-wife. But one shouldn't be cruel; he meant well. And she had never shouted at Prize. 'I'm afraid I can't very well get out of it. The Exhibition, you see, is my ... is my—' She broke off, put a hand to her mouth, but the laughter forced its way through her fingers. 'My baby! Oh, oh, ha ha ha! My baby! Ha ha ha ha!'

Once again she was convulsed with helpless laughter, just as she'd been in the pub the other day, *drawn spades at twenty paces.* She must be off her rocker, lurching between extremes of emotion like this. It was like walking a tightrope. One wrong step and she'd fall to her doom. But it was never ending, this tightrope, stretching back into ten years of wasted endeavour, stretching ahead into unknown territory, a world of nappies and sleepless nights which was totally alien to her. How would she ever cope with a baby? No wonder she was hooting with laughter. Her life was ludicrous.

All round the staff room, curious faces were turned towards her, but Terry, like a shaggy dog, was standing guard valiantly. It was just his eyes, watching, that expressed misgiving.

NINETEEN

GWEN SLIPPED INTO the house. Downstairs was all in darkness. Basil must have gone up. She closed the door quietly, bolted it, put on the chain. This took longer than she had expected. She seemed to be having problems with her coordination. Anyone would think she was tipsy. All she'd had was two glasses of wine. Or was it three? She seemed vaguely to remember a third – it had, after all, been a very long meeting. But it couldn't have been four. It couldn't possibly have been four. She would never be so debauched as to drink *four* glasses of wine in *one* evening.

She hung up her coat. It fell on the floor. She bent over to pick it up. Goodness, it was a long way down! Perhaps if she put the light on it might help. It wasn't as if Basil wouldn't know what time she had got in: he would know to the exact minute. All this creeping around in the dark was fooling nobody.

Slowly she climbed the stairs. It had indeed been a long meeting. But at last they were getting organized. They were to start collecting exhibits next week. Tickets were to be printed. A preliminary sketch had been made on the back of a pub menu as to how the space inside the village hall might best be utilized. It had been suggested that, were exhibits particularly thin on the ground, then children's artwork would be used to fill in the gaps, as well as handicrafts. Whatever the case, there was to be a kids' corner where children could experiment. Of course, this would require even more volunteers. They had bandied names about. *Would Dean? Would Amanda? Well, I'm not sure.* Gwen had not held out much hope.

Basil was in the bathroom with the tap running, which drove Amanda mad. ('Don't you realize how precious water is?' 'More precious than ketchup?' Basil could be acerbic at times. 'Or is it one rule for me and another for you?' 'You're just a profligate pig!' *Profligate*, no less! There were times when one's faith in the education system was vindicated.) Gwen tiptoed past the bathroom, past Amanda's room, noted the light under Dean's door. (Why was he still up? She had been under the impression that teenagers needed lots of sleep. He would stunt his growth if he wasn't careful – if, that was, his growth had not already been irrevocably stunted.)

In the master bedroom, she quickly slipped out of her clothes in the light from the bedside lamps, pulled on her nightdress and dressing gown. She could pretend that she had been home for ages, that she had been sitting waiting for him to finish his protracted ablutions. It might just work.

Oh, but look, she sighed: there were Basil's clothes, willy-nilly all over the floor. He was as bad as Dean.

She began picking them up, feeling absolved from guilt, on a firmer footing. She would not pass any comment, she decided, as she stretched to retrieve one of Basil's rolled-up socks that had got lost under the bed, holding it between the tips of her thumb and forefinger. She would just let him watch as she tidied up after him; she would let him listen to her pointed silence.

As she dropped the sock into the washing basket, Basil loomed up in the doorway, came shuffling into the room. He was wearing paisley pyjamas and had trodden down the backs of his slippers, which never ceased to irritate her.

'So you're home at last,' he grumbled. '*Newsnight's* been finished ages.'

Newsnight was Basil's curfew, except at the weekend when it wasn't on. On Fridays he stayed up to watch that review programme – why he bothered, she did not know, as he only got het up and began shouting at the television, especially if Germaine Greer was on.

'That bloody woman!' (Yet another *bloody woman*.)

'If you'd actually listen, Basil, you would realize that what she is saying makes perfect sense.'

'Nothing that woman says ever makes sense. She has only one agenda, and that's hating men. She's a frigid Australian b—'

'*Basil!*'

139

Basil sat on the edge of the bed and kicked off his slippers. Gwen averted her eyes from the sight of his feet.

'What have you been *doing* all this time, Gwendolen?'

'You know very well what I've been doing. We've been having a committee meeting.' She dropped his shirt into the basket with a flourish, moved to straighten his slippers, lining them up neatly by the bed, pulling up the trodden-down backs. 'There's a lot to discuss, a lot to be arranged.'

Basil looked at her, suspicious. 'Have you been *drinking?*'

'Of course not.' *Oh, you barefaced fibber!* 'Well, maybe a glass of wine. One can hardly sit there with nothing when one is in a pub.'

Gwen unfastened the cord of her dressing gown with a sinking feeling, changed her mind, retied it, pulled it tight, turned to the dressing table, sat down. She knew only too well what would happen next. It was always the same. Having told a little white lie – completely harmless – she would now feel an irresistible urge to confess some other misdemeanour in recompense. It was a bit like that dream she sometimes had, the one where she was sweeping dust under the carpet (a ridiculous dream: as if she would ever do something like that!). She would be there, in the dream, holding up a rug, sweeping dust under it; but as soon as she started sweeping under on one side, the dust came leaking out on the other. And so it went on, from one side to the other, *sweep sweep sweep, leak leak leak*, until she woke up in a cold sweat.

'I think you should know, Basil ...' She picked up a bottle of perfume, turned it round, put it back down again. *Please don't do this, please don't.* 'I had to tell Lydia about Richard.'

There. It was done.

She turned the perfume round again, moved it a centimetre closer to the mirror. Out of the corner of her eye, she could see the reflection of Basil sitting in bed. A tuft of hair was sticking up on the left of his head. It always stuck up.

He was not happy. She could see that a mile off. But now she had confessed, she actually felt better. It was a weight off her mind. She had been fretting about it these past few days. Richard was, after all, Basil's business. Basil had a right to know.

'It was impossible not to tell her, Basil.' She moved the perfume bottle back to its original position and turned round on her stool to face the music. 'If you must know, Lydia is pregnant, and was under the impression that Richard was the father.'

'You mean Richard ... and that woman...?' Basil's eyes widened. He groaned, ran his hand through his hair, making more tufts stick up. 'Will that boy stop at nothing? Is he determined to make me a laughing stock?'

'Make *you* a—'

'He is my son. What he does reflects on me.'

'He's a grown man. He can do what he likes.'

'But ... but....' Basil groaned again.

Gwen got to her feet, had to put out a hand to steady herself. Catching the movement, Basil stopped groaning and looked at her charily.

'Are you *sure* you're not drunk?'

'Of course I'm—' Gwen was negotiating the acres of carpet between the dressing table and the bed. Who would have thought it was so far across – and so slippery! 'I'm not drunk.' Whoops, best hold on to the wardrobe, the floor had started swaying....

Basil gave her another suspicious look, but then his eyes glazed over. Gwen could see another groan working its way up from deep inside his chest. 'That boy ... that woman.... But, for pity's sake, Gwendolen, was it really necessary to tell her *everything*?'

'How else could I convince her? She was so certain that the baby was Richard's.' Gwen struggled to get her arms out of her dressing gown. 'Anyone would think you were ashamed, Basil – as if it was Richard's fault.' *Gosh, I must be tipsy after all; I'd never talk to him like this normally.*

'What are you going on about, Gwendolen?'

'Richard didn't *ask* to be ill, Basil. He couldn't help it. There was nothing he could have done.'

'I don't wish to discuss it. Now will you please get into bed and turn that lamp off. You know I can't sleep with the light on.'

'Yes, Basil.'

The conversation was over. The conversation was always over – hardly got going – when Richard's illness cropped up. One might have been forgiven for thinking that Basil didn't care, but that was just silly, Gwen told herself as she climbed into bed. Basil had his own way of dealing with things, that was all.

She reached to turn the light off, settled herself, wondered if she would have a headache in the morning (*four glasses!*), felt Basil's hand creeping along her thigh, said automatically, 'Oh, Basil, not now, this nightdress is clean on, I thought you wanted to sleep?' She barely noticed Basil's hand disengage, her mind racing, going from Richard to Lydia to Lydia's baby. Did Lydia have any idea how her life would be turned upside down?

Sleepless nights, smelly nappies, puke: thank goodness, said Gwen, *I am past all that … though when I say, past it … I am not quite at that stage yet, am I? If there was to be a little accident … it's not beyond the bounds of possibility, even at my age … and they have such tiny fingers, such tiny toes. I am not that much older than Lydia … first words, first steps … but, no, I couldn't, it's not practicable … and I shudder to think what people would say. Anyway, there is hardly likely to be an accident of that sort unless we— One never knows if he's sulking or if he feels he's done his duty, made the effort, and that it's my lookout if I push him away. Why do I push him away? What sort of wife does that make me?*

She shifted her position, tried to dampen down her rampaging thoughts. Basil had his back to her. Sulking or not, she knew from experience that he would soon be asleep and snoring. She would never drop off once he started snoring. But at least in the dark (be thankful for small mercies) one couldn't see the hair on his head sticking up in tufts; nor did one have to face the sight of all that chest hair in the V of his pyjama jacket (why did it make one think of lawnmowers?). Perhaps tonight for a change he would keep to his own side of the bed, wouldn't prod her with his feet (why were men's feet so ugly: so pale, bony, misshapen – and so cold?)

Gwen sighed, turned on her side. Wasn't alcohol supposed to make one sleepy? Instead, she was wide awake. She wondered if she dared switch on the lamp and read a chapter of her book. If Basil was asleep she would get away with it, but if he wasn't she would never near the end of it. ('I've got work in the morning…how can I manage on two hours' sleep ... why must you read that trash anyway ... that light is hurting my eyes....')

Be fair, Gwen said to herself, *he is a good man at heart. He has taken care of me, of Dean and Amanda too. How many men would have taken on a task like that?*

She ought to feel grateful, she told herself. She ought not to feel trapped, to feel that the walls were closing in on her. *Perhaps it is my fault,* she whispered. *Perhaps if I tried harder, if I was more amenable.* Her first husband, in the latter stages of their marriage, had got into the habit of describing her as—

But no, no, she couldn't think about him, wouldn't, mustn't! It brought the walls that much closer; they threatened to smother her, to crush her; she had to push, push, push to keep them at bay – to keep *him* at bay, his smiles and jokes and affability, everyone's friend—

But to be fair, Basil could be charming too when he wanted. Perhaps not so much in the days when he'd been wooing her (it had been business-like), but what about the proposal on Westminster Bridge? They had been in London for the day, sightseeing, a meal, the theatre. Basil had not gone down on one knee when the time came (and thank goodness for that, on Westminster Bridge), but his eyes had shone with an eager light. It was later – much later – that she had begun to wonder if the shining eyes had been for her, or if he had actually been looking over her shoulder, indulging in fantasies of demolishing the Houses of Parliament and replacing them with a nice modern shopping centre—

Oh, I'm so cruel, I shouldn't, I really shouldn't.

But there was no getting away from the fact that Basil did like demolishing things. Terry might be an unfortunate little man, but he did have a point there. The Houses of Parliament were safe but closer to home Basil had decimated the town centre, flattened all those picturesque old buildings, built concrete monstrosities in their place, filled in the lovely lido, turned it into a car park. What a fuss there had been over the swimming pool, such a broo-ha-ha! She had begun to dread going into town. It had been the only topic of conversation in Waitrose. But the more people protested, the more Basil had dug in his heels. He *did* know best; they *would* listen to reason. He was stubborn, so very stubborn.

Gwen sighed again, twisting round to lie flat on her back, staring up into the dark which covered her like a shroud. *Why did I accept him? If he's that bad, why did I say yes?*

But her head had been in the clouds on Westminster Bridge – almost literally so after stepping off that giant wheel.

What a horrendous experience that was. I kept my eyes shut nearly the whole time. I've never liked heights. I prefer to keep my feet firmly on the ground.

She closed her eyes as she had done on the wheel, shutting out the dark and the encroaching walls but not shutting out a voice that seemed to whisper by the bedside, faint and indistinct like the wind round the windows: *a mistake ... mistake ... mistake...?*

But, really, what else could I have done? I'd been abandoned, I was on my own, I had two children. I couldn't have coped all alone. I needed a man. I had to take Basil when the chance came. I had to. There was no other choice ... no choice ... no choice....

TWENTY

DRIVING OUT OF the college car park, Lydia joined what was known as the ring road, which carved its way through the middle of the town, cutting it in two. She drove in a twilight convoy before turning onto a smaller road that led to the council estate. She had been weighing this sortie in her mind for several days. It was not that she owed Richard an apology as such; she was simply dissatisfied with the way things had been left. She had said some things at their last meeting which, given what she now knew, might be construed as insensitive. Not that Richard came out of it (she resisted calling 'it' *the affair*) smelling of roses, but what else could one expect? He was a man – and a very young man at that. But if she now offered an olive branch, they could at least part as friends.

The car juddered and lurched; the wheels thudded into pot holes. Terry was right. The road surfaces were appalling, but perhaps the residents didn't notice or didn't care. Most of them never bothered to vote, Terry said.

Parking by the flats – Jubilee House – Lydia got out of her car and locked the door. She looked round suspiciously. Would her car be safe here? Would she come back to find it gone, the windows smashed, the wheels missing? Nigel had called the people who lived on council estates *trash*; criminality was part of their culture, he had said. But did that say more about Nigel than it did about the inhabitants of council estates? Had Nigel, in fact, been a fascist and she'd never noticed?

What did that say about *her*?

Terry would never use the word *trash* in reference to human beings, she thought, as she picked her way along a cracked pavement to the door of Jubilee House. But why think about Terry? It was getting to be a habit.

The door to the flats was ajar, propped open by a pile of free newspapers. Lydia hesitated, looking into the dingy entrance hall. A flight of stairs led up into the gloom. Was this a good idea? She didn't even know which flat was Richard's. She'd heard Gwen speak of Jubilee House, but hadn't liked to ask for a complete address. It did not seem appropriate, after making such a fool of herself where Richard was concerned. Perhaps the buzzers might work. She could buzz a few flats, might strike lucky. But it was quite possible that Richard was not in. She had no idea what shift he was working this week.

She turned to go back, experienced a sense of relief, but then she was struck by the thought of what her mother's ghost might say later: something along the lines of, *That's always been the problem with you, my girl. You never see things through. You never stick at anything.* Well, noodles to her. This time she *would* see it through.

Pushing the door fully open, Lydia stepped over the free papers and into the hall. There was some post on the floor, junk mail by the look of it. She bent down, sorted through it. *Mr Richard Collier, Flat 7, Jubilee House, Tudor Avenue.*

She found flat seven upstairs. There was no bell. She banged on the door, waited. A TV was blaring inside.

I'm wasting my time, she said, staring at the mucky door, the lopsided plastic number seven, *but at least I've done my bit, I've made the attempt, tried to—*

The door opened. Richard stood there with tousled hair, a grubby T-shirt, baggy boxer shorts, bare feet. He looked like he had just woken up.

'You,' he said.

'Hello, Richard. Aren't you going to invite me in?' She surprised herself with her insouciance. Not quite the femme fatale, but definitely high-handed. 'I've brought up your post.' She barged past him, giving him no option.

Richard's main room was something of a tip. She surveyed it warily. The sagging sofa and stained carpet were decorated with takeout cartons, beer cans, CDs and DVDs and their covers, copies of *Auto Trader, Zoo* and *Nuts*, several TV guides, plates, mugs and cutlery, not to mention bills, bank statements, wage slips, final demands and a football. The curtains were half-pulled. Possibly they stayed that way permanently. A print of a Monet painting of London hung on the wall: left by a previous tenant, perhaps – or did Richard have a dash of culture in him? The huge widescreen HDTV was shiny and new. On screen, Anne Robinson was insulting a contestant on her quiz show.

She watched as Richard grabbed the remote, turned the TV down but not off. Even caught off guard in this dishevelled, torpid state, there was a latent energy about him. He was, she thought, like a phoenix rising from the ashes – the ashes being the detritus littering the room. One could imagine him stretching his new wings, smoothing his fiery feathers—

But this was not useful. She had not come here to indulge in flights of fancy (though she must make a mental note of the idea for future reference: the phoenix and the detritus of daily life; it would make a most interesting subject). She had to keep her wits about her if she wanted to survive this awkward encounter.

'Take a pew.' Richard grinned. 'If you can find a space.'

Lydia bit her tongue. The phrase *look at the state of this place* was not exactly conducive to a congenial conversation, and anyway it reminded her of her mother.

'Tea? Coffee?' he said.

'Tea would be nice.'

He disappeared through a doorway, leaving Lydia to contemplate the sofa and wonder if she dare take her life in her hands by sitting on it. It looked like it might collapse at any moment.

Richard's head popped round the corner before she could decide. 'Milk's sour, sorry.'

'Lemon?'

'Yeah, right, like I've got lemons. Beer do you?'

'Yes. Why not?' Make yourself agreeable, she told herself.

He soon reappeared, handed her in turn a glass and a can of lager. His own can he put down on the floor before sweeping off some of the flotsam from the sofa.

'There. Now you can sit.'

'Thanks,' she said drily. The sofa squealed, sagged some more, but seemed inclined to hold her weight.

Richard sat at the opposite end, propped his feet on the football, opened his can with a blunt thumb, took a long swig of lager.

Lydia inspected her glass. It was surprisingly clean – pristine, even. She could see Anne Robinson's face through it, distorted by the pattern of dimples. Pouring her drink, she gazed around the room again.

'It's a bit untidy.' Richard had obviously noted her perusal.

'A bit?'

'So what? It's better than going to the other extreme, like my neurotic stepmother.'

'You think Gwen is neurotic?'

'Don't you? Have you seen her place? She cleans to excess.'

He had a point, Lydia admitted, but one could not say so. One had to keep solidarity with Gwen.

She watched as Richard picked a scab on his knee. His hairy knee. He had rather hairy legs, like a satyr's. One could imagine him frolicking in an Ancient Greek forest—

She reined herself in. This was not helping. Richard looked nothing remotely like a satyr, or a phoenix – or even St George, for that matter. And if he kept poking at that scab, he would make it bleed.

'You banked one hundred and fifty pounds,' mumbled Anne Robinson as the pause stretched out between them. 'That's pathetic. You need to do much better than that.'

'So ...' Richard turned his attention from his scab to Lydia. 'Is this a social call, or...?'

She braced herself. 'I hadn't seen you for a while—'

'Missed me?'

'—and I knew you wouldn't—'

'Wouldn't what?'

'—make the first move, so—'

'You want to make a move on me?'

'—as it seems I may owe you—'

'Owe me what? Twenty quid for services rendered?'

'—an apology—'

Richard looked at her sidelong. 'Oh? Why's that?'

'Last time we met, I may have—'

'May have?'

'May have,' she repeated, 'been a bit hasty—'

'Hasty? Is that what you call it?'

'Will you please stop interrupting! You are not making it any easier.'

She waited for him to ask what it was he was not making easy, but he said nothing, swigging his lager and looking at her speculatively.

Her courage deserted her. She was trespassing – in more ways than one. She wished she hadn't come.

But now that she was here.... In for a penny, and all that.

'This baby.' She laid a hand on her stomach, an unconscious movement. 'I know now ... I mean, I realize it's ... I know that you ... can't....'

Richard choked, eyes bulging as he stared at her, coughing and spluttering. He jumped to his feet, lashed out at the football, sending it hurtling across the room. It narrowly missed Anne Robinson's glowering face, smacked into the wall behind the TV, rebounded, went bouncing behind the sofa.

'Fucking hell! Fuck's sake!' He was pacing up and down, oblivious to the detritus on the floor, treading and trampling, knuckles slowly whitening as he crushed the can in his hand. Lager was forced out, ran across his fist, dribbled onto the carpet. He almost lost his footing on a copy of *Zoo*, then turned to face her, his cheeks flushed.

'Who told you?'

'Your ... er ... Gwen....'

'Gwen!'

'She ... er ... let it slip.'

'Fuck's sake!'

'I warned you.' Lydia heard a disembodied voice in her ear. 'Don't say I didn't. But would you listen? You had to go your own sweet way, just as you always do, and now look—'

'Oh, shut up!'

Richard stopped his pacing, turned to look down at her, frowning, puzzled. 'What did you say?'

'Nothing. I—'

'He thinks you're talking to yourself!' the ghost jeered.

With the ghost in one ear and Richard staring at her as if she was mad, it was desperation that made her bark out, 'Sit down!'

To her amazement, Richard obeyed. He looked more shell-shocked than angry now. In the sudden silence, the muted TV sounded very loud. 'You are the weakest link – goodbye!'

Lydia took a deep breath. She needed to conduct proceedings on her terms. The final parting must be effected gracefully.

'You could have told me yourself,' she said, business-like. 'It would have saved a lot of bother and misunderstanding.'

'It has nothing to do with you.'

'Maybe not, but if it's any consolation, I do understand what it's—'

'Had cancer lately, have you?'

'Prize had cancer. That's why he was put to sleep.'

'Are you suggesting I should be put to sleep too? Are you comparing me to a fucking *dog*?'

'You should be so lucky.' She bit her lip, avoiding his eye. He would think she was being flippant. It would hardly be tactful to tell him she wasn't.

Staring at the floor, she became aware of spots of blood in a trail across the carpet. He must have cut himself when he was rampaging around the room.

'Your foot is bleeding,' she said helpfully, plastering over her gaffe.

'What? Oh. Yeah.' He hauled his foot up, resting his ankle on his knee, probed the wound, frowning, distracted, wiping his fingers on his already grubby T-shirt. The sole of his foot was brown with dirt, Lydia noted. The toenails needed clipping.

But those were details, unimportant. She needed to get this parley over with, to draw a line under Richard. That was her only aim.

'Am I right in thinking you are fighting fit now, that the cancer has gone?' she said conversationally.

'Yes, it's gone. And so's one of my bollocks.'

'Ah.' (Whoops.)

He appeared to be absorbed with his foot. 'They told me I could have a fake one if I wanted – a sort of giant marble, I suppose you'd call it. Their name for it was a pro ... a pros....'

'A prosthesis.'

'That's the word.' He sniffed. 'I told them to get stuffed.'

'I see.'

'*I see?*' He gave her a black look. 'What does that mean, *I see?* Why say it in such a parsimonious tone of voice?'

'I think you mean *sanctimonious* rather than *parsimonious*.'

'How do you know what I mean? You haven't got a fucking clue about me!'

'Then explain.'

'Easy for you to say. Easy for you to sit there and go *explain, explain, explain*. I *can't* explain, that's just the point.'

'But wouldn't it have been better to....' She faltered, but there was no going back now. It was like walking out onto thin ice: you had to keep going until you'd reached the safety of the other side. 'Wouldn't it have been better to have the prosthesis? Wasn't that the sensible option?'

'Maybe I didn't want to be sensible. Maybe I wasn't in the mood for it. How would you have felt, being poked and prodded and pumped full of drugs, being hacked apart by a bunch of quacks?' He returned to his foot, squeezing the wound, making it bleed, watching with a closed-up expression as the blood dripped. 'I was losing something that was a part of me,' he muttered. 'Some poxy marble couldn't make up for that.' He squeezed harder, grimaced, said through clenched teeth, 'I'll tell you what it was like. I'll tell you how I felt. Pissed off, is how. Cheated. It was like I was being punished for something I hadn't done. It was like I was being singled out. The last thing I needed was to have to decide whether or not to have a giant marble sewn into my scrotum.'

He put his foot back on the floor, picked up his half-squashed can. She watched as he gulped lager, saw his Adam's apple bobbing up and down as he swallowed, was aware of his eyes swivelling towards her. His frown had been smoothed away. The streetwise jack-the-lad expression was back. 'I don't suppose,' he said speculatively, 'you fancy a quick shag, for old times' sake?'

151

She had been on the verge of feeling sorry for him. She had seemed to glimpse beneath the surface a different Richard, lost, alone, afraid. She had almost been able to smell that clinical hospital smell. She had imagined a bearded doctor wielding a sinister hypodermic. 'It's only a testicle, Mr Collier.' The lacerating banality of professionalism, ripping one's world apart. *It was like I was being punished for something I hadn't done.* But he must have been, at his age, almost as innocent as Prize, who'd never harmed anyone, who'd never even barked at the postman, let alone bitten him.

But Richard had to spoil it. He had to revert to type. The facile suggestion of sex wiped away her incipient compassion.

He seemed to read the anger in her face, said hurriedly, 'I'll put a clean sheet on the bed and everything.'

'And you'll keep your clothes on and tell me not to touch you,' she sneered. She was taken aback by the vitriol in her voice, but what was even worse were the sudden doubts in her mind, wondering what Prize might have said if he could have talked (there had been times when she had thought he was about to). Would Prize too in his fear have made cheap jokes and facile remarks about sex, spoiling the dignity of his dumbness? The thought made her lash out. 'Just because you've had *cancer*!' she seethed. 'You think you can use *that* to get a woman into bed!'

'Can't blame a bloke for—'

'You think you can snap your fingers and—'

'Jesus Christ, I only *asked*, there's no need to bite my—'

'As if you're such a catch, as if you're anything to write home about! An oik, a slob, someone who lives in a tip, who works in a warehouse, who drives a rust bucket, who deals in drugs—'

'Hang on a minute!' said Richard, growing heated. 'Who said anything about drugs? I like the odd smoke now and again but that doesn't make me—'

'You use people. You use women. Sandra—'

'Oh, right. I wondered when we'd get round to—'

'Sandra!'

'I explained about that, I told you I was—'

'*Sandra!*'

'Just because you're fucking *jealous*!'

With a shock of surprise, Lydia realized they were both on their feet facing each other – yelling at each other. Richard was looming over her but she refused to give ground. She had an overwhelming urge to harangue, lambast, wound. She could barely see him through the red mist. He might have been anyone, any man; he might have been shorter, stockier, with the build of a rugby player.

'Women are just playthings to you.'

'That's crap, that's so—'

'You don't give a damn about anybody's feelings.'

'Who the hell do you—'

'You don't care how much you hurt people. You have no compunction.'

'No *compunction*? I don't even know what the fuck that *means*!'

'You have no respect.'

'Respect! You talk about respect!'

He took a step towards her and suddenly she felt fear. It was like being doused in ice water. Her anger was extinguished. She backed away, felt the wall behind her, pressed herself against it, watching Richard warily through narrowed eyes. (Richard, this was Richard, she had nothing to fear from Richard.)

'You don't know me, you haven't a clue!' he said, animated. 'Of course I respect women. I love women. I love everything about them. I love their legs, their tits, their eyes, their hair, the curve of their neck, the dimple at the base of their back—'

'Objects,' Lydia whispered, thinking of her stumpy neck, too-long legs, saggy breasts. 'You see women as objects.'

'That's not true. It's just not true. Try to understand. It needn't have anything to do with looks, with her body. It might be the way she talks, or the way she walks, or the clothes she wears. It might be the fact that she's confident and knows what she wants; or maybe she's shy and you have to coax the words out. I love it all. I love the way a girl gets into your head. She might be nobody, a complete stranger, someone you see in the street, but you wonder who she is and where she's going and what she does all day. And if she stops and talks to you, then it's the way she looks at you, as if everything is possible, or nothing. She might invite you in; she might slam the door in your face; she might string you along: it doesn't matter, it's all brilliant, it makes you feel alive, even when she blanks you, when she looks at you like dirt; when she's way out of your league and you don't stand a chance: it just gives you a buzz knowing that she's out there, that a girl like that really exists. And what gets me – what really gets me – is that half the time they don't even know how wonderful they are. Like you—'

He swung round to face her and she felt herself sliding down the wall, pressed her palms hard against it, propping herself up.

'—you, with your charity shop clothes and avant-garde ways. Sometimes I think you don't even realize how fantastic you are, so droll and original and sexy. I love the way you spar with me, I love the way you have me in stitches, I love the way you do my head in. I didn't think I'd ever stand a chance, a bloke like me. I thought you'd laugh in my face, and … and … And why haven't you told me to shut up? You usually tell me to shut up. You don't usually let me get away with anything.'

He peered at her uncertainly. As he did so, he seemed to be hearing his own words – the flood of words – echoing in his head. She watched him colour up, watched him turn away abruptly, watched as he grabbed the remote, pressing the buttons convulsively, frowning as if it required all his concentration to change channels.

She stayed where she was, frozen in position. His words were echoing in *her* head, too: *droll, fantastic, sexy*. He didn't know what he was talking about. He must be off his rocker. The cancer must have eaten his brain.

The TV suddenly boomed out, making her jump. Adverts were on: biscuits, washing powder, shampoo. Not just any old biscuits, the finest biscuits, biscuits that tasted better than anything else in the universe, one bite made you melt inside (or so you'd think judging by the way the actress on screen was romping on a bed). And the washing powder, making clothes whiter than white, fresh as a summer meadow, softer than feathers – and all with fifty per cent less impact on the environment! Shampoo, also, which transformed your hair, made it shine like burnished metal, made it toss and tumble as (for some reason) you jerked your head about like a demented chicken in glorious slow motion.

People advertised themselves too, thought Lydia as she peeled herself away from the wall now that Richard had thrown away the remote and gone to stand in the window, wrenching open the curtains, staring out into the dusk. People advertised themselves, represented themselves as talented, gorgeous, the world's experts in everything under the sun, CVs as long as your arm.

I do it as well, she admitted. *But I don't convince anyone, let alone myself. I am not a coolly competent teacher; I am not a well-balanced, independent woman; still less am I a femme fatale. I am in fact rather plain-looking, nearly forty, damaged (beyond repair?), the world expert in nothing, with no talents to speak of except a penchant for painting pictures no one ever wants to look at.*

And as for Richard—

She looked at him standing in the window with the twilight sky behind, the glow from a street lamp giving him a sort of angelic radiance. But he wasn't an angel. He wasn't talented, gorgeous or the world's expert. He didn't shine like burnished metal, wasn't new or improved or fifty per cent better. She pictured him instead – the pictures rising unbidden in her mind – waiting forlornly in a hospital corridor or lying in a hospital bed with tubes attached. She thought of him as scarred and damaged too, a boy whose boasting and bluster couldn't quite paper over the cracks.

She could not have said what prompted her to cross the room, to put her arms round him. It was instinctive, a reflex action, with nothing of the femme fatale in it. He gave a start of surprise, turned towards her; but he did not pull away.

He said after a pause, 'Er, why are you hugging me – or shouldn't I ask?'

'Pity, of course,' she said. Pity for him? Or for herself? Or was it more like desperation, clinging on to something, anything, as she tried to weather the storm?

'About Sandra—' he began.

'I don't need to know about Sandra. It's none of my business.'

'She got the wrong idea, that's all. I mean, I like her, but ...'

'But what?'

'It wasn't as if I was trying to take her for a ride or anything. Things just got out of hand. And I don't deliberately go out of my

155

way to hoodwink people about … about my mutilation. It's just easier not to have to explain. It sort of kills the mood, if I start explaining.'

'I see.'

'Do you?' His muffled voice grew anxious. 'You do realize that if you tell anyone about any of this, I will never speak to you again?'

'Promises, promises.'

There was another pause. His body, which had been tense in her arms, now began to relax. She could smell washing powder on his clothes, beer on his breath. The television boomed and burbled, filling the silence.

'I can feel your bump,' he said at last.

'Nonsense. There is no bump.' It was her turn to be anxious now, reminded of the child growing inside her. 'Not yet,' she whispered. 'No bump yet.'

'I don't suppose you're going to tell me who the father is?'

'You suppose correctly,' she said in a tone that might have been called *droll*, which might have been mistaken for *sexy*.

'For what it's worth….' He was hesitant. 'I'd give anything for it to be mine.'

'Is there no chance, then, of you ever…?'

'There were supposed to be ways and means. Contingency plans were put in place. But … well, things don't always work out.' His voice was bleak.

'You could always,' she said very slowly, 'be godfather to my production.'

She felt him shaking with laughter. 'What, an oik like me? A slob? A— What else was it?' The laughter drained away. He said cautiously, quietly, 'You're serious?'

'Absolutely. I shall need all the help I can get.'

'Well, in that case … I mean, yeah, thanks, I'd … I'd love to.' Another pause, then, 'Um….'

'What?'

'Are you going to let me go? Or do we stay like this all night?'

It was an awkward moment. For a second as they pulled apart their arms got entangled, then they suddenly sprang away from each other like strangers who'd collided on the pavement. They hung their heads, avoiding each other's eyes. Richard, a sheepish grin on his face, aimed a casual kick at the sofa, mistimed it, stubbed his toe.

'Ouch! Ow! Shit!'

She laughed, making her way to the door.

'You are laughing at my pain! That's harsh!'

'Yes, it is, isn't it,' she said, closing the door behind her.

Picking her way downstairs, she tried but failed to put her thoughts in order. By some miracle, her car was where she had left it, unmolested. As she unlocked the door, it occurred to her that whatever you might say about Richard, it had to be admitted that he was nothing like Nigel. Not all men were like Nigel.

Holding on to this discovery, she started the engine and drove off into the twilight.

TWENTY-ONE

CHARLEY'S HOUSE WAS massive. It could easily accommodate half the population of the college: which was just as well, seeing as half the college appeared to have turned up. Dean had thought (secretly) that it must be something of an accolade to get an invite to one of Charley's legendary depraved parties, but he realized now that it would have been an affront *not* to have been invited.

Charley was in transit through the spacious hallway when Dean ventured in through the open front door.

'Hey, Morley! You've come! Nice one! Grab yourself a drink or whatever. There's booze, pills, weed. I'll be back down in a sec. I'm just going to get some more CDs.'

Charley bounded up the stairs, leaving Dean to make his way along a corridor where people were standing chatting, laughing, smoking, drinking. From a room on the left came the sound of music. Girls were shrieking, boys guffawing.

Where was the booze? If there *was* any booze. He'd heard people at college sniggering. 'Booze, pills and weed. Ha, ha! What he means is cola, aspirin and tea leaves in your tobacco.' But the sniggering people might be those who never got invited, so possibly their opinion should be discounted. At the very least Dean was counting on booze. He needed booze. He'd made his mind up to get drunk. It was to be an experiment. He'd never been drunk, not properly, and it was important to experience these things. (The pills and the weed could wait for another day: it didn't do to mix up your experiments.)

In the kitchen, Ash was sorting through a promising array of bottles on the table. The back door was wide open like the front. There were people in the garden, some playing football, others trying to push each other into the pond.

'Morley, have some single malt!' Ash waved a bottle under Dean's nose. 'Charley's old man's got loads of the stuff.'

'Won't he be angry if we drink it all?' asked Dean doubtfully, imagining Basil's reaction if anyone helped themselves to *his* whisky.

'No, man, he's cool. He likes it when Charley drinks all his booze. He thinks it's good for Charley's development and crap like that. That's why Charley has all these parties. He has to. His parents went away once and he *didn't* have a party and they thought there must be something wrong with him. They wanted him to see a shrink and everything, innit.' Ash poured a large glug of whisky into a wine glass and handed it to Dean. 'It's sick, man. Try it.'

Dean held the glass up, sniffed. What was single malt, anyway? How did it differ from ordinary whisky? 'Is this one measure or two?' he asked Ash. 'How many units is it?'

'Units? What are units? Morley, man, you're such a geek!' Ash lowered his voice, said reverently, 'Mike Somerville's got some skunk.'

'And? So?' Dean hoped he looked suitably unimpressed.

Ash tittered. 'Bet you don't even know what skunk is, innit.'

'Of course I know what it is!' Dean was scathing. Did they think he was thick? Had they never heard of the internet? Were they strangers to Wikipedia? Freak he might be, but he wasn't *stupid*.

Ash was sorting through the bottles again. 'Here, Morley, what can I give that Cally bird to get her pissed? I'm gonna get her pissed and then try it on. Think it'll work?'

Dean drained his glass. His face twisted with the taste of the whisky, the fire of it; but it was the thought of Cally that made his heart race. She must be here, then; but where?

'I reckon she fancies me, man, innit!' Ash grinned lasciviously.

Dean experienced a strong urge to find some of Mike Somerville's precious skunk and stuff it down Ash's throat until he choked on it. It was unexpected, this compulsion for violence. Did it mean he was already a little drunk? Was it a symptom?

'What's eating you, Morley?'

'Nothing.' Dean squeezed his fists tighter. 'Why do you talk in that stupid accent and say *innit* all the time? You don't talk like that to your mum and dad. You talk posh to your mum and dad, I've heard you.'

'Ah, man, you don't get it.' Ash's grin faded. For a moment he looked like he really might be choking. 'It's not easy, know what I'm saying? You've got your mates, you've got your folks, you've got about a million relatives, you've got the mosque, too; and it feels like they've all got a piece of you, and they're all pulling you in different directions. Half the time I don't even know who I am, I don't know who I'm meant to *be*, know what I mean, Morley?'

For a split second, Dean thought he *did* know what Ash meant. It was as if there was a different Ash locked up inside Ash's body, the way the real Dean Morley was hidden away inside *him*. You could almost see the different Ash peeping out as he spoke.

But then the lascivious grin snapped back into place and the illusion (it had to be an illusion, right?) was shattered.

'Anyway, fuck all that, Morley. I'm going to look for Cally.' He held up both his hands. There was a glass in each, filled with some reddish potion. 'I reckon this stuff will do the business. This'll get her pissed.'

The urge to do some severe damage to Ash came back, even stronger than before, but Ash was already on his way out of the room. He was lucky, muttered Dean.

Picking out a bottle, Dean poured himself a glass of something green. It tasted of peppermint. You could get drunk and freshen your breath at the same time: ingenious!

Cradling his glass, he set off on a tour of the house. Cally had to be around somewhere. He needed to warn her about Ash.

First of all he stepped outside. Charley was now in the garden with the football-playing lads. They had stripped off their shirts, showing off. Pathetic, thought Dean, who wouldn't have lowered himself. Apart from anything else, it was March, freezing cold, the wind gusting. And anyway, they weren't impressing anyone. There *were* some girls down by the garden shed, drinking wine, giggling, but they seemed entirely indifferent to the footballers, shirts or no shirts.

Interesting, thought Dean, sipping his mouthwash cordial. It was obviously not enough to simply strip off: you needed something else, too – the sort of something that Richard had got. *Charisma* for want of a better word. It was a very crude sort of charisma, appealed to people's baser instincts, but the problem was, so few people saw through it. They didn't stop to think that it was brain power that had created the world's civilizations, not brawn and blarney. Mind you, Dean added, taking a last glance at the foot-ballers, Charley was fooling himself if he thought his chunky frame was all brawn. *Flab* would be nearer the mark. And he had spots on his back. *At least my spots*, said Dean, turning away in disdain, *are confined to my face. And even those have all gone. Well, nearly.*

Passing back through the kitchen, Dean helped himself to more mouthwash liqueur then went to check out the dining room. This was Mike Somerville's room. Any room with Mike Somerville in it became Mike Somerville's room: that was the way he was. He was a bit like Richard, only grungier. Dean watched from the doorway with a curl of his lip as Mike and his mates sat around the table smoking dope and playing cards – playing for money, of course, because Mike was such a poseur. Everything about him was a pose: the way he was slumped in his chair, the way he fanned his cards out using only one hand, the way he held the joint between his lips, the way his trousers were half way down his thighs. Girls were grouped round him, some were draped over him. Little did they know, said Dean to himself, that smoking dope was not only giving Mike lung cancer, it was also destroying his short-term memory. By the time he was twenty-five (if he lived that long), he'd be a zombie with no idea who he was or where he was going. So much for Mike Somerville.

Next door in the living room, the curtains were closed and the noise intense (hip-hop on the stereo, people shouting over the top of it). There was no room to move and no sign of Cally. Where was she?

Back out in the hallway, a hand appeared as if from nowhere and grabbed his arm. 'Dean! Dean! I want to talk to you! Dean!'

It was Sandra. He tried to twist his arm away, but she was clinging like a limpet.

'Dean! Dean!'

He looked more closely. She looked dishevelled and rather red-faced. Her eyes were rolling. Perhaps getting drunk was not such a good idea – even for experimental purposes – if it turned you into a shambolic mess like this.

'Dean! Dean! Are you listening? Where's Richard? Where is he?'

'I don't know and I don't—' He tried again to prise her fingers off his arm '—care.'

'Why won't he talk to me, Dean? Why won't he answer my calls? Tell me! You must know! He's *your* brother!'

'He is *not* my brother!' As fast as he removed one hand, she clamped the other in its place. It was like wrestling with an octopus – and it made his flesh crawl, being pawed and groped: being *touched*.

'What have I done wrong, Dean? I don't understand what I've done wrong!'

She was starting to frighten him. Well, not *frighten* exactly (he wasn't a wimp, he wasn't frightened of *girls* … well, not much, anyway), but it was like she wasn't even human – as if she'd been taken over by some alien virus. All this *Dean, Dean*: it was setting his teeth on edge. He'd had enough of it.

'Ouch! Ow! Dean, you're hurting me! Ow!'

'Then get *off* me! Leave me *alone*!'

'But I want to talk—'

'Well, I don't. I hate Richard – and I hate you!'

He had to be brutal in the end: there was no other way. Suddenly Sandra was in a heap on the floor, grizzling like a baby. He backed away, stumbled against the stairs, turned and fled up them, putting distance between himself and the alien virus.

The upstairs corridor was empty. It was quieter up here, too. Dean moved stealthily, warily. The bathroom door was open; all the other doors were shut. One door had a sign on it: *Charley's Room, Keep Out*. Dean wrinkled his nose. How juvenile. He must remember that, mock Charley about it later. And perhaps if he had a quick look round inside, there might be other evidence he could use against Charley.

Dean opened the door, stepped into the room, and—

'Oh, sorry. Sorry—'

He stepped quickly out again, pulled the door shut. How embarrassing! But how was he supposed to know there'd be people in there? John Beresford, by the looks of it, rolling around on Charley's bed with that girl who was supposed to be a right slapper. Mind you, John Beresford was no better. He shagged anything with a pulse: girls, boys, his dog. That was what people said, anyway. Not that people were exactly reliable when it came to things like that, but even if John Beresford didn't *do it* with animals, he was certainly *acting* like one, snogging that girl right there in Charley's room when anyone could walk in and see. They could have found somewhere a bit more *private*.

Dean opened another door, took refuge in a different room. This was a flashy, flaunty sort of room. There was a massive wardrobe, a huge bed, mirrors, plush carpet, a window festooned with curtains. It had to be Charley's parents' room. They were like that, Charley's parents: over-the-top, in-your-face. And that bed.... Dean found he couldn't keep his eyes off it, couldn't help but imagine Charley's mum and dad rolling around on it the way John Beresford and the slapper were rolling around next door.

Dean slid slowly down with his back to the door, sat on the floor with his head in his hands. Sex. It was everywhere. You couldn't get away from it. And it was vile. Odious. Charley's parents flaunting, John Beresford rolling, Ash leering – not to mention Sandra, reduced to a quivering wreck. The worst of it was, Dean admitted with a groan, he had been sullied by it too. He had been touched, fingered, fouled, despoiled by the panther. He could never go back; he'd never be free of it now.

He scrambled to his feet. He felt sick, needed something to settle his stomach: more of that mouthwash liqueur would do, the whole bottle for choice. Forget about the experiment and measuring the units. He'd lost count anyway.

Down in the kitchen, he dosed himself with medicinal mouthwash and glanced out of the window. The garden was empty now, the football abandoned in the middle of the lawn. Dean went out, wanting to be on his own. He was beginning to think that coming to Charley's party had not been a good idea.

There were some glasses and bottles down by the shed where the giggling girls had been. The shed door was ajar. A bolthole, thought Dean. Somewhere to sit and sort himself out, take stock of his experiment, produce some preliminary findings, make a few mental notes for later.

He opened the shed door – and there was Cally, sitting on top of a stack of garden chairs, a bottle in her hand. There were sacks of compost and wood chips, garden furniture nestling against a lawn-mower. Gardening tools were hanging from hooks, shelves were laden with pots, containers, plant food. No room to swing a cat, as his mother would have said (his mother was always saying ridiculous things like that with no thought as to what the words actually meant: why would anyone want to swing a cat in the first place, and if they did, wouldn't the RSPCA have something to say about it?).

It was too late to beat a retreat. He would have to brave it out, talk if necessary. After all, he'd *wanted* to find her earlier, he'd actively been seeking her out; but now that he'd found her, he didn't know what to say.

He felt unsteady on his legs – the alcohol, of course, but also Cally, staring at him: improbable and unscientific as it sounded, there really did seem to be some correlation between her looking at him and the fact that his knees had turned to jelly.

He sat down on a plastic sack of compost as a gust of wind caught the door and blew it shut with a crash. They were suddenly alone together, cut off from the garden, the party – from the whole of the rest of the world. Daylight came in through cracks in the wooden walls, but it was very dim in the shed. There was a strong musty smell from the bag of compost. Spiders' webs dangled.

Dean was not sure that he liked this situation. It made him nervous.

'Why have you upset Sandra?' Cally spoke at last, rather guarded.

'I didn't. I haven't.'

'She says you won't talk to her. She says you were rude and walked away. She was crying.'

'She wouldn't leave me alone. She kept going on and on about Richard.'

'Oh. I see.' There was a pause, then Cally added, 'I think he's dumped her. She won't say.'

Dean's eyes moved rapidly from side to side, looking at everything except *her*: he dared not look at *her*. He knew that she was watching him, knew that he was blushing. He wished he was back in the old days, playing mummies and daddies. He'd never felt awkward with her then.

'What are you drinking?' she said after another long pause. She was less frosty now.

'It's ... er ... peppermint. Like mouthwash.'

'Crème de menthe.'

'Oh.'

'I've got a WKD Blue.'

'Oh.'

'I'm squiffy. Are you? I smoked some stuff. Mike Somerville gave it me. I like Mike Somerville.'

Mike Somerville's a poseur. He's destroying his brain, turning into a zombie. Don't like Mike Somerville. Like me instead: me, me, me.

'I don't like Ash so much. He's a bit weird. He kept trying to give me drinks. He's your mate, isn't he?'

'N-not ... not really.' *I don't have any mates. I'm too much of a freak.* Dean took a deep breath, held it, afraid to say anything in case it was the wrong thing. 'H-how do you *know*?' he ventured at last, letting out his breath at the same time.

'How do I know what?'

'That you're ... squiffy. Drunk.'

'Oh, that.' Cally giggled. 'I just feel as if I am. I've had three WKDs and half a spliff.'

'Alcohol depresses the central nervous system.' Dean remembered the notes he'd made before coming to the party, notes for his experiment. It was easier, somehow, to quote his notes than to think of anything original to say. 'It takes ninety minutes for the liver to metabolize one ounce. The effects of alcohol include impaired coordination, s-slurred speech, p-p-poor judgment ... euphoria ... emotional ... um, um ... emotional d-d-disregulation....' Dean faltered. His cheeks were burning up. She was still staring at him.

Her pupils were big and black and round, mesmerizing, you couldn't escape them. '... memory lapse ...' he muttered. 'Memory lapse, r-respiratory f-f-failure ... c-c-coma ... d-death....'

'What is all that?'

'Research. For my experiment.'

'What experiment?'

'It's ... er ... it's nothing. It doesn't matter.'

She got up, came and sat next to him on an upturned terracotta pot. She was so close, the shed so confined, that he was in danger of touching her if he so much as moved a muscle. Not that he didn't *want* to touch her, but there was the question of personal space (his as well as hers). Also, he was worried about what it would *feel* like, touching her – her touching him. What if he didn't like it? How could he possibly enjoy it when his head was full of the most vile, putrid things: the musty compost, the tattered webs; John Beresford rolling around on Charley's bed like a witless animal; the panther toying with him like a cat with a mouse? What if he'd been spoiled? What if he turned out to be a freak in this as in so much else? He'd wanted to kiss Cally's *feet*, for goodness' sake. That couldn't be normal – could it?

'Dean?'

'What?' His voice sounded weirder than ever, a sort of hoarse whisper: a fake voice to go with his fake face.

'You're very clever, aren't you?'

'I know.' She'd noticed. *She'd noticed*!

'Dean?'

'Uh?' He grunted, couldn't find any words – couldn't *think* of any words.

'Can I ask you something? It's sort of ... personal.'

'Uh.'

'Do you ever see your father? Your real father, I mean. Mr Collier is your stepfather, isn't he?'

'My f-father ran off, left us. He ran off with his secretary – I mean his business partner's wife. I hate him.' There were lots of words in stock on this subject – too many, in fact. None of them would be of any use in making Cally think better of him.

'Do you ever see him?'

'Not if I can— No.'

'That's ... that's how I used to feel about my mother. It's how I still feel, sometimes. My mother gave me away, she didn't want me, left Grandma to look after me. My mother's a hippy with no sense of responsibility. That's what Grandma says. But—' Cally lowered her voice, leant closer. 'I found out something. My mother tried to see me. Grandma stopped her. At first, I was glad. But now I wonder if ...'

She was breathing heavily, her chest going up and down. It was making him dizzy – or was that down to the mouthwash liqueur?

... poor judgment ... emotional disregulation....

'Dean?'

'Huh?'

'Do you ... do you think I'm like my mother? Sometimes I think I am. Sometimes I *want* to be. Other times I think I'm more like Grandma. But most of the time I think I'm not like anybody. I don't fit in. When I was at my old school, I thought it was because I was in the wrong place. I thought if I went to the college in town I'd feel different – like I belonged. But I don't. I don't feel different.'

She was looking at him intensely – anxiously – her eyes big and luminous. He wished he could answer her questions, but even if he'd known the right words he wouldn't have been able to speak because there was something wrong with his heart. It was going like the clappers, pumping blood like mad – but pumping it to all the wrong places. His brain was getting nothing, was being starved, turning to mush.

'I often feel,' Cally continued in the same breathless voice, 'as if I can only be my real self when I'm with the horses. It's like ... like the horses are my only friends. Do you understand, Dean? Do you?'

'The horse. *Equus ferus caballus.*' He was on safer ground here, didn't have to think, the words came by themselves: Wikipedia was coming into its own. His eyes had swum as he read about horses on the internet, thinking of Cally in her jodhpurs, wondering what it would be like to be Cally's horse, to be ridden by her. His eyes were swimming now, for that matter. He couldn't focus. And his heart—

...respiratory failure ... coma ... death....

He shook his head, trying to clear it of the fog. But perhaps it

167

wasn't his eyes so much; perhaps it was because it was so gloomy in here; perhaps that was why he couldn't see. And his heart: well, it might be in overdrive, but it was still working. He wasn't dead yet; not even in a coma.

'*Equus ferus caballus*,' he repeated. 'A single-hoofed mammal, domesticated around 4000BC. Horses have a well-developed sense of b-balance, can s-sleep both standing up and lying down....'

'Oh Dean!' Cally's eyes shone ever brighter. 'So you do understand! I guessed that you would. Grandma doesn't get it at all. She says horses are there for our convenience, not to make friends with – but then she says that about people, too. Only people with breeding are worth getting to know, she says.'

'*Equus. Equus ferus.*'

'Mmm, yes! I like it when you say that, Dean! You sound so clever, so brainy! I'm not clever at all. I'm not level-headed, either. It's because my father had dreadlocks.' She leant even closer, whispered, 'I feel sad sometimes. I can't help it. Grandma says it's a congenital weakness, a blemish in the blood stock. One shouldn't give in to it. One should fight it.'

'Unhappiness, depression,' said Dean. 'Feelings of....' He took a deep breath, then rattled the words off. 'Feelings of sadness-anxiety-emptiness-hopelessness-worthlessness—' It seemed to be pointless, unhappiness: a waste of evolution. He had wanted to find out why it even existed. And so, as with horses, the internet had prepared him, given him the right words. It was like fate, as if his whole life had been leading up to this moment, everything falling into place. 'Feelings, er, feelings....' He stammered, trying to remember his lines. 'Feelings associated with ... with chemical changes in the brain, substances such as serotonin, dopamine, norep – nor – nor—'

'Yes!' cried Cally. 'Yes! But it never *feels* like that, does it! It never feels like chemicals. That's what's so beastly about it. I'm so glad you know, Dean. I'm so glad you understand. Somehow I knew you would, ever since that day when I saw you on the pub car park in your Morris kit. You looked so strong and sensible. You looked so ... so *fit*! It made me feel all ... all gooey inside—' She broke off, put her hand to her mouth, giggling. 'Oh God! Listen to me! I sound like such an idiot! How *embarrassing*!'

He didn't think she was an idiot. He might have done, once, in the days of mummies and daddies. Not now. But he couldn't tell her that because his heart was going off the scale. The pressure was building up inside him. He felt as if he might explode at any moment. His knee was touching hers, their thighs were rubbing together, their elbows clashing, their shoulders butting against each other. It was sending him loopy. But if he was quick, there'd be time for one last experiment – one last, desperate experiment before he—

He took hold of her hands, drew her even closer. Lips to her lips. His chest against hers. Arms round her.

So *this* was how it felt. Not foul, not vile, not odious, but—

... *impaired coordination ... emotional disregulation ... euphoria....*

This was it. The end.

His heart really was exploding now.

TWENTY-TWO

COLLECTING FOR THE Exhibition was a thankless task, Gwen said to herself as she trudged along High Street past the church, weary. One could be forgiven for thinking that art had not been invented in these parts. She had a most meagre return after three hours of trekking round the village. An old lady in one of the bungalows had lent a portrait of Princess Diana composed of different coloured foil wrappers ('It's taken me ten years, dearie. You *will* be careful with it, won't you? What? What did you say? You'll have to speak up, dearie. It's no good, you're mumbling. I haven't got my hearing aid in.') Mrs Wetherby had produced some embroidery. Mrs Pole had nothing to offer – nothing except a cup of tea and a chat. The chat had lasted three-quarters of an hour. Mrs Pole, thought Gwen wryly, had undoubtedly raised gossip to an art form, but it was not the sort of art that could be displayed in the village hall.

At this rate there was not going to be a lot to see – and less than a month to go! As she knocked on the pub door, her feelings of agitation grew. What was the point in the clocks going forward, what was the use of all the extra hours of daylight, when it was all going to waste?

There came the sound of a key turning in the lock, then the door opened to reveal the Stasi.

'Oh, there you are, Gwen! We thought you'd got lost!'

Gwen followed the Stasi into the lounge bar. The bar lights were off, the pub being shut at this hour of the afternoon. It gave their meeting an illicit air, thought Gwen as she plonked her offerings on the table and sank thankfully into a chair: as if they had gathered to drink moonshine, looking over their shoulders for any sign of the revenue officers.

The turnout was poorer than usual. No sign of Dick Emery or Sandra. Apart from Gwen and the Stasi, only Lydia and Terry had turned up. Terry, of course, was not technically a member of the committee but he was becoming something of a fixture. One assumed, Gwen said to herself, watching the pair out of the corner of her eye as she eased her feet out of her shoes and raised her aching ankles to rest on the shelf under the table, one assumed that Lydia had a soft spot for the man, though one failed to see why. Then again, Lydia was a bit of a mystery all round. Full of surprises. Who'd have thought she would … and with Richard, of all people. One had imagined that she would have grown out of that sort of thing at her age.

The Stasi, examining the contributions that Gwen had brought, snatched up the collage of foil wrappers. Gwen winced. (*You will be careful with it, dearie.*)

'Isn't Lady Di a bit old hat – a bit twentieth century?' said the Stasi.

'I was under the impression,' said Terry rather shyly, 'that the whole point of the Exhibition was to give people the opportunity to express themselves, to show that art is not just something *other people* do, but that there's an artist inside every one of us.'

'That's all very well,' said the Stasi, waving Princess Diana back and forth, 'but what exactly *is* art? I wish Sandra was here. She could tell us.'

'Where is Sandra?' asked Gwen, hoping to imply by her rather strained question that the Stasi should put the foil picture down before she did it permanent damage.

'Boyfriend trouble,' said the Stasi confidingly. 'I had to send her home last night. She was a bit tearful. *He's not worth it*, I told her: *no man is worth it*.' She cocked an eye at Terry, seeming to suggest she thought him more unworthy than most. 'We had a bit of a heart-to-heart, if I'm honest. I gave her some advice. You know how it is, people do tend to confide in me. I suppose it's because I'm such a good listener, ha ha ha!'

Gwen glanced across at Lydia, sitting hunched and withdrawn, and it suddenly occurred to her that there might be more to Sandra's boyfriend trouble than met the eye. If Lydia had been entangled with Richard, and Richard was entangled with Sandra.... But, really, one didn't like to dwell on other people's ... well, *entanglements*: not in broad daylight. There was something indecent about it.

The Stasi, to Gwen's relief, replaced the foil picture on the table and waved her hands in the air instead, saying, 'I suppose we could call it an *arts and crafts* Exhibition, and then we could include more of Jean's embroidery and Old George's wood carving too.'

'But George said he doesn't—'

'That's just his little joke. I know better, ha ha ha!'

Lydia moved impatiently in her seat, spoke for the first time. 'I had rather hoped, having spent so much time on this Exhibition, that it would be ... *special* in some way.'

'It will be special,' said the Stasi confidently.

'But will it make a *difference?*' cried Lydia.

'Is that want we want?' The Stasi was doubtful. 'To make a difference?'

'It is what *I* want,' said Lydia. 'I want not to have wasted my time.'

'You will be proving that art is for everyone, not just for some self-proclaimed elite,' Terry interjected. 'That will be the difference.'

'But when it's all over,' said Lydia, 'will anything have actually changed?'

'It's not easy to change things,' said Terry.

Lydia rounded on him. 'Are you saying that it's pointless? Are you saying that we might as well not bother?'

'Of course not. But it doesn't come easy. I should know. It's a struggle even to get people to come out and vote. Most people – ordinary people – are too busy trying to survive. They don't have time for widening their cultural horizons, let alone to consider the eclectic questions of society. Ordinary people have been fucked over by the ruling classes for so long they hardly know their arses from their elbows.'

Gwen felt her hand twitch. She had a good mind to box Terry's ears. There was no need for bad language. And the conversation was rather drifting from the point. He was going on now about working at the grass roots, effecting change from below, which had nothing to do with the Exhibition. It was, in fact, politics. Why did he feel the need to reduce everything to *politics*? No wonder Basil gnashed his teeth whenever Terry's name was mentioned.

Gwen stole a glance at Terry: the baggy jumper, the grizzled beard, the air – really – of neglect. Was it possible – was one meant to assume – that *he* was the father of Lydia's baby? But if that was the case, why had Lydia been so convinced that the baby was Richard's?

Thinking of her visit to Mrs Pole earlier, Gwen shuddered to think what the village gossips would make of Lydia's pregnancy. It would be grist to their mill, Mrs Pole's in particular. She had been disappointed by the death of *that fat, smelly dog*, which had closed off one line of attack, but there were others. Miss Taylor frequented charity shops. Miss Taylor had gentlemen callers. Several credible witnesses attested to the fact that Miss Taylor *talked to herself*. It only went to show that—

Gwen wrinkled her nose, not sure what it went to show. Mrs Pole tended to lead one up the garden path and then leave one standing. If one was honest, one shouldn't just sit there and let oneself be swept along by it all. One should nail one's colours to the mast. One needn't be a shrinking violet all of the time.

She felt the blood rush to her cheeks, remembering one occasion at least when she had been quite the opposite of a shrinking violet – only a few hours ago, too! Had she really told Basil that she would be busy collecting for the Exhibition all afternoon and that if he wanted his supper on time he might consider lifting a finger for once? But if one had the temerity to do *that*, then surely one could venture to say to Mrs Pole, *Oh, Lydia Taylor? I quite like Lydia Taylor, actually....*

Gwen looked again, sidelong, at Terry, someone who did – it had to be said – nail his colours to the mast; someone who was not afraid to irritate people (imagine Mrs Pole's face if one admitted to *liking* Lydia Taylor).

'... I'm not sure. What do you think, Gwen?'

'I'm sorry? Excuse me?' Gwen looked up, realizing that she had stopped paying attention to the conversation some time ago. Lydia was staring at her expectantly. 'What do I think of what?'

'Terry's suggestion of standing for the parish council.'

'It would be a start,' said Terry. 'One small step.'

Gwen stifled a sigh. This was what happened if one took one's eye off the ball for even a second. The conversation not only drifted, it became completely irrelevant.

Lydia seemed to interpret Gwen's silence as disapproval. 'No, Gwen's right. I couldn't. I've no experience. I've no interest in politics.'

But Gwen, slowly cottoning on, suddenly saw light at the end of the tunnel. There was only one vacancy on the parish council, Imelda Darkley had said so. If someone else was to fill that vacancy, then she – Gwen – would be free not to.

'I think it's a marvellous idea, just the thing!'

'Do you really?' Lydia was dubious.

'What about me?' The Stasi was not one to be left out of things. 'Couldn't I stand too?'

'Why not?' exclaimed Gwen delightedly. 'The more the merrier!'

'Then it's settled,' said the Stasi, but at that moment a lugubrious voice from behind the bar interrupted her.

'Before you get any ideas like that, dearest, you might consider focussing on your own business for a change. It's five past seven.' It was the landlord, tousle-haired, grumpy, glowering at his wife.

'I'm in a meeting,' snapped the Stasi. 'Can't you see?'

'But it's your turn,' said the landlord through gritted teeth, 'to open up.'

'It won't hurt for you to do it. It's not as if you've anything else to do.'

The landlord snatched a bunch of keys from the bar and stomped off to unlock the door. Doing as he's told, thought Gwen. She looked with grudging admiration at the Stasi, who did not seem in the least put out by her husband's bad mood, as if it simply didn't matter. It was enough to make one envious.

Old George was waiting on the doorstep. 'About time,' he said as he came in, taking off his coat. 'And is there anyone serving, or is that too much to ask?'

The landlord had gone straight back upstairs, so the Stasi was forced to get up and go behind the bar.

'We're having a meeting, George. It's important.'

'Oh aye. And what's it about, this meeting?'

'We've all decided,' said the Stasi, handing him his bottle of light ale, throwing money in the till, 'to stand for the parish council – the whole committee is going to stand.'

All? thought Gwen in sudden panic. But that wasn't the idea—

George took a long swig of his drink, looking through at them from the public bar as the Stasi began to turn on the lights. 'Well,' he said at last, smacking his lips, 'that'll put the cat among the pigeons, that will. There'll be ructions, mark my words. But I'll vote for you. We could do with some fresh blood. It's about time that lot—' He jerked his head vaguely, '—were put in their place. About time indeed.'

Gwen's heart sank. The tunnel closed round her again. The light at the end was snuffed out. And now, her hopes dashed, she had to go home to see about supper – and face Basil.

TWENTY-THREE

LYDIA OPENED HER front door.

'Richard,' she said drily. 'What an unexpected surprise.'

'Don't sound too pleased to see me.'

'To what do I owe this honour?'

'Look, do we really have to conduct this conversation—'

'Conversation?'

'Is that not what this is? Is it not what mates do?'

'Mates?'

'Mates, friends, whatever. Are you going to let me in or what? I can feel beady Wetherby eyes on my back.'

Lydia stood aside so he could enter the cottage.

In the main room he ranged about like a beast in a cage, picking things up, putting them down, peering out of the window. It looked like he had come straight from work. He was wearing chunky boots, heavy-duty trousers, a mucky T-shirt.

'Tea?' Lydia suggested, watching him from the doorway.

'What about beer?'

'No beer.'

'Gin, then.'

'No gin.'

'Blimey. What's got into you?' And then he laughed, pointing at her stomach. 'Oh, I get it. *That's* got into you.'

'I've given up booze for the duration. Turned over a new leaf. No gin, no silliness—'

'No fun?' Richard cocked an eye.

'I do hope,' said Lydia, 'that you haven't got any daft ideas that we might—' She was uncomfortably aware that – sod's law – she was wearing the same clothes – the same jeans, the very same jumper – as the day after Boxing Day.

'You think I'm here for…?' Richard guffawed. 'Course not! Do me a favour! We've given all that up. It's in the past.' He began fiddling with her canvases, turning them round, bending down to squint at them – almost as if he was interested. 'I've come to say hello to my godson, that's all. How is he?'

'Until there is evidence to the contrary, *he* is an *it*.' She moved to join him, slapped his hand as he reached for another canvas. 'Leave those alone.'

'Ouch! That hurt!' He shook his hand, blew on it, an injured look on his face. 'I don't understand why you have all your paintings stacked facing the wall. Don't you like them or something?'

'One is never satisfied with one's work—'

'Oh, isn't one?' he mocked.

'But it's not that. I would never get any peace if they were there looking at me all the time. My head is full enough as it is without that lot crowding in.'

'Oh, here's a good one!' He had sidled back to the paintings, hoisted up a canvas. 'It's old St George!'

Lydia made a grab for her painting, but Richard twisted away from her, inspecting it with a critical eye.

'I like the dragon – though I'm not sure what Lady Darkness will make of it. She might not think that red scales suit her, nor a tail.'

'She will never see it. I've decided not to show it.'

'After all my hard work?' Richard held the painting at arm's length, closed one eye. 'You could have given me biceps. And a decent six-pack.'

'It's a depiction of you as you are, not the muscleman you'd like to be. You don't have a six-pack.' Lydia cornered him, snatched the painting – and at the same moment seemed to snatch, as if from thin air, the germ of an idea. 'This is too conventional,' she said thoughtfully, putting the painting aside. 'Far too conventional.'

'You're saying I'm conventional?'

'Not you. I am not talking about you. I am referring to the theme, the motif.'

'What is convention, anyway? If anything, I'd say that picture is decidedly *un*conventional.'

Lydia, running with her new idea, ignored him. 'The whole scheme is fallacious. The representation of heroism in such simplistic terms is not authentic. The dragons we *really* contend with are all in our own heads.'

'You've lost me.'

'I've had an idea!' cried Lydia, the germ growing, blossoming, new vistas opening up in her mind. 'A much better way of symbolizing heroism. You can help.'

She outlined her proposal.

'No. No way. Definitely not.' Richard looked alarmed; backed away from her towards the door as if he thought she was about to pounce on him right then and there. 'I'm not doing it.'

I must strike whilst the iron is hot, thought Lydia, *before the inspiration withers and dies; before I lose my nerve.* 'Look, Richard—' She took his hand.

He snatched it away. 'I'm not doing it,' he reiterated. 'You must be out of your tiny mind if you think I would. No way am I posing in the buff.'

'But don't you see? This is exactly the idea I was looking for. It will be simple yet profound, will make a valid point whilst simultaneously shaking the observer out of his complacency.'

'At my expense. I'll be a standing joke!'

'That's just what we want!'

'It's now what *I* want!'

'The aim would be to get a response – any response – from the observer! To make people sit up and think! They won't need to know it is you, of course. It will be a generic male form. Impressionistic. Idealized. I'll give you muscles, I'll even give you a six-pack—'

'And a second bollock?'

'No, of course not, that would spoil the whole thing. Your missing testicle is the *point* of the exercise. I'm thinking Marc Quinn. I'm thinking *Alison Lapper Pregnant*. On a smaller scale of course, but it will be—'

'Porn. That's what it will be. A naked body equals porn.'

'Don't be ridiculous! It won't have any reference to sex, except in an abstract sense. It will be a statement about body fascism. A celebration of our differences. An assertion that disfigurement—'

'Disfigurement? Well, thanks a lot—'

'You know what I mean.'

'It's only a testicle. I'm not the Elephant Man.'

'Only a testicle?' She remembered the word he'd used that day in his flat: *mutilation.* 'There's nothing *only* about it in your mind. You see yourself as the Elephant Man. And that's what we will be exploring: what is in the mind, people's perceptions of others, our own perceptions of ourselves.'

'I knew it was a mistake coming here.' Richard had his back against the door, but the door was shut. There was no escape. 'I should have steered clear.'

'It was serendipity. You came in order to inspire me.'

'You're a loony. Barking mad.'

'It will help you, too. It will help you to feel more at ease about yourself. All you do at the moment is avoid the issue. You even hide it from the women you sleep with.'

'I told you about that, I—'

'Excuses, excuses! All that talk about it being too much bother, not knowing the right words: that is simply a pretext. The real reason for your reticence is that you're ashamed, you're embarrassed, you're—'

'Oh. Right. So now you claim to know me better than I know myself, is that it?'

'That's exactly it. Take Sandra, for instance—'

'I've dumped Sandra.'

'And why?'

'Because ... because she's a kid. Too young for me. And ... well, I told you all about that before.'

'Precisely! It was getting to the point where you would have to confide in her. Rather than face up to it, you dump her!'

'Crap! You're talking crap! I don't even fancy her!'

'Are you sure? Anyway, there will be other Sandras, other situations in which you will shy away from being honest.'

'You don't know what you're talking about. And another thing. This painting you're planning—'

'You are changing the subject, avoiding the issue. There won't be a painting unless you agree to it first.'

'I still think it will look a bit dodgy.'

'So what? If people choose to regard it in a sexual way, won't that be a vindication of our aims?'

'*Our* aims, now, is it?'

'It is what we want: for the observer to see beyond the so-called deformity – to look at the subject as a person in his own right, not a victim or a patient.'

'That's all very well, but there's not going to be a picture, I'm not doing it: I am not standing around for hours in my birthday suit so you can paint my bits.'

'You won't need to stand around. All I need are some photos to work from. But if you're too much of a wimp even to pose for some photos ...' She used cunning, looked him in the eye, approaching him like a matador waving a cloak as he stood trapped by the door.

He met her eyes. 'You think I couldn't do it, don't you? You think I haven't got the balls. I mean, I haven't, but I have, if you get me.'

'Then you agree, you'll do it?'

'No.' He slipped out of the gap between her and the door, went and sat on the sofa.

She turned, resting her bum against the door, watched him scratch his stubbly cheek, avoiding her eye now. 'You have no self-confidence,' she said. 'That's your problem. You always take the easy option. Sex with no strings, that job in the warehouse—'

'I *like* working in a warehouse; it's where I *want* to work. The money's good for one thing. And if you think it's *easy* work—' He went silent as she came and sat next to him. He looked at her warily.

'It might not be easy work physically,' she said, 'but it is not challenging. You don't have to use your brain. Does it not bother you, the things your father says, that you're a disappointment?' She was goading him, distracting him with the matador's cloak.

'Dad would never be happy, no matter what I did. He'd never be proud of me. Even if I became Prime Minister – even if I won a Nobel Prize – he'd still think I'd fallen short in some way. I learned ages ago that it's useless trying to impress him. I learned it when I was about five.' He moved a safe distance from her, shuffling along the sofa. 'There won't be any painting.'

'There will.'

'Won't.'

'Will.'

'Won't.'

Lydia jumped to her feet. 'Get your clothes off, chop-chop, there's no time to waste!'

Richard jumped up too. 'You can whistle. I'm not doing it. That's final.'

'Yes you are!'

'No I'm not!'

They faced each other, standing in front of the fireplace (there was no fire: it was a bright March morning, the sort of morning on which she would have taken Prize for a long ramble – in the old days). Richard, tall and gangly, seemed almost to reach to the ceiling, but she was not frightened of him as she'd been that day in his flat. He was not like Nigel. Nigel was an aberration. Why had it taken her so long to learn that lesson? Looking at Richard, so young and full of sparkle, she was overcome by a feeling that she had wasted her life, that Nigel had been with her not for ten years but for twenty. She was old now, middle-aged, worn out like the rug they were standing on, fraying in places, walked all over. Her enthusiasm drained away. Her great idea withered in the cold light of day. She was deluding herself if she thought – at her time of life – that she could produce anything worthwhile, the tour de force she craved.

'You're right,' she said wearily. 'There won't be a painting. Apart from anything else, I could never get it ready in time. And ... well, it's just pointless....'

'There's ages yet before the Exhibition.' Richard was guarded. 'It can't take *that* long to dash off a masterpiece.'

'I said nothing about it being a masterpiece.'

'Profound, then. You said it would be profound – make people think.'

'I may have exaggerated. It's not as if I have much skill—'

'Now who's lacking in self-confidence? Takes one to know one, I say. Pot. Kettle. Black.'

'There's no point in discussing this,' she said, taking refuge behind his reticence. 'You are not interested. You said so.'

'I thought you were meant to be persuading me different.'

'What are you saying?' she asked warily.

'Who am I to stand in the way of art? That is what I'm saying.' He didn't sound reticent now. He sounded reckless, as if he was going out on a limb. 'Get your camera. And quick, before I change my mind.'

'I'll be right back,' she said. 'Don't move.'

But, fetching her camera from upstairs, fresh doubts assailed her. How could she be sure that her idea was not simply some wild flight of fantasy? Goading Richard, she had lost sight of reality. Had she hoist herself with her own petard?

Hesitating on the stairs, she tried to gee herself along. She had seen naked men before. She had been in far more intimate situations – with Richard himself, for one. But the real problem was the one he had put his finger on: she had no faith in herself. She had only run with the idea because she had banked on Richard refusing to cooperate. Why, for that matter, *was* he cooperating? Did he feel *sorry* for her? Was that what her life had come to?

Masterpiece, he had called it. The word made her tremble. What if she was overreaching herself? What if she failed? But it wasn't just *her* painting now. She had made it Richard's too. She couldn't afford to fail. There was nothing for it but to take a deep breath and go on.

Richard was waiting for her. He had taken his clothes off, was hiding, coy, behind the sofa, had his hands cupped over his genitals for good measure.

He had drawn the curtains. She opened them.

'What are you doing?' he asked anxiously.

'I need the light.'

'I was only thinking of your reputation. You know what the Wetherbys are like, the world's original nosey neighbours.'

'You'll just have to hope they're not watching. Now come out from behind that sofa.'

At the drop of a hat, she thought as she watched him shuffle onto the rug, he would have run a mile. It was only bloody-mindedness that was keeping him going.

But the same was true of her.

Oh Lord! I don't want to look! What if he is horribly disfigured? But if I use the viewfinder, then it's the camera looking at him, not me. The camera is cold, rational, detached.

She raised the camera. The air of tension made her hand shake. She had to use her other hand to steady it.

'You might want to ...' she began.

'What?' he said defensively.

'Move your hands.'

'Oh. Right.'

He was avoiding her eyes – raised a hand in front of his face, in fact, shielding himself, a gesture that made him look strangely vulnerable.

She fiddled with her camera, trying to remember how to operate it. It had been years since she'd used it. Nigel, she remembered, had been apt to get impatient. 'How many more times? *This* button, not *that* one. No, no, no: that's the zoom, you don't want the zoom. Oh, for pity's sake, women and technology: it's a recipe for disaster.'

'Have you finished?' asked Richard fretfully. 'I'm freezing my balls off here.' He laughed: a very thin, strained sort of laugh. 'Freezing my balls off. Get it? It's a joke. I've been thinking up jokes. Working on a routine. A way of telling people – girls, I mean: women. A way of telling them that I'm one bollock short of a set – since you reckon it has to be done. I don't want to get all heavy so I thought I could use something like this. I say, "What have Richard Collier and Adolf Hitler got in common?" And she says, "They're both megalomaniacs who want to take over the world?" And I say, "Close, but ..."'

'But what?'

'You know. That's when I spit it out. Confess. That's the punch line.'

Lydia, changing her position, lining up another shot, said speculatively, 'I am not, I must admit, an expert in male physiognomy. I have not had much experience—'

'That's what *you* say,' said Richard from behind his hand.

'—but do you really think,' Lydia continued, 'that anyone would actually notice?'

'What do you mean? It's pretty obvious ...' He spread his fingers, peeped through them. 'Isn't it?'

'Not to me. But like I said ...'

The camera clicked. Richard's fingers snapped shut.

'I don't see,' said Lydia as she crouched down to get a different angle, 'that you have anything to worry about. You are young, you are what might loosely be termed good-looking, you—'

'You're just buttering me up.'

'Am I?'

'Taking the piss.'

'Really?'

'I'm just me. Nobody special. A bit of a comedian. Rich Collier, always up for a laugh, always out for some fun. But that's not the same as ...'

'The same as what?'

'Well, I'm not exactly ... *boyfriend material* ... or however you want to put it.'

'Do you want to be boyfriend material?'

'No. Course not. Don't be daft. Well ... maybe. Sometimes. If I met the right girl, I'd like to ... to know I had it in me.'

'Well, you do. You do have it in you.'

'You think?'

'That day at your flat: I saw a different side to you.'

'I thought we'd agreed never to mention that again? Anyway, that was with you. I can talk to you. Most girls wouldn't be interested in ... in all that stuff.'

'You'd be surprised.' Lydia pressed the button one last time, stood up. 'There. I've finished.'

'Thank fuck for that.' Richard could not get into his clothes quick enough. 'Remind me,' he said from inside his T-shirt, searching for the arm holes, 'never, ever to come visiting you ever again.'

TWENTY-FOUR

GWEN RESISTED ONCE more the urge to pinch herself, making do instead with a sidelong glance at Basil pushing the shopping trolley beside her.

Basil in Waitrose. Basil pushing the trolley. Basil helping with the shopping.

What on earth was going on?

The only drawback was that his presence was so discombobulating that she was making a hash of her slick and well-practised Waitrose routine. On a good day she could be up and down the aisles and out in twenty minutes. Today she was having to go back for things – they'd skipped one aisle completely – and she found herself comparing price labels uneasily, wondering if Basil would notice that she occasionally preferred brand names to own-label.

She nudged the trolley, steering Basil surreptitiously back towards the aisle they had missed, wondering what people would think, seeing them together. Notice would be taken. Comments would be made. It would be all round the village. 'Did you see ... could you believe your eyes ... Basil in Waitrose ... well I never, what is the world coming to?' They would assume it was down to her, assume that she was a fish-wife, had nagged her poor husband into submission.

They had already run into Mr Wetherby, although he had been more interested in his own woes than in Basil. The staff in Waitrose, he complained, insisted on moving everything around. They did it to annoy him. They probably thought it was funny. It wasn't. Where, for instance, were the tins of baked beans? They used to be here. Now they weren't. It was a disgrace. He had a good mind to complain to the manager or write to the papers: he wasn't going to stand for it.

'That man,' Basil had said, watching as Mr Wetherby scuttled off to buttonhole a passing assistant, 'is a menace.'

But Gwen had thought that Mr Wetherby looked rather pitiable today: a forlorn figure haunting the aisles like a lost soul, searching for baked beans as if they were the Holy Grail. 'Twenty minutes,' he'd wailed, 'twenty minutes I've been in here, and blow me if I can find them. I really don't know what I'm going to do.'

'Gwen! Just the person!'

A trumpeting voice jolted Gwen back into the present. A tall, imposing figure came swooping down on her like a vast black bat. Even Basil flinched.

'Have you heard the latest, Gwen? You must have heard!'

'Hello, Imelda. Have I heard what?'

'It's *inconceivable*, that's what it is. Who *do* they think they are? I've never known the like, people putting themselves forward for the parish council without so much as a by-your-leave!'

'Oh, *that*...' Lady Darkley's booming voice caused heads to turn, eyes to stare. It was most discomfiting. But, flanked by Basil, protected by the ramparts of the shopping trolley, Gwen felt unusually bold. She ventured to say, 'I suppose you won't need me, now that there are more than enough people to fill the vacancy?'

'Oh no. No, no, no. You must stand. I insist. Surely you've handed in your nomination papers by now? No? I tell you what I'll do. I'll pop round later and collect them, save you a job.'

'Well, if you think—'

'It's horrendous, Gwen, absolutely horrendous. As if Smithson retiring wasn't bad enough, now I've got Pendleton being awkward. "I haven't got time to go canvassing and delivering leaflets," he said. "My dear Ronald," I told him, "we won't be canvassing, don't be ridiculous. It's not a popularity contest. Everyone knows that we are the fit and proper people to run the parish council. We've been doing it for years. We are ordained." But no, he won't have it, silly little man. The upshot is, I shall probably need *two* replacements. You, of course. And for the other, I've told Margaret Pole she will have to step in. Whatever happens, I am not – I repeat *not* – having

those people on my parish council: that arty-farty woman who
looks like she gets her clothes from a jumble sale, and that public
house woman – so common. She's only been in the village five
minutes—'

'That's democracy for you!' said Basil, breaking into the monologue impatiently.

Gwen drew breath. How reckless, interrupting Imelda Darkley!
Did Basil realize he was taking his life in his hands?

'Democracy, Basil? Piffle! What's democracy got to do with it?
We don't need democracy on the parish council. It's a nonsense!'
Lady Darkley fixed her eyes on him. 'I don't suppose there's
anything *you* can do? Put a stop to this pantomime? It's a criminal
waste of money as much as anything, all those ballot papers and so
on and so forth.'

'Oh, I can't be seen to interfere,' said Basil loftily. 'Everything has
to be done according to procedure. Elections have to be conducted
properly, all correct and above board.'

'What you mean is, you can't be bothered. You don't want the
trouble. Well. You are always quick enough to interfere when it
suits you. What about that swimming pool? It didn't even belong to
you. It was paid for by public subscription. There was a covenant
on the land. But that didn't stop you. You bulldozed the pool and
built a car park, and to the devil with *procedure!*'

'That was completely different. Covenants are not worth the
paper they're written on—'

'There was the old museum, too,' Lady Darkley went on,
ignoring him. 'You closed that without consulting anyone—'

'The museum wasn't paying its way, it was surplus—'

'You closed it down and then – surprise, surprise – it burnt to the
ground just as people were trying to get it listed. Very convenient
for you, I must say.'

'I hope you're not suggesting....' Basil spluttered and stuttered,
going red in the face.

Gwen felt faint. Basil going red was an ominous sign. There was
going to be the most terrible scene, right here in public, in
Waitrose, next to the fresh fruit and veg – unless she did something
quick! She looked round desperately for inspiration. All she could

come up with were some laminated boards under Imelda Darkley's arm.

'What are those?' she asked brightly.

'What are what? Oh, these.' Lady Darkley, who seemed quite impervious to Basil's wrath, held the boards up. Written on the first one, in large capital letters, was WARNING: BULL IN FIELD. 'I've just collected these. I'm going to put them up in Stonepit Meadow to discourage the ramblers. I've tried chaining up the kissing gates but they just climb over the fences.'

'You can't do that!' Basil's voice was rather strangulated. 'You can't chain up gates and put up notices! It's a public right of way!'

'Don't be silly, Basil. I'm not having people traipsing across Stonepit Meadow where I can see them from my lounge. They can walk on the roads, if they must walk at all. Now, Gwen, about those nomination papers.'

'I'll have them ready, Imelda.'

Basil cleared his throat, a sign of imminent danger.

Gwen jumped in again, wishing she could think of some way of terminating the conversation. 'How is Cally?'

'My dear woman, how would I know? That gal is a law unto herself. Now, another thing while I remember: about this Exhibition—'

Gwen felt a chill of fear. What was coming next?

'Am I right in thinking that jumble-sale woman is involved in all that nonsense? The public house woman, too, from what one hears.'

'They have helped out a little—'

'Yes, I thought so. Well, I've a good mind to put a stop to it. It's not the sort of thing we want to encourage in the village.'

'You can't, you mustn't!' Gwen was appalled: appalled at Imelda Darkley's suggestion, appalled too at her own brass neck, daring to contradict the queen of the village. But she had no choice. She couldn't rely on Basil, who wouldn't have defended the Exhibition even if he hadn't been choking with rage. If the Exhibition was to be saved, it would be down to her – if she could only find the nerve.

She took a deep breath. 'I'm afraid ... I mean, it's all arranged now, the notices have gone out and it's been advertised in the local paper. The tickets have been printed, too.'

'Hmm.' Lady Darkley's eyes narrowed. 'Well, if you're sure. I don't suppose there can be *too* much harm in it if you're involved, Gwen. But you can tell that jumble-sale woman that I've got my eye on her – the public house woman, too. You can tell them just what I think of this parish council business. I haven't finished with them yet, you can be sure of that!'

With that final warning, Lady Darkley swept off, cutting a swathe through the other shoppers, swatting them aside with her laminated signs.

Gwen's heart was doing somersaults. She needed to sit down – to lie down. A darkened room. A cold compress. But there was the shopping to do, Basil to deal with, nowhere to hide in the wide vistas of Waitrose.

Steam was coming out of Basil's ears. 'That woman! Who does she think she is? What she said about the museum: that was slander!'

'Well, Basil, it was your own fault,' said Gwen impetuously, not having the strength to pick her words carefully. 'You wouldn't keep your mouth shut.'

'Me! Me, keep my mouth shut!' Basil glowered at her, eyes nearly popping out of his head.

This is quite ridiculous, thought Gwen. *Rowing in public – in Waitrose – by the cauliflowers. Which reminds me....*

She reached out, plucked a cauliflower, dropped it in the trolley. This simple, practical act calmed her. She began to breathe again.

'This parish council business,' Basil said. 'I absolutely forbid it. I won't let you do it.'

'Don't be silly, Basil.' She rather liked the sound of that: *don't be silly, Basil*. If it was good enough for Lady Darkley, why should it not be good enough for her? 'Don't be silly, Basil. There's no way I can get out of it now. Anyway, I shan't get elected so there's no need to worry.' (Who would vote for a newcomer, twice married; a fish-wife who bullied her husband into going shopping?)

Easing Basil aside, Gwen took control of the shopping trolley, wheeled it up the fruit and veg aisle, paused, picked over the

Golden Delicious, decided against them, set off again, all the while bracing herself for the inevitable outburst. But to her surprise, Basil – stomping along beside her – kept his peace. Basil showing forbearance? Whatever next!

'This way, Basil. Come along.' Gwen turned into another aisle, back on track now, slipping into the well-worn groove of her shopping routine. She reached for some tins of Heinz baked beans (they were in the same pace they'd always been – Mr Wetherby must be going potty in his old age), ignoring the discount brand, waited for Basil to pass comment, daring him.

But all he said as they moved on again was, 'You are becoming very bossy, Gwendolen.'

He sounded (and looked) sulky, resentful, but was there something else too, some other element in his tone of voice, in the way he was plodding along beside her. One might almost have thought that he was quite pleased beneath that bluff exterior, as if he quite liked her being bossy once in a while. But that couldn't be right; she must be imagining it.

Gwen slowly got her breathing back under control, felt her heart slowing to its normal rate. The dizziness faded away. She must gainsay Basil more often if this was the effect it had. And had she not saved the Exhibition single-handedly? She was actually looking forward to the Exhibition. She had not realized how much until now. And there was not long to go, Easter almost upon them, the opening ceremony just round the corner.

She experienced a surge of excitement, felt like hopping and skipping around the aisles, singing too. But of course she didn't. One couldn't very well do something like that in Waitrose.

TWENTY-FIVE

THEY CALLED IT Good Friday, but Dean could not see anything good about it. For one thing, he'd been bullied into turning out and dancing with the Morris men in honour of the Exhibition. Dean didn't give a fig for the poxy Exhibition. He had better things to do with his time, like staying in bed (this was meant to be a holiday) or thinking about Cally.

Actually, he *was* thinking about Cally. He couldn't not think about Cally: he'd tried and it didn't work.

On the whole, though, he was rather proud of himself. He'd gritted his teeth, got on with the job; hadn't sulked like a little kid, hadn't said *do I have to* even once. Quite a crowd had gathered in front of the village hall and he hated being stared at, but he had acquitted himself well, proved there was something he was good at, something that the gawpers wouldn't have the first clue about. Plus, he looked good in his Morris kit. Cally had said so. *Fit*, she had said: *fit*.

Cally! Why wasn't she here?

Amanda, of course, had to do her best to burst his bubble. 'You were out of sync in the middle section, Dean. The others were waving their handkerchiefs when you were still twizzling.' She sounded smug. He despised her.

'I wasn't out of sync. It was the others. What do you know about it anyway?'

'She's right, though.' Another know-all butted in. 'Even I could see it – once she'd pointed it out, like.'

Dean glowered at Old George. It was none of his business. He was just an old curmudgeon, the sort who shouted at kids playing in the street and claimed they were making too much noise (Dean

191

had a long memory). Why was George talking to Amanda anyway? Was he some sort of paedophile? Serve Amanda right if he was.

Dean wiped his face on his sleeve. He was hot and sweaty after his exertions, and it was a warm day. The sun was shining, making his head ache. He needed a drink and a rest. Why were they all standing around like lemons? Where was Cally? She'd said she'd be here. But then Lady Darkley hadn't shown up yet, either.

Another time he'd have gone home and changed, but he desperately wanted Cally to see him in his Morris kit again – although, now he came to think about it, she'd been quite drunk when she'd said that stuff about him looking fit: drunk *and* stoned. What if she—

But the kiss! The kiss! He couldn't be mistaken about that, could he?

Only why hadn't she called or texted since then? Was she really not here yet – really, really, *really* not?

He looked round, searching the crowd. His mother was waving to him (God, how *embarrassing*); Basil had shown up too (you didn't like to even begin imagining what he was thinking: the word *sissified* probably came into it somewhere). Sandra was nearby (he was so over Sandra, she was nothing compared to Cally). The squire, perspiring freely, looked like a dumpling in his white Morris kit. The panther was wearing some sort of poncho, it looked ridiculous (but best not to think about the panther). Mr Armitage from college was with her; you'd have thought he'd have known better (though he *was* a bit weird). The withered old Wetherbys had staggered down from their house on Well Lane (shouldn't they be in a home at their age?). Mrs nosey-parker Pole was ear-bending the vicar. A girl reporter from the local paper was making notes: there was a photographer with her (he hadn't taken any pictures of the dancing, had he?). There were people, people, people everywhere you looked (it was almost as if this stupid Exhibition was actually *important*), but there was no sign of the one person he most wanted to see. Cally really, really, really wasn't there.

No Richard, either, but that was a bonus. Perhaps he was avoiding Sandra. Rumour was they'd split up.

All heads turned at the sound of a car engine. A massive four-by-four came hurtling down High Street and screeched to a halt outside the pub, all but blocking the road. Lady Darkley got out on one side, done up in her best tweed and green wellies, a chunky handbag dangling off her arm. Cally got out on the other side.

Cally.

Dean broke out in a fresh sweat. His heart moved up a gear.

Cally.

And she was looking at him – *smiling* at him. Oh shit! Surely the human body wasn't designed to cope with such stress. All his systems were overloading.

'Nice of her to show up,' said Old George drily.

'Nice of who to show up?' Dean couldn't take his eyes off Cally.

'*Her*. Lady Darkness. Kept us waiting long enough.'

'Cally's had her hair done,' said Amanda. 'It doesn't suit her.'

Dean ignored this. Amanda didn't know what she was talking about. Cally's hair looked brilliant, just like a pop star's. He would tell her so when he got the chance (good job Amanda had pointed it out).

But it was impossible to get near Cally in the crush. The crowd was surging towards the village hall where there was a ribbon tied across the doorway. Lady Darkley moved up to it, flanked by Dick Emery on one side, Mrs Pole on the other. The Stasi was elbowed out of the way, the panther was ignored. Silence fell. Dick Emery stepped forward.

'A short prayer.'

The prayer ended. 'And now,' said Dick Emery, 'if I might ask Lady Darkley to say a few words.'

'A few words, my arse,' said Old George at Dean's side. 'Why don't they just get on with it?'

Lady Darkley's voice boomed out, so loud it rocked you back on your heels. Dean tried to make out what she was going on about. 'I will begin, if I may, by saying what a great honour it is for you to have me here today....' Dean blinked. She hadn't *really* said that, had she?

At last the ribbon was cut. There was a round of applause. Dean watched his mother step forward, invite Lady Darkley to enter the village hall. Typical that his mother had been saddled with the job of showing that old dragon around. Obviously no one else had volunteered. Lady Darkley led the way, her sidekick Mrs Pole stuck to her like a limpet. Dean's mother followed. The other members of the committee came next, with Dick Emery bringing up the rear. At the very last moment – just before the ribbon was replaced to keep out the hoi-polloi during the 'royal' visit – Cally slipped in behind them all. *Cheeky*, thought Dean admiringly. Then: *why did she do that, why didn't she come to find me?*

Dark clouds of suspicion began to gather in his mind. He tried to fight his way towards the front of the crowd so he could see better. It was not easy. Everyone else seemed to have the same idea.

If she smiles at me again, said Dean, *then everything's all right. If she doesn't....*

But that didn't bear thinking about.

He finally reached the front row only to find, to his annoyance, that his sister and Old George had followed in his wake. They stood either side of him as he craned his neck over the ribbon. Amanda had somehow got her hands on an Exhibition catalogue and she began to read aloud from it.

'*...an array of home-grown talent, a panoply of artistic endeavour, an affirmation of the central importance of creativity in all our lives—*'

'Shut up,' said Dean.

'*Exhibits numbers one to four*,' Amanda continued, doing that thing where she raised her eyebrows and looked excessively pleased with herself so that you ground your teeth and wished that sororicide was legal (sororicide was a good word, it deserved to be used more often). '*Exhibits numbers one to four: fine pieces of needlework from the skilful hands of Mrs Jean Wetherby of Well Lane....*'

'Sewing!' Lady Darkley had obviously reached exhibits one to four. She had her glasses out but was not wearing them, was holding them up to her eyes like binoculars. She looked less than impressed with what she was seeing.

'It's embroidery,' Dean heard his mother say.

'I daresay it is, but my dear Gwen, sewing is not art. It's drudgery. I'm surprised at Jean Wetherby. I didn't know she *sewed*.'

Lady Darkley swept on, dismissing Mrs Wetherby's embroidery.

'*Exhibits five and six,*' read Amanda. '*Hand-crafted pottery courtesy of Mr Roscoe Mainwaring....*'

Dean scowled, leaning as far as he dared over the ribbon. Why wasn't Cally looking at him? She was talking to Sandra. What were they saying? Was Sandra still banging on about Richard: *why doesn't he text me, I'm so in love, blah-blah-blah?* It was time she got over it. It wasn't as if Richard was anything special – apart from the fact that all the girls fancied him – half the boys, too, or so you'd think, the way they went on, as if he was a superhero or something.

But wait a second: *all* the girls?

Not Cally.

Surely not Cally.

But if she did … if she *did*! Oh God … oh shit … it was too horrible to think about. If Cally *did* fancy Richard then that would be it, Dean would lose all faith in humanity for ever. Not that he had much faith in them to start with. People were so shallow, so annoying. Old George and Amanda, for instance, talking across him as if he wasn't even there.

'Well, girl, what's next? What other delights do we have in store?'

'*Exhibits twelve to sixteen,*' Amanda read, then exclaimed, 'Oh, this should be good. It's Mum's stuff.'

Dean, still following Cally with his eyes, allowed himself a quick glance at his mother's work as Amanda continued to read from the catalogue.

'Number twelve is entitled *A Woman's Work,*' said Amanda. 'Number thirteen: *Divine Inspiration.* Number fourteen: *Feeding Time At The Zoo.* Number fifteen: *They're Here....*'

The 'royal' party was now at the far end of the hall. His mother's paintings were on display facing the entrance but they were so far away it was difficult to make anything out for certain. Was that a kitchen in the first picture? But it was so cluttered and untidy, crockery and utensils everywhere, it couldn't possibly be drawn from life: his mother would have had an apoplectic fit if her kitchen had ever looked like that. The next picture was of what looked like psychedelic banana splits – but he must be wrong, it couldn't be banana splits, no one in their right mind would do a painting of banana splits. Then there was one of baby birds sitting on fluffy clouds – drowning in them, it looked like, from this distance, except that the clouds resembled mashed potato more than anything.

'I think Mum's gone round the twist,' said Amanda.

The 'royal' party had been inspecting Gwen's paintings for some time. At last Lady Darkley's voice came trumpeting down the hall.

'Hmmm. Rather avant-garde for you, Gwen. That one there makes me feel rather itchy. It looks like millions of creepy-crawlies climbing all over each other. I suppose it's what they call *abstract*. Nice try, though. Seven out of ten for effort.'

The 'royal' party moved on, went out of sight behind the display boards, but Lady Darkley's voice could still be heard, reverberating around the hall. 'Yes, yes, very good, good, good.' She seemed to have speeded up now. Probably bored, thought Dean. Who wouldn't be?

'*Exhibit thirty-one*,' read Amanda. '*The Queen of Hearts. Foil on card. Mrs Green, The Bungalows.*'

'Ah. Diana Spencer.' There was an ominous tone to Lady Darkley's disembodied voice. 'Not a good likeness, I have to say. Not a good subject, for that matter. Couldn't stand the woman. All me, me, me. Egotistic. Manipulative.'

'Oh, I agree, all me, me, me, I always said so myself.' Mrs Pole was like an echo.

'Not a nice family, the Spencers. Troublemakers. I won't speak to Charles Spencer any more, won't have anything to do with him.'

'Like she's ever even met him,' muttered Amanda.

'Wouldn't put it past her,' said George. 'Very pushy, Lady Darkness. Bet she used to slobber all over him, until Lady Di began to ruffle a few feathers and they decided to bump her off.'

'That's just a conspiracy theory,' said Dean, feeling the need to enlighten George on this subject: people couldn't be allowed to live in ignorance *all* their lives. 'Conspiracy theories aren't true.'

'And how would you know, boy?'

'I looked at the evidence. I went on the internet and—'

'The interweb? You don't want to take no notice of the interweb.

It's all propaganda. You mark my words, Lady Di was bumped off. Secret Service, it was. They're allowed to kill people if it's on foreign soil.'

Dean opened his mouth to reply, was about to point out that using a double negative as George had just done gave his sentence the opposite meaning to that intended, but then, glancing at George – glinting eyes, stubborn jaw – Dean had second thoughts, decided to keep quiet. Some people got a bit uppity when you took the trouble to point out where they were going wrong. You'd have thought they'd be grateful, but—

'Shut up, you two,' said Amanda. 'Listen!'

'... but what is it meant to *be*?' The 'royal' party had obviously moved closer. They were still out of sight, but Lady Darkley's voice was loud and clear, must have been audible even to those right at the back of the crowd outside. 'There's nothing there. It's just different shades of white.'

'What is it she's looking at, girl?' said George, nudging Amanda.

'*Exhibits forty to forty-six*,' read Amanda. '*Paintings by Lydia Taylor.*'

'Morris dancing, you say? It's meant to be Morris dancing, is it? Well, I'm sorry, but this sort of thing infuriates me. A child could do better. It's meant to be modern, I suppose, like those pickled animals or that dreadful woman with her unmade bed. That's not art. It's an insult to my intelligence. It drags this country's name through the dirt. And this.... What's this called? What? Well, for a start, there aren't any black panthers in England, so what's the point in a picture like that? I'm not even going to look at it, it only encourages more of the same nonsense. Oh, and here's another one. I thought we'd finished. What's this one—?'

A sudden silence fell. People looked at one another. It wasn't like Lady Darkley to be lost for words. What was going on?

The silence stretched out. You could have heard a pin drop.

Old George nudged Amanda again. 'Well?'

Amanda consulted the catalogue. 'It says here, *Beauty in the Eye of the Beholder.*'

'And what's that mean when it's at home?'

Amanda shrugged. 'How should I know?'

The silence was abruptly broken. '*WHAT* is the meaning of this?' It was like a sudden explosion, made people jump, cower, cringe.

'Quick, you young 'uns!' said Old George. 'There's a window round the side. We can see what's happening. Follow me!'

Several other people seemed to have the same idea at the same moment. It began as a casual stroll, one or two amongst the crowd heading towards the corner of the village hall as if they were simply stretching their legs. Within seconds it had become a mad scramble, people pushing and shoving and climbing over each other to get at the narrow window round the side. Old George forged ahead, bony elbows flying, Dean hanging on his coat tails, Amanda tagging on behind. The crowd pressed and squeezed. Thirty or more pairs of eyes strained to see through the miry window.

Dean found himself squashed right up against the glass. He peered through the dirt. The 'royal' party was gathered in front of the last of the display boards where, presumably, the panther's pictures were on show. Dean could make out one with swirls of white and hints of shadow; another where dark shapes seemed to be flitting across a patchwork-quilt landscape. But Lady Darkley was not looking at those. She was standing in front of a different painting. She had her back to the window so you couldn't see her expression. Next to her, Mrs Pole was like a startled rabbit. Dick Emery was rubbing his hands together, uneasy. His mother, Dean noted, looked decidedly sheepish, hovering on the very edge of the little group.

'Huh! It's only a picture of someone with no clothes on.' Old George sounded disappointed. 'Not even a woman, neither. And there was I thinking it would be something juicy.'

Amanda had her head on one side, contemplating the picture which they could only half see. 'Men are ridiculous,' she announced. 'They look ridiculous, is what I mean. It's no wonder they don't go round with their bits on show.'

Dean had an urge to rub Amanda's nose in the dirt on the window. Men were *not* ridiculous, *she* was ridiculous. Though he did sometimes wonder – not that he'd ever mention it or anything – but he *did* wonder if his own bits weren't … well … *lopsided* … and perhaps slightly …

But yeah, well, anyway: how would Amanda have liked it if it had been women's bits on display? Women's bits were ridiculous, if anything was.

Except they weren't. They were ... were.... Words failed him.

The picture being of no interest, Dean tried to locate Cally instead. He could just see the top of her head (was she really that tall?) and one of her legs (her legs...), but the rest of her was hidden by the ample figure of the Stasi. Dean wondered what Cally thought of the painting. Did she have the same opinion as Amanda? It was a worrying thought.

'This is beyond the pale!' Lady Darkley's voice, though muffled by the glass of the window, was still eminently audible. 'Male *pudenda* is most *definitely* not art! It's smut. Pure smut!'

'Don't know why she's getting so het up,' muttered George. 'It's only a John Thomas. She's seen plenty of them in her time, from what I've heard.'

'It's depraved! It's outrageous! I won't have it! My grandfather built this village hall and I won't have it defiled by this filth!'

'T'weren't her grandfather as built the hall,' muttered George. 'It was old Lord Darkley's grandfather, nothing to do with her. She was a nobody afore she married Lord Darkley. Ann Smith, she was called. *Imelda?* Pah!'

'Is nobody going to do anything about it?' trumpeted Lady Darkley. 'In that case, I will! Down with it!'

She lunged for the painting, but at the same moment the panther jumped forward, barring the way.

'Oh no you don't! You're not touching *my* work!' she cried.

Dean goggled as a most undignified struggle ensued, Lady Darkley doing her best to get her hands on the painting, the panther fending her off. Old George was chuckling, the crowd *oohing* and *aahing*.

'Ladies, ladies!' Dick Emery stepped forward, wringing his hands. The two women ignored him.

'I'll thank you to get *out* of my way!' bellowed Lady Darkley, raising her handbag and giving the panther a thwack across the shoulder. The crowd gasped.

Someone pushed to the front of the little group inside. It was Mr

Armitage from college, Dean realized. He hadn't known Mr Armitage was even in the hall. You tended to overlook Mr Armitage most of the time. Not now. He was blazing with anger.

'Stop! How dare you! You can't treat a pregnant woman like that!'

'Pregnant? Did he say pregnant?' There was a buzz in the crowd.

Old George tittered. 'This just gets better 'n' better. Like the telly, this is.'

'Pregnant, is she?' Lady Darkley took a step back – not, thought Dean, due to any solicitude over the panther's condition; more because, with Mr Armitage now also in the way, her path to the porno painting was well and truly blocked. 'Pregnant? Well, that doesn't surprise me. I've heard all about her loose morals. As if we hadn't got enough single mothers sponging off the state – and to have one in *my* village!'

'She's got a head of steam now!' said George delightedly. 'There'll be no stopping her!'

'It's a scandal, the things that go on in this country nowadays, an absolute scandal!' Lady Darkley tiraded. 'Harold Wilson is behind it: Harold Wilson, I tell you. He wreaked havoc on this country. Anything went in the sixties: drugs, permissiveness—'

Who was Harold Wilson? Dean wondered. Would he be on the internet?

'—absolutely anything. It was shameful!'

'And Europe,' murmured Mrs Pole, who was staring up at Lady Darkley with a mix of awe and wonder. 'There's Europe, too.'

'Europe my fanny!' thundered Lady Darkley. (Another gasp from the crowd.) 'Why did we bother fighting the war if we were just going to hand the country over to the Germans afterwards? That was Harold Wilson, too—'

'No it weren't,' said Old George. 'It was Ted Heath, not Harold Wilson. She don't know she's talking about. Never has.'

Dean looked at George, indignant. Harold Wilson, Ted Heath – Dick Emery, for that matter: who were these people, and how come some old relic like George knew more about them than he did? It wasn't right; it made Dean feel almost as if he was *ignorant*. His fingers itched for Wikipedia.

'He should never have been allowed to get away with it, he should have been … should have …' Lady Darkley faltered.

'Put on trial?' suggested Mrs Pole demurely. 'A traitor?'

'I may have misjudged old widow Pole,' murmured George. 'She's a bit of a shit-stirrer on the quiet.'

'He *was* a traitor,' Lady Darkley resumed. 'He was in the pay of Moscow, everyone knows that. And this is what it's led to: filth like this on open display where anyone can see it!'

Lady Darkley made a sudden lunge towards the painting but Mr Armitage stood his ground. You would never have guessed he had it in him, thought Dean.

'It's all right, Terry,' the panther was saying now. 'Let her take the painting if she objects to it so much.'

'I will *not* let her take it!' cried Mr Armitage. 'She's just a bigoted, parasitical, proto-fascist—'

'Please, please, ladies and gentlemen.' The vicar stepped forward again, raising his hands in a sign of peace, his face twitching, a nervous smile coming and going. 'If we could conduct proceedings with a little more decorum. I'm sure with a little calm and rational discussion we can reach a consensus that will—'

'*Consensus!*' Lady Darkley swung round, bore down on him, steamrollering. The vicar backed away in alarm. 'What are you blithering on about, you silly little man? You should be taking the lead! You should be making a stand! What else is a vicar for if not to uphold Christian values?'

'And morals,' Mrs Pole added pertly.

The vicar flinched. 'Well … er … yes, of course … but things are … things are not … always … so … clear-cut. Different points of view, different outlooks, and so on.'

'Points of view? *Points of view!* I have never heard such balderdash! Where in the Bible does it say that one should daub one's walls with filth and obscenity? Is peddling pornography the Christian way? Is this what the Church of England has come to? If you are not careful, you will be turning into one of those happy-clappy, wishy-washy, flower-power vicars!'

'I … I …' Dick Emery looked at that moment as if he very much wished he wasn't any sort of vicar at all – not that he even looked much like a human being, thought Dean, with eyes popping out in alarm, a head jerking like a chicken's, teeth sticking further and further out as he was driven back against the wall by the force of Lady Darkley's onslaught.

'Let me tell you here and now, my good man, I won't have *that* sort of nonsense in *my* church. You had better buck up your ideas. Now do as you're told and come away from this ... this *Exhibition*. I wash my hands of it!'

Lady Darkley spun round to leave – but caught sight of the panther again as she did so. She paused, fixing the panther with a baleful stare. Dean could feel the intensity of it even from outside the hall, but unlike the vicar, the panther stood her ground, looking Lady Darkley in the eye.

Dean trembled. Anything might happen. Weren't there nuclear shelters for this sort of contingency?

'You!' Lady Darkley spat. 'You're behind all this. Don't think you've fooled me for one moment. I know. I know. And to have the effrontery – the brass neck – to stand for the parish council, too! I've never heard anything like it, you ... you ... you snake in the grass!'

With that, she swept past the panther and the other committee members, Mrs Pole trip-trapping behind her. Dick Emery, after a moment's shilly-shallying, looked apologetically at the committee, spread his arms as if to say *what can I do?* and hurried after the two women.

The crowd of spectators was already on the move, dashing back round to the front of the village hall. Dean was caught up in the stampede, bundled along until he found himself by the front door just as the vicar was leaving.

A voice beside him – Old George again – said quietly but very distinctly, 'Ooh, you are awful – but I like you.'

To Dean's astonishment, the vicar went bright red and almost tripped over his own feet in his eagerness to get away.

Lady Darkley cut a swathe through the crowd, people falling back as if at the onset of an enraged bull – all except for the reporter girl who was too busy scribbling in her notebook to realize her peril. The photographer was backing away, click-clicking at top speed, continuing to do so as Lady Darkley bore down on the reporter and gave her a hefty shove in passing so that she went sprawling across the grass, her notepad and pen flying away over the heads of the crowd.

Lady Darkley opened the door of her four-by-four, then turned back to face the crowd, eyes blazing.

'You haven't heard the last of this!'

The car door slammed. The engine roared. Gears crunched. Doing a U-turn in the road, Lady Darkley zigzagged along the High Street past the pub, accelerated up the hill, swerved left, cutting across the green, her wheels slicing through the turf and gouging up great divots of mud. Then her car turned a corner and was gone, zooming off at twice the speed limit in the direction of Overbourne Hall.

Dean let out his breath. All around him there was a buzz of conversation, people talking in little groups, gesticulating, eyes wide with wonder, faces expressing shock, consternation. One voice suddenly rose above the hubbub: Old George's. 'Isn't it about time that pub was open?'

The landlord in his Morris gear said with feeling, 'That sounds like a very good idea.'

But Dean just stood there, blinking in the sunshine (it was bright enough to make your eyes water). He felt crushed, for as Lady Darkley had been getting into her monster car on one side, Cally had got in on the other – and she had not given him so much as a glance.

TWENTY-SIX

THE PUB COULD never have seen such trade, thought Lydia as she pushed her way through the crowd – two-thirds of the village at least. The landlord was working flat out, still in his Morris gear, sweating profusely. *Alas*, she said to him silently, *no time for ogling the female customers today, but think of the profits!*

'Lydia! Lydia! Over here!'

There was an incredible babble, everyone talking at cross purposes, but the Stasi's unmistakable voice rose above the noise, calling Lydia to a table in one corner of the room. Lydia pushed and shoved to reach it, Terry trotting at her heels. She resisted the temptation to pat his head and call him a good boy, even though in the village hall he *had* been a good boy and barked at the nasty woman.

'We're having an emergency meeting,' the Stasi greeted her. 'To decide what to do.'

The landlady was enjoying this, thought Lydia: such drama, and to be in the thick of it! All her Christmases had come at once. But one shouldn't begrudge people their little pleasures.

'Is this all of us?' asked Lydia, taking a seat and looking round at the depleted group.

'Dick Emery has defected,' said Gwen. (*She would never call him* Dick Emery *usually: not in public, not out loud*, thought Lydia. Even Gwen was over-excited.)

'Sandra's on guard duty,' added the Stasi.

'Guard duty?'

'At the village hall,' Gwen explained. 'In case Imelda Darkley comes back and tries to close the Exhibition down.'

'Would she really do that?'

'I wouldn't put it past her,' sighed Gwen.

'How can we stop her? What can we do?' cried the Stasi. 'We must make plans!'

'Perhaps, all things considered,' said Gwen, diffident, hopeful, 'we should call the whole thing off?'

Anything to keep the peace, thought Lydia: but wasn't there something to be said for taking the path of least resistance? One didn't exactly *enjoy* being called a snake in the grass, even in the cause of art, not to mention having one's private business – the baby – broadcast to all and sundry.

Terry leaned forward in his chair. 'You mustn't let the likes of her—' he jerked his head in the direction in which Lady Darkley's four-by-four had disappeared '—walk all over you! Keep the Exhibition open, I say!'

'Yes, we must give people a chance to visit,' said the Stasi. 'It will be in the local paper after this, perhaps on local TV too. People will flock.'

'In that case,' said Gwen, 'perhaps we ought to ... take down the, er, the controversial ... picture....'

'We can't do that!' cried the Stasi. 'That's the one everyone will want to see!' She paused, looked sidelong at Lydia. 'Who,' she said slyly, 'did you get to model for that painting? Who is Mr One-Ball? The face is rather blurred.'

'It is meant to be,' said Lydia. 'It is abstract. Symbolic.'

'But you can tell us, Lydia! We won't let the cat out of the bag!'

'It's no one,' said Lydia, almost speaking the truth. She always felt a certain detachment from her paintings once they were finished, but with this particular work she felt she had hardly been involved at any point during the creative process. It had painted itself, so to speak: the paint had all but flowed onto the canvas of its own accord as if it had nothing to do with her – or with Richard.

But this was not the time or place to start discussing her work, with half the village listening, people hanging on their every word, wondering what would happen next. More drama perhaps? Was it worth sticking round for?

'There can't be many people,' the Stasi mused, 'with only one testicle.'

'More than you'd think.' Lydia tried to control her irritation. 'Hitler only had one ball,' she added and suddenly laughed, remembering Richard stripped and shivering in her little cottage, making pathetic jokes as a fig leaf to cover his embarrassment.

Gwen interrupted. 'Oh, Lydia, *really*!'

The tone of exasperation was out of character, but Gwen, of course, would know exactly who Mr One-Ball was, or at least she would have a very good idea. Jokes about it would seem to her to be in very poor taste.

'We need to decide what to *do*,' Gwen wailed.

'You're right, Gwen, of course.' Lydia was contrite. After all, heaven forefend that she should start acting like a *snake in the grass*.

'It seems to me,' said Terry, who could be relied on to be pragmatic, 'that the Exhibition needs protecting. If you want to keep it up and running, you will need to keep Lady Darkley and her cronies out. There will need to be someone on duty – on guard – day and night.'

'Day *and* night?' repeated Gwen plaintively.

'We can draw up a rota!' exclaimed the Stasi. 'I'm good at rotas, just ask my staff. There are four of us including Terry, plus Sandra of course, and … and you'll help, won't you, George?' Her eagle eyes had spied George loitering in the crowd.

'No I will not!' said George. 'That there Exhibition is a load of old tat!'

'But I thought you were on our side, George!'

'I'm not on nobody's side, me. I like a quiet life. You can count me out.'

'Quiet life!' It was Gwen's daughter piping up, Lydia noted: rather a precocious child. What was her name again? One forgot these things. 'That's not what you said outside, George. Better than telly, *you* said.'

'Never mind what I said!'

'I thought better of you, George, I really did,' sighed Lydia.

'Now then, missus, don't you start. I'll still vote for you in the elections. I'm not voting for old widow Pole, not when she stole my horse manure right from under my nose! I'll vote for you, missus, and for all of you, but that's as far as I go.'

'But what about Imelda Darkley?' said Gwen. 'We can't just ignore her!'

'Oh can't we?' said George mulishly. 'Let me tell you about Lady High-and-Mighty Darkley – or Ann Smith, as I like to call her: it's her name. When she was first married, she used to go hunting—'

'What has this got to do with—' the Stasi began, but George silenced her with a glare.

'As I say, she used to go hunting when she first got married. Now, being in the saddle all day, all those fine ladies, they don't have time or opportunity to go to the loo. So what they used to do is, they shit in their jodhpurs—'

'George! Must you?' Gwen looked pained: you could almost see her temples throbbing with it.

'You're making that up!' shrieked the Stasi excitedly. 'It's revolting!'

'They shit in their jodhpurs,' George repeated, 'and then they pat it all round their thighs, nice and neat.'

'I don't believe that for one moment,' said Lydia.

George turned his baleful stare on her – then, unexpectedly, he grinned. 'Never mind if you believe it or not. All I'm saying is that she shits just like the rest of us. She's not some angel out of heaven. She don't intimidate me. Never has. If she crosses my path, I just picture her patting her jodhpurs and I laugh.'

It might have worked, thought Lydia as she watched George pushing his way to the bar to fetch another light ale, *it might have protected me. But all I could do at the time was wonder if she was right, if my pictures are pointless. Do they strike a chord; or am I waving in the dark?*

'Never mind,' said the Stasi. 'We don't need George anyway. There are still enough of us for a rota. If, that is—' She glanced at Lydia. '—in your condition.' She nudged Lydia with her elbow. 'You're a dark horse! Fancy not telling us, ha ha ha!'

Gwen sat there expressionless – rather magnificent in a way, thought Lydia. You'd never guess that she'd known about the baby for ages. How many other secrets had she got tucked away in that head of hers? So many people talked to her, she made time for them all – even that dreadful Pole woman. And yet she always seemed the most straightforward and transparent of women.

'Quite a surprise, this baby, with you being single and every-thing.' The Stasi was like a dog with a bone. Ears were flapping on all sides. 'I can't imagine who Daddy is!'

Terry stirred in his chair and blurted out, 'Not that it's any of your business, but the baby is mine!'

Lydia gaped at him. Was he out of his mind? He had gone bright red, looked shifty – as if he was regretting his words now. But it was too late, the damage had been done.

There was a fresh buzz of conversation (what was it George had said about all this being better than telly?). Lydia knew that she was being discussed all round the pub. However, talk soon turned back to more interesting matters (Lady Darkley's ballyhoo); there was no sense of outrage, no whiff of scandal, as there might have been if the baby's *real* father had become known – or even if it had been Richard's. The Stasi had already lost interest, was busy drawing up a rota: who was to follow who on guard and when.

Lydia had had enough. It was high time, she decided, for the snake in the grass to slither quietly away. As she pushed her way out of the pub, she was aware of Terry trotting at her heels. She no longer felt like patting him.

Out in the street she rounded on him. 'What were you thinking? I am fed up of people meddling in my life! This baby has nothing to do with anyone except me!'

He looked crestfallen in his shapeless waterproof, old cords, scuffed shoes. 'I ... I was only trying to help, to stop all the hurtful conjecture.'

'I don't need your help, I don't need anyone, I am better off alone. Apart from anything else, what you said in there is patently ridiculous, impossible. There is no way the child could be yours! We have never even—'

'I know! I know that we have never! But that doesn't mean I wouldn't want to, wouldn't *like* to!' His face was even redder now than it had been in the pub. She could almost feel the heat coming off his cheeks. With an air of desperation, he shouted, 'I think you're wonderful, the most wonderful woman in the world!'

Abruptly, he turned and fled, heading for his battered old Renault in the village hall car park. Lydia was left standing in the middle of the road, mouth agape, staring after him.

TWENTY-SEVEN

'Hasn't this gone on long enough?'

Basil looked at his wife down the length of the table, an aggrieved expression on his face. Dean stifled a sigh. This continued wrangling was putting him off his lunch. Adults could be so childish. You wouldn't catch him sulking and grousing and being a misery, not now he was eighteen-and-a-half. He hadn't said *do I have to* in weeks.

Amanda, of course, didn't seem to notice the strained atmosphere, or if she did, it didn't stop her from stuffing her face. She'd end up as fat as a pig, if there was any justice in the world.

But where was the justice in finding a girl then losing her? He hadn't seen Cally in days; there'd been no word. It must all be over. She'd dumped him, and that was cause enough to put you off your soup even without the bickering, his mother and Basil going on and on almost as if they were enjoying themselves – which would be just too, too weird.

'It's the principle of the thing, Basil.'

'What principle?'

'Well, freedom of speech and so forth.'

'Never mind freedom of speech. I've had the *Daily Mail* at my front door, Gwendolen: the *Daily Mail*!'

Dean crumbled his roll, listening, watching his soup go cold. They were talking absolute nonsense. Could they not *hear* what they were saying? He began silently to annotate.

'It's all down to that arty woman.' (Basil, arbitrarily judgmental as usual.)

'What woman?' (Mother being deliberately obtuse. She must know how *irritating* that was.)

'You know what woman' (Stating the obvious.) 'Lydia What's-her-name.' (Pretending he'd forgotten.) 'Dragging you down the pub at all hours for those meetings.' (Outrageous exaggeration.) 'You'll be turning into an alcoholic next!' (Ditto, plus breathtaking hypocrisy.)

'One small glass of wine now and again hardly constitutes alcoholism.' (So prim.)

'Well, I don't know about that, but there is certainly something … different about you just lately, Gwendolen.' (Hmm, he could have a point there.) 'A certain contrariness.' (The trademark Basil frown – and yet, oddly, his tone of voice didn't quite match it. What was going on?) 'That woman leads people astray. She is not in her right mind.'

'Nonsense, Basil!'

'You think her behaviour defensible? Seducing a boy young enough to be her son—'

A warning 'Basil!' stopped his stepfather in his tracks. Silence fell. Dean stirred his soup with a growing sense of unease. This talk of seduction: it was rather too close to the bone. Had the panther said something? But if she had, Basil would have passed some comment or other by now, Dean was sure of it, and as for his mother…. But what other explanation could there be, unless … unless … unless the panther had seduced *someone else*?

Dean watched his mother get to her feet. Nothing more was to be said about the seduction business, that was obvious. Perhaps it was for the best with Amanda sitting there listening. Amanda was already too much of a know-all as it was.

'I'm due down at the village hall for guard duty. If any of you want pudding—'

'Dessert,' Basil corrected her.

'If any of you want *pudding*, you can get it yourselves. Have you finished with that soup, Dean?'

Gwen swept up the plates, cutlery, uneaten rolls and went through to the kitchen. Basil, heaving himself out of his chair, picked up the salt cellar, using it (Dean conjectured) as a transparent excuse to follow Gwen and continue the argument in private.

With Basil out of the way, Amanda leaned across the table and whispered, 'Oh my *God*! Did you hear that bit about Lydia Taylor? It's Richard: it *has* to be Richard!'

'What are you *talking* about?'

'Richard has been doing it with Lydia Taylor!'

'*Doing it!*' Dean mocked such a juvenile euphemism.

'Yes, *doing it*. Sexual intercourse. Copulation.'

Copulation! What sort of word was *copulation*? She was *such* a smart arse. 'There's no evidence whatsoever. You are not being scientific.'

'I am using my powers of deduction. Who else can it be? Who does Miss Taylor hang round with? There's that beardy lecturer from your college, but he's not young enough to be her son. Richard is.'

'But no one would … with *Richard*—'

'Get real, Dean. Richard could charm his way into bed with *anyone*.'

Richard? Charm? She had to be joking.

'Lydia Taylor's all right for her age,' Amanda continued. 'Richard would *so* go there if he got the chance. He's such a slag.'

'But she's—'

'She's what? Go on, Dean! I bet you'd do her!'

'No I *wouldn't*!' Dean felt his cheeks burning, the trauma of that terrible night with the panther coming back to haunt him. Whatever happened, Amanda mustn't be allowed to find out about *that*. He grabbed the pepper pot, began examining it, twisting it round, just to show how cool and nonchalant he was, uninterested in her chit-chat.

'Copulation,' he muttered derisively. 'What a stupid word.'

'It's just sex, Dean,' said Amanda loftily. 'Nothing to be embarrassed about.'

'I'm not embarrassed.'

'Yes you are. You've gone bright red.'

'No I haven't! Anyway, shut up!'

'Embarrassed because you're a virgin. Everyone says you're a virgin.'

Dean ground his teeth, straining every fibre to think of a

crushing riposte, but nothing would come. How did she do it? How did she *always* manage to have the last word? One day he'd—

He would have liked nothing better than to put her straight, tell her that he wasn't a virgin, that he'd done it (*copulated*): but that would let too many cats out of too many bags. He decided to make himself scarce instead, before Basil saw the mess on the table (ground pepper everywhere). But as he made his getaway he ran slap-bang into Basil coming out of the kitchen. Basil had a flask in his hand.

'Ah, Dean. Your mother has forgotten her coffee. Take it down to her, will you?'

'Do I have—' Dean stopped himself just in time. How easy it was to slip back into bad habits! He grabbed the flask. 'All right, I'll do it.' He curled his lip disdainfully (you couldn't be civil to Basil, it wasn't appropriate).

As he skulked down Well Lane, Dean tried to come up with a way of murdering Amanda without anyone suspecting – though it might, he thought suddenly, be better to deal with Richard first. Why did Richard have to stick his oar into *everything*? You couldn't even be *raped* without that bastard wanting a slice of the action (a slice of the panther). And what if Cally…? Oh shit! It didn't bear thinking about!

That miserable old git Mr Wetherby was sitting outside the door of the village hall on a camp chair, representing the forces of darkness (the forces of Lady Darkness, that was). Dean loitered, gathering courage to run the gauntlet. Old Wetherby was sure to make some sort of remark. Several remarks, knowing him.

Dean debated. Did his mother *really* need a flask of coffee? Perhaps if he shouted loud enough she would come out and get it. Or was she not allowed to leave her post inside the door? Would old Wetherby take advantage, nip into the hall and start demolishing the Exhibition? As he dithered, he saw Charley and Ash unexpectedly walk up.

'All right, Morley! What you doing with that flask?' said Charley.

'Got any crème de menthe in it?' asked Ash, grinning.

'Crème de menthe?' said Charley. 'What you on about?'

'Didn't you see him, man? At your party? He got wasted on crème de menthe! It was wicked!'

Dean scowled. 'What are you two doing in the village?'

'We've come to see the Exhibition.'

'It's famous, innit. It's been on the local news and everything: *village at war over art Exhibition* and all that.'

'We've heard—' said Charley, lowering his voice but going no further.

'Yeah, man, we've heard—' Ash looked all round and whispered, 'They say there's pictures of naked women on show: muffs, tits, clits, the lot. Oh man, if I could just—'

A voice behind them said, 'Hi, boys. What are you plotting?'

All three turned. Charley and Ash looked very shamefaced. Dean suspected he did too, but it wasn't his fault; he wasn't the one who'd been talking about naked women.

'Hi, Sandra.'

'All right, Sandra.'

'Charley and Ash have come to see the Exhibition.' Dean got in first, hoping to drop them in it. 'They think there's—'

'Shut up, Morley! We haven't come for the Exhibition, don't be a dork!'

'Oh, but you should!' exclaimed Sandra. 'There are some fantastic pictures, you'll love it. Come on, I'll take you. I'm going in anyway, to see if Mrs Collier needs anything.'

'She needs this.' Dean offloaded the flask, shoving it into Sandra's hands.

'Oh. OK.' Sandra looked expectantly at Charley and Ash. 'Well? Are you coming? It's not just paintings, there's pottery too, and needle-work, and there's a lovely picture of Princess Di made out of foil.'

Charley and Ash were backing away.

'We gotta go, we're busy.'

'Busy doing what?' Sandra enquired.

'Yeah, Ash, busy doing what?' Charley put the onus on his friend.

'We're … er … we're going swimming.'

Sandra raised an eyebrow. 'The swimming pool's closed. Demolished.'

'Yeah, I *know* that,' stuttered Ash, 'but … er … we *would* have gone swimming, if it was still there: that's what I meant to say. I was being ironic, innit. We'd have gone swimming if Morley's dad hadn't tarmacked it over.'

'He is *not* my dad!'

'Dad, stepdad: same thing.'

Dean sighed, but it wasn't worth the bother pointing out to them that he and Basil Collier had no genetic connection whatsoever. They could believe what they liked, he didn't care. What was the point in anything, anyway, when you'd been dumped? He turned to go, drag his heels back up Well Lane, but Sandra called him back. She wanted news of Richard. Richard, bloody Richard, who stuck his oar into everything, who could charm any girl into bed. But not Cally. Surely not Cally.

Dean grimaced, bunched his fists. 'Richard is a bastard.'

'No he's not!' said Sandra indignantly. 'He's funny and exciting and—'

'And he's been copulating with Miss Taylor,' Dean interrupted, fed up of hearing how wonderful Richard was. (*Copulating?* That was Amanda's fault, her and her hoity-toity words.)

Sandra blanched, staring at him.

Charley's eyes were popping out of his head. 'No way, Morley! Your brother's shagging Miss Taylor? This is brilliant!'

'You all right, Sandra?' Ash was peering at her. 'You've gone a funny colour.'

Sandra ignored Ash, and said to Dean, 'I thought you were all right, Dean. I thought you were different. But you're just as bad as the others, making sick jokes and … and … and *telling lies*!'

'I'm not telling lies, it's….' Dean dried up, the look on Sandra's face giving him pause for thought. He wondered if he should take it back about Richard and Lydia Taylor, admit that it wasn't a fully fledged scientific fact, but if there was one thing you could say about Amanda it was that she knew it all. If she thought it was true, then it probably was.

'Miss Taylor!' Sandra's voice rose, wavered, cracked. 'Miss *Taylor*! But she's so … so old! She wears charity shop clothes! And … and I *liked* her, I thought she was really *nice*!'

215

'Now then, Sandra,' said Charley, putting an avuncular arm round her shoulders. 'Don't upset yourself—'

'Get off me, you creep!' Sandra twisted away from him, eyes blazing. 'You are such a pervert, I don't know why I ever wasted my time on you! And you—' She turned on Dean. 'I hate you! I hate you!' She flung the flask at him, went running down the hill past the church and around the corner.

Slowly Dean bent down to pick up the flask. It made an ominous tinkling sound. Broken. Guess who'd get the blame for that? What was it with people, why did they have to shoot the messenger? And with Charley and Ash lapping it up – that old git Wetherby, too – it would be all round the village, all round college before you knew it. Richard, showing him up yet again.

Dean turned his back on them without another word and set off for home.

'It's not my fault,' he muttered as he retraced his steps up Well Lane, clutching the broken flask to his chest. 'It's not my fault.'

GWEN THOUGHT LONGINGLY of her warm and comfortable bed as she headed down Well Lane for the late shift. Most of the houses and cottages were in darkness. Lights showed in a couple of windows. Street lamps were few and far between.

She would never have admitted it to Basil, but she was having serious doubts about the wisdom of carrying on with this siege or stand-off or whatever one liked to call it. It was all very well sitting on the door during the day. One would have had to do that anyway, and one was kept busy, the Exhibition being something of a hit. Guarding the place at night seemed rather excessive and was horribly inconvenient – although, unfortunately, she could see why it was necessary. Lady Darkley, being on the village hall committee, was bound to have access to a spare set of keys and she might strike at any time, night or day. It was such a nuisance.

Gwen took over from the Stasi, as required by the rota. Watching the landlady toddle back to the pub, Gwen said, *I must stop calling her the Stasi. It will slip out in conversation one day and that would be disastrous.*

Gwen unpacked her little bag, placing her pillow on the plastic chair, pulling out her packet of sandwiches along with a blanket, a torch and a flask of tea (a new flask, Dean had broken the old one: typical Dean). She took a peek outside where Jean Wetherby was sitting on a camp chair huddled in her duffle coat. Gwen could not fathom why the forces of darkness thought it necessary to keep vigil all night as well. Poor Jean looked perished. It was only April, after all. Being so thin and bony, one would feel the cold. Was it really fair to lumber her with the late shift at her age? All the same, Gwen took comfort in the older woman's presence: it was much preferable to being alone.

Gwen settled on her chair in the pool of light by the door. Glancing over her shoulder, she thought of all the exhibits in the darkness of the hall, her own paintings amongst them. There was no doubt the Exhibition had been a runaway success. People had come flocking, as the Stasi had predicted. Lydia had been the star, of course. One couldn't really begrudge her. Her work *was* rather impressive – such use of colour, such intricate detail, such *imagination* – though what had possessed her to paint Richard in the ... well, in the *nude* (not to put too fine a point on it), what had possessed her was a mystery. Something to do with the dignity of man, one gathered, but, really, one couldn't even begin to understand; and one didn't like to be caught staring at a picture like that. Luckily, Richard's name had been kept out of it despite all the fuss and palaver (and despite the Stasi's best detective work). One had to be thankful for small mercies. Basil would have—

But one did not like to think of what Basil would have done.

Gwen yawned, covering her mouth with her hand. What time was it? Not yet one o'clock. Hours to go. And poor Jean outside: she had to be chilled to the marrow. How long was she here for? One could ask her ... couldn't one? They might be on opposite sides, but that didn't mean one had to be *churlish*.

'Jean?' Gwen opened the door a little wider. 'Jean? What time do you finish?'

'I? Oh. Five. Hmm. Yes. Five.'

'Five o'clock! Oh, poor you! I'm off at three. I hand over to Sandra at three.'

'Ah. Hmm.'

The ice broken, Gwen moved nearer the door, and Mrs Wetherby shuffled her chair a little closer too. They were able to conduct a conversation of sorts (Jean Wetherby was hard work at the best of times). It was better than sitting there yawning and trying to prop one's eyes open. It helped pass the time.

The clock struck one, then two. It grew very cold, very still. Their whispered voices sounded loud, so they lowered them yet further – as if afraid of disturbing ... what? Not people, not at this time of night. Everyone with any sense was locked away, tucked up in bed. The pub lights were off, the cottages opposite all in darkness. There might, perhaps, be ghosts abroad, with the churchyard so close, but one didn't really believe in ghosts. What else might be lurking in the shadows? Dean had said something about panthers. One wouldn't normally take any notice, but this was a different world, a world one barely recognized. Even the street lamps seemed dimmer at this hour, the circles of light round them slowly contracting, the darkness closing in.

Gwen would have liked to have shut the hall door, but it would hardly be fair on poor Jean.

'I do think it's a bit off, Jean, making you sit here all night in the cold and dark.'

'Oh. Hmm. Yes. But Donald … and Imelda….'

Yes, thought Gwen impatiently, pulling her blanket closer round her shoulders. Wasn't that always the way? There was always a *but*. But Donald, but Imelda – but Basil, too; not to mention Lydia and the Stasi. Why did one try so hard to please people all the time? In the bright light of day, one hardly gave it a thought, it seemed eminently sensible. It was only now, in the middle of the night – two o'clock – that one began to wonder if it was worth it. But how did one put all this into words?

'All this fuss, Jean,' Gwen hazarded. 'And over what? A little Exhibition. Nothing.'

'Not nothing. I—'

'Well, I suppose you're right, it's not exactly nothing.'

'And, hmm, yes.'

'Oh, I agree, Jean. But, you see, we didn't set out to….' Gwen paused, tried to put her thoughts in order. If one wasn't careful, one could easily end up like poor Jean Wetherby, never a sentence finished. 'It was not part of the plan,' Gwen said, picking her words, 'to *upset* anyone.'

Mrs Wetherby raised a bony claw, pointing into the shadows of the village hall. 'That painting.'

'I know what you mean, Jean. I have my doubts about it too.'

'But it's … I….'

'You?'

'Had.'

'You had?'

'Mastectomy.'

'Oh, Jean! I didn't know! I'm so ...' *So sorry?* Was that the best she could do? Gwen shook her head, exasperated. Words at this time of night were so small and hollow, scraped clean of almost all meaning. Yet what else could one rely on, when even the street lamps didn't keep back the creeping darkness? 'I'm so sorry. I can see why that painting would bring it all back.'

'Donald....'

'Donald found it difficult, I presume.'

'He never ...'

'Never?'

'Touched me. Afterwards.'

'Oh. Oh, I see. Well, it ... it takes time, I suppose: time to get used to it, I mean.' And yet, thought Gwen, when one looked at that picture of Richard one didn't really notice the afflicted area – one didn't notice his *private parts* (to put it bluntly). There was, in fact, something rather majestic about the way he gazed out of the painting (the sharp, clear eyes were most definitely Richard's eyes, despite the rather blurred face). He looked like some primeval explorer surveying a wide vista of uncharted lands, lands never trodden by the feet of man. One felt that it would never have occurred to such a heroic figure to worry about being, well, *nude*. But one could hardly say something like that out loud – not when one was reputedly so sensible, a woman who kept her feet on the ground. And, it had to be admitted, there might be people who didn't see the painting in quite the same way, people who didn't think of the wide vistas but who looked for the flaws and imperfections, for something to criticize; someone like Donald Wetherby, for instance. He had never been the most tolerant of men. But surely even Donald would come round in the end, when it was his own wife; when one had made a vow, a commitment; when common decency came into play?

'But it must take time to adjust,' Gwen murmured. 'How long is it, Jean – if you don't mind me asking – since...?' (One had never heard a whisper; even Mrs Pole must be in the dark about this.)

'1974.'

'1974! But ... but Jean! That's nearly forty years ago! And in all that time Donald has never ... never...?'

'Mmm. Forty years. Never.'

Mrs Wetherby folded her hands in her lap, sitting upright in her chair. Dignified, thought Gwen. And once upon a time she had been proud, too – rather too proud, by all accounts: a snooty woman. Had they cut away all that, too, when they sliced into her with their knives all those years ago? And to think that Donald, that lecherous little gnome—

But one shouldn't judge. One didn't know the particulars. One's own marriage must look very different to outsiders.

Gwen wondered if Jean had ever spoken about this before; or had she been waiting forty years to do so, waiting for a sign? It might never have happened had they not been sitting here in the dead of night, alone. It might never have happened but for Lydia's painting. That had been the sign Jean Wetherby needed. Was that what Lydia had intended: to strip away the surface and expose the flaws and disfigurements in everyone? It was remarkably clever – and terribly dangerous. But one had to admit that one saw the world in a different light because of it. One saw Jean Wetherby in a different light. One would never have guessed what was behind the familiar facade. One had thought of Jean as an emaciated old sparrow who had not completed a sentence for – well, for forty years.

'Oh, Jean! What are we doing? We should ...' Gwen groped for the right words, but what was the use when they were all so hollow and scraped – when Jean was out there and she herself in here? 'We should all be on the same side. We are on the same side, really.'

'But—'

'Yes. Yes, I see.' It always came down to that in the end: but Donald, but Basil, but Imelda. And yet *they* were people too: Donald and Basil and Imelda. What had Donald seen, looking at Lydia's powerful painting: his own wife, perhaps, who he hadn't been able to bring himself to touch for forty years? What had Imelda seen? What had been reflected back at her? One would never know. That was the tragedy of it.

'There are no sides, Jean: that's how I see it. There are no sides. It's more like ... like a *web* we fall into. Threads attach. We are caught – cradled, yes; but there is no escape either.' *I am talking nonsense*, Gwen said to herself. *Even I don't know what I am trying to say. Oh Lydia, you have a lot to answer for, stripping us bare like this!*

Mrs Wetherby, leaning across, patted Gwen's hand as it rested on the arm of her chair: a curiously decisive gesture for one who was usually so hesitant. Her skin was cold to the touch, and papery; her fingers bony.

She is comforting me, thought Gwen with surprise. *And there was I, feeling sorry for her. But she has had the right idea all along. What is the use of saying anything – of finishing a sentence – when a pat on the hand is more eloquent than all the words in the world?*

'My word!' Gwen gathered herself, spoke brightly, clearly, defying the shadows. 'The things one finds oneself talking about at half past two in the morning! I feel quite parched after all that. How would you like a cup of tea, Jean, and a sandwich?'

Gwen reached for her flask.

TWENTY-NINE

LYDIA WOKE FROM a deep sleep to the sound of someone hammering on her door, making enough noise to wake the dead. She did feel half dead, too, as she prised herself out of bed, glancing bleary eyed at the clock. Was it really half past four?

Bang-bang-bang. Bang-bang-bang. Insistent. Urgent. And a voice – no, two voices: 'Lydia! Lydia!' If they carried on like that, they'd wake the Wetherbys, and then there'd be hell to pay.

Pulling on her dressing gown, she hurried barefoot downstairs, unbolted the door.

Gwen and the Stasi were on the doorstep wearing a motley collection of clothes as if they'd both got hurriedly dressed in the dark. Gwen's hair was tousled. The Stasi looked pasty-faced without her make-up. Both had bags under their eyes. The nightly vigils were taking their toll.

'Oh, Lydia, at last! Thank goodness. You must come at once—'

'It's the forces of darkness!' The Stasi jumped in, her voice echoing to the sky in the dead quiet of the sleeping village. 'They've broken in – they're in there now. Heaven alone knows what they're going to do.'

'What?' Lydia's mind was still slumbering.

'The forces of darkness!' cried the Stasi. 'Lady Darkley, Mrs Pole and the others. They're in the village hall! I was asleep in bed. I heard a noise. I looked out, and there they were! I said to my husband, I said—'

'Never mind that,' said Gwen, interrupting in a most un-Gwen-like way. 'We must get down there as quickly as we can!'

It was an emergency, Lydia realized as her brain at last clicked

223

into gear. She reached for the nearest footwear – a pair of flip-flops – and without further ado followed Gwen and the Stasi down Well Lane at full speed.

There was a flickering light ahead and, as they rounded the bend in the road and the pub and the village hall came into view, Lydia saw that a bonfire had been lit on the grassy space between the two buildings. All the lights were ablaze in the village hall. The doors were wide open. Mrs Wetherby stood nearby with her camp chair, wringing her hands. Lady Darkley's four-by-four was parked slap-bang in the middle of the road. Some people from the cottages opposite, most in night attire, had come out to see what all the noise was. The pub landlord, in a vest, pyjama trousers and wellington boots, was talking to Old George who was dressed as always in his cap, cardigan and old cords (did he go to bed in them?). Sandra, standing alone, was in floods of tears.

'Sandra, my dear!' Gwen hurried to put an arm around the distressed girl. 'You were on guard, weren't you? Did they hurt you? Oh you poor thing!'

'I ...'sobbed Sandra. 'I ...'

'What are they burning?' asked Lydia anxiously.

'Your picture, missus,' said Old George. 'The one of the nudey man.'

'But they can't do that!'

'Why didn't you do something to stop them, you useless lump?' The Stasi was lambasting her husband, punching and slapping. 'Why didn't you *do* something!'

The landlord seemed immune to the violence – or else he was used to it. 'Not me. I'm steering clear of that lot in there. You should have stayed here instead of running off, then *you* could have done something.'

'But I had to fetch Gwen and Lydia, you stupid idiot!' Smack, slap, thump. 'And now they're burning down our Exhibition! All our hard work, going up in flames!'

'It's only the one painting they've burned,' said George placidly. 'The rest of the bonfire's some rubbish Lady Darkness had in her car, and one or two of them display boards from the hall. Most of your so-called Exhibition is over there on the grass.'

George pointed. Lydia saw, strewn on the ground, a jumble of paintings, pottery, photographs, all the precious artwork and handicrafts tossed aside: Gwen's pictures, Roscoe Mainwaring's pots, the foil Diana glinting in the dancing firelight. Hours of work and dedication – people's pride and joy – treated like rubbish, left to rot.

Worst of all, though, was the thought of her painting, gone for good. She had never produced a work so quickly, so easily – and yet every moment had been filled with a fizzing sense of achievement. For once (and once only?), she had been able to seize the idea in her head and reproduce it exactly on the canvas. She had not really thought in terms of a subject or a composition; she had been consumed by the form, the colours, the energy. It had taken shape as if by magic, a figure stepping out of a golden mist like a summer's dawn, a simple human figure in which was distilled (she had felt) all the grandeur and nobility of one of those colossal statues of Ramses III at Luxor. She had never dared believe that she was capable of such a creation.

And now the picture had been burnt to cinders. She was back to square one, bereft. It felt as if a black pit had opened up inside her. It was like being catapulted back to the worst moments after Prize's death.

'Thought you'd make a fresh start, did you?' Her mother's ghost was at her elbow to rub it in. 'Ha! You'll never change now, not at your time of life. You've missed the bus, my girl. And you're not fit to be around people. Look at the chaos you've caused! Just look!'

Lydia did not want to look; did not want to see the fire burning, the people staring; did not want to hear the clattering and banging coming from inside the village hall, or the sound of Sandra sobbing as Gwen comforted her.

'There, there. It's not your fault, Sandra. We should never have left you on your own, a young girl like you.'

'But it *is* my fault!' cried Sandra. 'It's all my fault! I let them in—'

'You did *what*?' The Stasi rounded on her. 'What are you saying, Sandra? Why would you go and do a stupid thing like that?'

'She's upset,' said Gwen. 'She doesn't know what she's saying.'

'I do know what I'm saying. It's all true. I waited until you'd gone, Mrs Collier, then I phoned her: I phoned Lady Darkley. I told

225

her to come at once. Mrs Wetherby tried to stop me, but I wouldn't listen. I didn't care.'

'Oh Sandra …' Gwen sighed.

'It's because of *her*!'

Lydia found an accusing finger pointing at her. All eyes turned to look.

'It's because of her! She slept with Richard. He was my boyfriend. And now he won't even talk to me. I wanted to make her pay. But … oh … oh….'

'Well, well.' The sardonic voice in Lydia's ear was complacent, smug. 'Didn't I tell you this would happen? I knew you'd end up a laughing stock. You've been acting like a trollop these last few months. Now the chickens are coming home to roost.'

Lydia closed her eyes for a moment, tried to pretend it was all a dream, but she could not block out the thumping and bumping from the village hall, the murmuring voices of the onlookers, or Sandra's weeping.

'I didn't know they'd *burn* things,' Sandra wailed. 'I didn't know they'd do that. They just ripped everything down, it was horrible. I wish I'd never … never….'

'Hush, now. It's all right, Sandra. We'll get everything sorted out, don't you worry.'

Lydia opened her eyes. Sandra was being led aside by Gwen and a police car was nosing up the hill past the church, blue lights flashing, dazzling in the dim twilight.

At that moment, Lady Darkley herself emerged from inside the village hall, followed by Mrs Pole and a couple of other stiff and starchy middle-aged women from the big houses on the Overbourne Road. They turned the lights off inside the hall and Lady Darkley locked the door.

'At last,' she said with satisfaction, 'at last we have restored some order!'

With the village hall lights off and the bonfire dying down, it became more obvious that dawn was at hand, the sky a murky grey, the air damp and chill. A new day was coming, but to Lydia it felt more like the end of things. She was like the ashes of the fire: burnt out, dried up, trampled in the mud. She wanted to go home, to run and hide, but one last little spark inside her told her to rescue her paintings first, to pick them off the grass before the dew ruined them. Her masterpiece had gone, and the rest seemed worthless, but it was better to save what she could than to be left with nothing.

As she sorted through the loot, she saw a policeman and a policewoman approach, steady and cautious, looking all round, taking it in.

'Morning. What's all this then?' said the policeman.

'We had reports of a disturbance,' said the policewoman.

'Not a disturbance,' trumpeted Lady Darkley. 'The restoration of law and order.'

The Stasi, of course, could not bear to be ignored. 'Excuse me, if I could just have a word—'

'And you are, madam?'

'I am a local businesswoman, a licencee, the organizer of this very popular and successful Exhibition. These people—these vandals—'

But she was outnumbered by Lady Darkley and her coven, her voice drowned out by their shrill voices. '... disgusting ... offensive ... filth ... nothing but pornography ... one has to draw a line ... common decency, Christian values....'

'Now then, ladies, one at a time, please.'

'Never mind *one at a time*,' trumpeted Lady Darkley. 'Do you know who I am? Let me tell you, young man—'

'It's PC Collins, if you please, madam.'

'Let me tell you, my late husband was very good friends with your chief constable, very good friends indeed. I would watch my Ps and Qs if I were you!'

Lydia had gathered all her paintings, found it was possible to slip quietly away now that all attention was focussed on the police officers and the group of women round them. But as she made her way up Well Lane, the voices pursued her, loud in the clammy air.

'... when I'm elected to the parish council, I will ...'

'... as if a woman like you – a *publican* – will ever get on the parish council....'

'... if I could just take a few details, madam....'

'... we hear far too much about rights and not enough about responsibility: write that in your little black book....'

And finally Lady Darkley's foghorn voice trumping the lot, blasting through the morning mist: 'Everyone can now see those people for what they are. They are finished, outcasts: nobody will want to know them! They won't be getting on the parish council, I assure you. We will get this ridiculous election over and then it will become clear who really runs this village!'

THIRTY

DEAN HAD THOUGHT it best not to go in his car, wanting to be inconspicuous, to see how the land lay, but having taken the footpath towards Overbourne Hall he'd found his way barred by chained gates and notices about bulls. He'd had to go the long way round, wading through beds of nettles, pushing past clinging brambles, ducking under low leafy branches. After about a hundred years (he let the exaggeration pass, he was in no mood for accuracy), he'd finally reached the rutted track which led to the back of the hall. He was hot, sweaty, worn out; wished he was back at home; just wanted to lie down and rest. But having come all this way, he couldn't turn back now. The possibility of seeing Cally spurred him on.

Overbourne Hall loomed ahead. It was a big, square, sandy-coloured building with many windows and crumbling stonework. Here at the back there were some brick-built additions, sheds and stables and so on. Somewhere, dogs were barking. This made Dean nervous. He did not like dogs. Dogs were insidious. They acted like they were stupid, but really they were very smart, very sneaky. You only had to look at the way they'd inveigled humans into 'domesticating' them, so that now they lived in the lap of luxury, lying around all day, getting fed at regular intervals – getting fat, too, if that mangy mutt of the panther's had been anything of an example. If dogs had been humans they'd have been labelled layabouts, dole scroungers, benefit cheats, but because dogs were dogs they got away with it. Dogs needed to be shown up for what they were. What people ought to do was—

But there was no time for that – no time to say what people ought to do: because he was here, he'd arrived.

Keeping close to the nearest wall, he edged his way into the stable yard, looking round warily. The barking dogs were still safely distant. The yard was empty apart from Lady Darkley's four-by-four parked over by the house. It was also filthy, full of dried mud and piles of horses' doings. Near at hand was a dark opening; old wooden doors, splintered and collapsing, hung off rusty hinges. There was a voice coming from inside: a woman's voice – a girl's voice – low and soothing. He couldn't make out the words.

He stepped inside. Slowly, his eyes got used to the shadows. It was a big barn-type place with compartments on the far side, and lots of corroded machinery and bales of hay stacked up. Daylight leaked in through holes in the roof. The voice was coming from inside one of the compartments. Cally's voice?

Yes, definitely Cally. Cally!

Propelled forward by an overwhelming desire to see her, Dean stumbled across the uneven floor towards the compartments and looked over a sort of gate or half-door. There she was, in a pair of old jodhpurs and a knitted jumper, brushing a horse with a large brush, talking to it (hadn't she said something about horses being her only friends?). Dean wasn't interested in the horse, wanted to ignore it – except you couldn't, it was so massive, so dangerous-looking, moving its lips most disconcertingly, and looking right at Dean with enormous, mocking eyes.

He took a step back, glanced nervously round. Was there anywhere he could hide if the great brute came at him? It was monstrous and it stank (mind you, the whole place stank; it was an unhygienic hovel). Horses ought to be securely chained, thought Dean. There ought to be a law—

Cally came out of the cubicle-thing. 'Dean! What are you doing here?'

She stood looking at him, waiting, guarded. The horse was also looking at him, stretching its neck over her shoulder. You got the impression that it hadn't yet made up its mind whether to kick down the door and charge, or simply toss its mane and not deign to notice him. It came across as very superior; and why shouldn't it, when it held all the cards? It was Cally's best friend, and she'd been talking to it, brushing it, stroking it.

Dean experienced a fierce spasm of jealousy which impelled him to speak. 'I've come to—' He stopped. His voice sounded ridiculous, all gravelly, but it was the only voice he had. He could either use it, or stand in silence like a moron. He began again. 'I've come to ... to see you.'

'That's nice,' Cally said. 'I was grooming my horse,' she added.

'Oh.'

'When I say *my* horse, he's not actually mine, he's Grandma's.'

'Oh.'

'Would you like to stroke him?'

'No.' *I'd rather stroke you.* 'Where have you *been*?'

'What do you mean, where have I been?'

'I haven't seen you.' It wasn't strictly true: he'd seen her at that stupid Exhibition last week but he'd not been able to get near her, he'd been forced to watch from afar whilst all round people had been carrying on like raving lunatics – all over a few paintings or something. 'You *ignored* me,' he accused her. 'At the village hall. You ignored me.'

'I didn't mean to. It was just, with everything going on and Grandma flipping her lid, I was so *embarrassed*. Anyway—' She wrinkled her nose. 'I thought you might have phoned or something. I thought you might have got in touch, after Charley's party.'

'*Me* phone *you*?'

'It's what boys do. They phone, they text, they run after you – they run after girls.'

'But I'm ...' *I'm not like other boys, I am a freak.* She knew that, didn't she?

A feeling of hopelessness swamped him. The real Dean Morley – somewhere deep inside – was screaming and shouting to be let out; but it was no good: he was trapped inside this useless body. Even speech was impossible right now, a simple thing like that. It hadn't been such a problem at Charley's party. It had been easy then. Well, not easy as such, but somehow, Dean remembered with a pang, he had got it right, been a hit with her. How had it happened? How had he managed it?

Maybe Cally would be better off with someone else, a proper boy, one who phoned and texted and ran after her – someone like Richard.

'Richard!' he muttered, grinding his teeth.

'What about Richard?'

He's a bastard, a half-wit, a diseased, debauched Neanderthal.
Except that nobody saw it, thought Dean with a sense of despair.
'Everyone likes Richard,' he said, unable to fight the injustice of it
any more. 'He's everyone's favourite.'

Cally pulled a face. 'He's so full of himself. I prefer quiet boys.
Shy boys.' She smiled at him significantly, then said, 'You've got bits
in your hair, Dean. Twigs. Burrs.'

She reached up, began picking things out of his hair (what were
burrs?).

'Your hair,' she said.

His hair, he thought unhappily: his unruly hair that never did as
it was told, that had bits in it – *burrs!*

'You hair looks good when it's all mussed up.' She was stroking
it.

She liked his hair! She preferred shy boys! She was *smiling* at
him! Oh God, oh shit.

'I like you, Dean. Do you like me?'

He nodded vigorously. There was no point trying to find the
right words. He was not sure that the right words had even been
invented.

'What shall we do now?'

'I....' He shook his head. Ideas were lacking.

'We could play mummies and daddies like in the old days. You
could smack my bottom the way you used to.' Her eyes twinkled;
he watched, enthralled. 'Or ...' she added.

'Yes?' he gasped.

'We could....'

'Yes?'

'We could kiss. Like in Charley's shed. Remember?'

Remember? He would never forget! But how had it happened,
how had he contrived it?

'We could kiss....' She was doing it, he didn't have to contrive
anything. 'And then you could do *this* ...'

'Oh....'

'And I could do *that* ...'

'*Oh!*' Now he came to think of it— '*Ooh!*' –she had always been the one who'd— '*Aah!*' – organized the games of mummies and daddies, too.

But this was a million times better than mummies and daddies. And that was no exaggeration.

His legs had turned to rubber. They began to give way. He grabbed hold of Cally, trying to stay on his feet, but she fell with him. They landed on something yielding and prickly. (What on earth was it? His brain groped.) Cally was with him, he had his arms round her, it had happened by magic. And oddly enough, even though she was on top of him, it felt as if a weight had been *lifted*. His heart was revving up in his chest like a souped-up engine, ready for anything. He felt different suddenly, like a whole new person – or should that be the *real* person, the *real* Dean Morley? Whatever was going on, it was obvious something had changed, because the old Dean – the hidebound Dean, the hopeless Dean – *that* Dean would never have allowed himself to fall headlong into such a hackneyed old cliché as to be rolling in the hay.

THIRTY-ONE

GWEN WAS HOOVERING the hallway when Richard let himself in.

She silenced the hoover. 'Richard. What are you doing here?'

'Been on nights. Can't sleep. Thought I'd pay my favourite step-mother a visit.'

'Tea?' she suggested.

He nodded, yawning.

She made tea. They took it outside as it was such a nice morning, sat on the patio, the May sunshine bright and warm, the few clouds high and white (nothing like mashed potato). Basil's garden, the *work in progress* in which progress was notably lacking, over-looked a patchwork of fields and a distant line of trees. Birdsong filled the air. The sound of the far-off motorway was a constant hum on the very edge of hearing.

Richard was yawning massively. It made one wonder how his jaw didn't crack. That jaw, and his cheeks, were dark with a day's growth of beard: like lichen, thought Gwen. One wanted to scrape it off. One wanted to comb his hair, trim his fingernails, polish him up. His trousers were filthy, could do with a wash. His boots – they had trampled dirt all through the house – were not much better. But it didn't end there, she thought with a feeling of despair, her fingers itching as she looked around, seeing the patio that could do with hosing down and scrubbing, the plastic chairs in need of soap and water and a scourer, the sun showing up smudges on the windows. The old compulsion to clean was coming back, threatening to take over. How could she protect herself from it now that the Exhibition was over?

She curled her itching fingers round her cup of tea, trying to steady herself.

'I've a—' Richard began, then stopped to yawn. (She wished he'd cover his mouth when he did that. He had nice teeth, though: got them from his father.)

'You've a what?'

'A bone to pick with you. Telling Lydia about … you know.'

'Ah.'

'You needn't get on your knees and beg. An abject apology will do.'

'But I had no choice, Richard. Lydia was under the impression … she thought she was carrying your …'

'Ironic, when you think about it. Do we know whose child it is? She wouldn't tell me.'

'Nor me. Terry claims responsibility, but …' Gwen shuddered. She did not like to think about it. It was too messy. She liked things neat, uncluttered, ordinary. Husband, wife; son, daughter.

But what about a husband who ran off with a floozy? What about a wife who remarried and acquired a non-neat stepson? That was verging on the messy. No amount of hoovering would clear that up.

'Terry.' Richard, leaning over to put his cup on the ground, looked up at her with a grin. 'One disapproves, does one?'

'One minds one's own business.'

'One didn't mind one's own business in the matter of my procreative potential, or lack thereof.'

'One has— I have explained about that.'

Another yawn displaced his grin. He stretched: arms, legs. 'I don't care. Tell who you like. Tell everyone.'

'I'm not sure that your father …' Gwen looked at him, shielding her eyes with her hand. 'You have changed your tune.'

'Yes, well, Lydia said …' Richard began, then tailed off.

'Hmm,' said Gwen thoughtfully. 'She does have that effect, doesn't she.'

'It was that painting,' he said, sitting back, tilting his head, squinting up at the sun. 'It made me feel … I don't know … *taller* or something. I wanted people to know it was me.'

'That painting has a lot to answer for.'

'Is it true that it's been destroyed?'

'I'm afraid so, yes.'

'And it was all down to Sandra, or so she says.'

'Then you two are…?'

'We have spoken.'

'Oh good. I am glad.'

'She told me in no uncertain terms what she thinks of me.'

'Ah.'

'I explained that Lydia was not to blame.'

'Very … noble … of you.' (Richard? *Noble?*)

'It's that painting. I have to live up to it now.'

'Not everyone admired it. Imelda Darkley for one. She called Lydia a *snake in the grass.*'

'How is dear old Lady Darkness? You have been crossed off her Christmas card list, I presume, since the iniquitous Exhibition?'

'Well, no, as it happens, I haven't.' (Imelda Darkley had telephoned. 'Gwen. So sorry you got mixed up in that farrago. They played on your good nature, I suppose. I don't hold it against you, not in the least. However, I think we have heard the last of them now. As soon as this ridiculous and unnecessary election is over, we can start putting the village to rights.')

'Don't tell me,' said Richard, 'that when you are on the parish council you will be aligning yourself with the forces of darkness?'

'I will not be on the parish council. No one is going to vote for me.' She lowered her hand, letting the sunlight dazzle her, the warmth of it caressing her skin. She wished the election was over, but at least there was not long to wait. After Thursday, she could start getting back to normal.

But what was normal? Cooking, cleaning, getting hysterical about dirt? Best not to think about it.

Gwen stirred. 'More tea, Richard?' But he had fallen asleep in the sunshine, slumped in his plastic chair, legs stretched out, his half-finished cup of tea on the patio beside him. Watching him sleep, Gwen was reminded that there had once been a time when he used to drive her up the wall. Taking her cue from Basil, she had treated him like an overgrown, unruly child. She had taken it for granted that he did not much like her, resented her taking his mother's place, thought her dull and frumpy and out of touch. And then one

236

day he had turned up out of the blue when she was up to her eyes in housework. She had been tearing her hair out, wishing him gone. 'Richard, I have just hoovered in here, will you please take those boots— Don't sit there with those dirty trousers— Must you wipe your nose on your—' She had been so anxious about her newly cleaned sitting room that she hadn't at first noticed the tears sliding down his cheeks.

Sitting on the patio in the May sunshine, Gwen could not help feeling a sense of achievement as she recalled that eventful visit, even if she had carried it off more by luck than judgment. Becoming aware that he was upset, she had been paralyzed with fear, not knowing what to do. The blatant tears, the runny nose, the way he was dribbling as he talked: he ought to have looked more childlike than ever, hunched up on the sofa, but that day he'd seemed more like a man, a stranger.

An undeveloped boy she could cope with. A sanitized husband was no threat. But a raw, undomesticated man! She had been so flustered that she barely recognized the sounds coming out of his mouth, had been unable to account for the word *sample* which had seemed to crop up again and again.

When finally it sank in, she had cowered in her chair, wanting to tidy it away, hoover it up, out of sight, out of mind. His illness should never be mentioned, must be left in the past. But suddenly that day she found herself face to face with it. His samples, he had been telling her, were all gone. There had been some accident: a power cut, the freezers had broken down, she couldn't remember now.

This is Basil's territory, she had said to herself. *I must delegate it to Basil.*

But when she had ventured to say as much, Richard had become violently agitated.

'You can't ... mustn't ... not Dad ... I've only told you ... there's no one else ... and ... court cases, compensation claims ... shit, fuck ... please don't ... he'll only think it's my fault ... the cancer was my fault too....'

One had said, 'Don't be ridiculous, Richard. Your father has never said anything of the sort. Of course he doesn't think that way.' But one had not exactly been able to convince oneself. Not that one had doubts about Basil's paternal feelings; one simply never went near the subject of Basil's *feelings* at all.

'That boy is impossible!' Basil complained, then and now. 'He won't let anyone do anything for him. He is stubborn.'

I wonder where he gets that *from*: those words had often been on the tip of one's tongue but – wisely – one had never spoken them aloud.

Looking at Richard sleeping on the patio, Gwen was at a loss to explain why he'd come to her that day. She remembered that he'd called her *Mum*, that it had slipped out more or less unnoticed. One had assumed at the time that one was merely a substitute for the dead parent Richard craved. Later, one had begun to wonder. From what one had gathered, Basil's first wife had been neither wifely nor maternal. One had, since then, never really minded when Richard called one *Mum*, even if it seemed little more than a joke. One could hardly explain this to Basil, however – not unless one wanted to risk being termed *silly* or *sentimental*.

Thinking about that day now, it was the sense of achievement, warranted or not, that one remembered best – that warmed one just as surely as the May sunshine. Until that day, for instance, one had never in one's whole life uttered the word *sperm*. One could recall a time when one hadn't even known such a word existed – when one wouldn't have *wanted* to know: a time when one was a dutiful, well-behaved little girl with pigtails and a brace on one's teeth.

The problem is, thought Gwen, *I am still that little girl. I still think of myself as having pigtails. I have never changed. I am like a butterfly that has never quite escaped its chrysalis. I am like a caterpillar ashamed of its wings.*

At times, she felt as if something different was just round the corner. That day with Richard. Her painting. Taking Basil shopping. Standing up to Imelda Darkley in Waitrose. But nothing ever quite came of it. And now that the excitement of the Exhibition was over, all that she had left was the nasty little sequel of the parish council election in which she was sure to be humiliated in some way or other.

And so life returned to normal. One put away one's paints. One would wash the patio, scrub the plastic chairs, clean the windows, go back to the endless grind of trying to make the house spic and span. Perhaps it was for the best. Probably it was for the best.

But, oh, if only...!

Silly woman that she was, she found herself dreaming of a different life. It was almost possible to do so with the sun shining and the birds singing and Richard sleeping peacefully in his chair. But on the edge of hearing the motorway droned on and on. It sounded to Gwen's ear like nothing so much as an everlasting hoover.

THIRTY-TWO

LYDIA PAUSED IN what she was doing, cocked her head, listened. Silence. No Prize, of course – she didn't expect to hear Prize anymore – but no ghost, either. Nothing. Just a strange fluttering sensation in her belly. The baby. An alien presence. Nothing to do with her. She had no feelings for it at all.

She looked down in the twilight of her room at the suitcase lying open on her bed, clothes piled higgledy-piggledy. The size of her task began to crush her. She had no choice but to leave, yet where could she go? And what about her furniture? She was so tired. Drained. All the life in her was being siphoned off by the baby. She was no longer in control even of her own body.

What a state to get into – and over something that had not actually happened.

Or had it?

She had been walking round the village to get a breath of air and clear her head, but without much success. It was odd how aimless walking seemed without a lead in your hand. She was starting to *waddle*, too. In the High Street, just past the church, she had met Mrs Pole coming the other way. Lydia had said 'good evening', because you had to be polite, you lived in a civilized country, there was no future in holding grudges. And then—

'Why don't you fuck off to the People's Republic of China, you communist whore.'

Lydia had been stunned, had stopped dead, turned round on the narrow pavement. 'Excuse me? *What* did you say?'

Mrs Pole had briefly looked back, dignified and frosty. 'I didn't say anything. Not a word. Do you really imagine I would want to

240

talk to *you*!' And she had gone on her way, disappeared into her cottage opposite the pub.

In the aftermath of this encounter, Lydia had rushed home, dragged the suitcase from under her bed, begun packing, but now she was beginning to wonder if the voice she had heard had been nothing but a hallucination. Was it really very likely that a woman such as Mrs Pole would use the word *whore* – let alone *fuck*?

But what did it matter if it had happened or not? The sentiment was there. The village was against her. She could imagine other frosty looks and muttered imprecations: poison pen letters, perhaps; bricks through her windows. She couldn't face it. She refused to stay and be trampled into the dirt. It was bad enough having Lady Darkley and her coven haunt her dreams, circling in tall black hats like witches round a huge bonfire where her wonderful painting curled and blackened amid the flames.

The sound of the doorbell made her jump. Who could it be at this hour? Was it starting already, the unrelenting persecution? Heart in her mouth, she crept towards the window, peered from one side, keeping out of sight. There was an unprepossessing figure on the doorstep. Pepper-and-salt pate, baggy anorak. Terry.

You are the most wonderful woman in the world.

She must have imagined that, too. The truth was, she was neither a communist whore nor a wonderful woman. She was nothing, nobody.

She flattened herself against the wall, waiting for him to go away.

'Hello? Anybody in? Lydia?' His voice came floating up the stairs.

Curses! He must have let himself in. Was nothing sacred? People were even invading her home now, her sanctum. She would have to go down and face him.

He was standing in the middle of the main room, looking round, indecision written all over his face.

'What are you doing here, Terry?'

'Oh, there you are. You made me jump.'

'Well?'

'I ... er ... came to see how ... how you— Your door was wide open.'

'Oh.' She must have left it open when she came in from her walk. She had lost her grip: that was becoming increasingly obvious.

'I was … er … worried,' he continued. 'Worried.'

'You needn't be. I don't want fuss, I don't want to be mollycoddled. I can do without charity and pity and people feeling sorry for me.'

'That's not how I—'

'I just want to be left alone. I am not a whore, neither am I wonderful, I am just me.'

Even in the half-light she could see him blush at the word *wonderful*. He must have said those things. It hadn't been her imagination. But he had mistaken her for someone else. He couldn't mean what he said. He didn't even know her. Perhaps, like so many men, he never looked beyond the end of his own nose, was only interested in himself. It must be that.

She gripped the back of the sofa, facing him across it. 'I am old, nearly forty. I have grey hairs, wrinkles, I am past it—' She stopped, caught her breath, felt in her belly the fluttering sensation again: *movement*. Not quite past it, then. But the baby would finish her off, she was sure of that.

'Forty?' Terry was saying. 'Forty's nothing. Forty's young.'

'I am pregnant,' she whispered. 'A pariah.'

'You are—'

'Finished. Washed up.'

There was a pause. She could see his eyes glinting in the gloom. 'My God, Lydia, what did Nigel *do* to you?'

'Nigel?' She licked her lips. The name seemed to leave a nasty taste on her tongue. Why was he talking about Nigel? He knew nothing about Nigel!

'Yes, Nigel,' he said, his voice suddenly tinged with the bombastic tone it acquired whenever he talked about the council, about Basil, about the ruling classes and the oppression of the poor. 'Nigel,' he repeated. 'The man you never mention except flippantly, in passing, as if he was of no importance; the man who is always coming between us.'

'Us?'

'Yes, us. You must realize how much I—'

'How much you...?'

'Like ... you.'

'Yes.' Of course she had realized. She wasn't stupid. And Terry, although he did not exactly wear his heart on his sleeve (he wasn't that sort; his sleeve was the sleeve of an anorak), had eyes that exposed him, eyes that followed you around, brown, watery eyes, legible and mournful.

Nigel's eyes had been different. They had been blue and diamond hard.

'I liked Nigel's eyes,' she said. 'People often remarked on his eyes.'

'His eyes?' said Terry dubiously.

'I put all my eggs in one basket. That is what people do when they are in ... when they ...'

'Love,' said Terry softly. 'In love.'

'Yes. That.' She took a deep breath, steadying herself. 'I should have read the signs.' *But I didn't*, she added silently. *That is what's so hard to take. That is why I feel ashamed. I was (am?) a clever, capable, independent woman, yet I let myself get trapped and I did nothing about it. If it had been someone else – some other woman – I would have been disdainful, disbelieving. Why didn't she stand up for herself? Why didn't she simply walk away? How could she be so gullible? She deserved to be a victim, for being so stupid!* 'Nigel was plausible. I believed in him. He made me laugh. He was charming, confident, virile: the complete man.'

'Are you sure?'

'It was all my fault. I was the one who stayed with him.'

'You are making excuses for him. What was he really like?'

'He was....'

'Yes?'

'He was ...' *Face it. Say it. Confess.* '... violent. A bully.'

'A Tory,' said Terry nastily.

That is his worst insult, thought Lydia, experiencing an unexpected and destabilizing emotion that she could not quite put her finger on. She wanted to laugh – or was it cry? Poor Terry. He was not sophisticated like Nigel. Nigel's insults had been more telling. She shuddered as a long-ago scene resurfaced in her mind, a certain restaurant, a certain waitress – little more than a girl. What was it she had done: brought the wrong mustard, spilt the wine? Nigel had eyeballed her. 'Are you congenitally incompetent, or is it something you've had to practise?' His aim had been sure, certain, deadly: it always was. Tears had sprung in the girl's eyes. She had crumbled in front of them. *I was naive*, thought Lydia, *young and naive. I laughed, I thought Nigel's remark witty, I disliked the waitress who was younger, prettier. I didn't realize that, looking at her as the tears sprang, I was looking into a mirror.*

'I thought he would change,' Lydia said out loud. 'I had changed, being with him. I was more confident, I felt worthy.'

'You were young?' suggested Terry. 'Inexperienced?'

'But I was not stupid. Yet I thought I could tap into the inner man, bring his gentler side to the fore.'

'I bet he didn't have a gentler side,' said Terry bitterly. 'I wish I'd met him. I'd have punched him on the nose.'

'Oh, Terry...!' She found herself laughing. It made her feel incredibly sad. 'Nigel would have flattened you. He was a big man, he played rugby.'

'I rather get the impression he is the sort of man who only picks on women.'

'He said it was because he cared: it showed how much he cared. You only get that worked up when it's something that matters.' He had said a lot of things, very reasonable things, the voice of authority. He had said she was wasting her time painting. He had told her it would never amount to anything. Those who can, he said, do; those who can't, teach. 'Which explains why you are a teacher, darling.'

'It is high time you forgot about Nigel.'

'Nigel is not my only error of judgment. I got embroiled with Richard Collier. I am old enough to be his mother.'

'That is what I like about you.'

'That I am old? That I slept with a man half my age?'

'That you dared to.'

'But there's the baby, too.'

'Our baby.'

'It is not your baby. Nor is it Richard's. It is—'

'That doesn't matter. It belongs to us.'

'There is no us.'

'Not yet.'

'How can there be when I am nothing, nobody, an empty shell?'

'You are not nobody. Look how you created that Exhibition. Look at the way you got people to rally round. You are an inspiration. That is why I like you. That is why I ... I love you.'

'But Terry, *I* don't love *you*.'

'Not at all? Not even a bit? Is there *nothing...*?'

'Your beard,' she conceded, whispering. 'I like men with beards.'

'That is a start. We can—'

'But your anorak. That anorak.'

She could hear him taking it off as she emerged from behind the sofa, feeling her way now that it had grown completely dark. Her groping hand met his. He gripped it.

'This could be a terrible mistake,' she said. Like Richard, like Dean, like Nigel.

'Look on it as an experiment. Two inert substances, coming together. Will there be...?'

'Will there be what?'

'A reaction ... a chemical ... reaction....'

His pullover was prickly against her cheek, his chest was heaving. Her fingers sought his face, as if to prove to herself that he was really there. She touched his bristly beard, his soft lips, felt his lips part as he spoke.

'Oxygen,' he muttered indistinctly.

'Oxygen?'

'Oxygen started as a waste gas. It was poison. Now we can't live without it. That is how things change. You see, we would not be here at all but for microscopic cyanobacteria millions of years ago, building stromatolites, excreting oxygen, paving the way for ... for.... What's so funny?'

She was rocking with laughter. 'Oh Terry, Terry! Is this the way you sweet-talk a woman?'

'I am no good at it. There is not much that I am good at. *Clueless*, my ex-wife called me.'

'Hush,' said Lydia, pressing her fingers against his lips. 'Hush.'

It was not the femme fatale talking. It was not even Miss Taylor from school. It was ordinary Lydia in her little old cottage, the Lydia who couldn't do and had to teach.

By the looks of things, she was going to have to teach Terry a thing or two.

The daylight woke her. She had forgotten to close the curtains. With spring getting on and the days drawing out, it got light early. Normally she'd still have been fast asleep at this time, but now she was wide awake and there could be no more hiding in her dreams.

She stared up at the sloping ceiling, aware of Terry sleeping beside her, snuffling slightly in a way that was reminiscent of Prize. But Prize was not here: Prize had gone, would never come back. It was Terry who was here.

She was still making up her mind if this was a good thing or not when she remembered what day it was. Thursday, the day of the election. If it was not one thing, it was another, she thought with a sinking feeling. Surely there was no real possibility of her becoming a parish councillor? It was the last thing she needed after the trauma of the Exhibition. She had enough on her plate with the baby, with Terry—

You're the most wonderful woman in the world.

Had he really said that? But Richard had said similar things in his cack-handed way, spinning a line, using fancy chat to get her into bed.

But what about that day in his flat? *You don't realize how fantastic you are, so droll and original and sexy.*

He couldn't have been talking about her. He couldn't have.

She thought of the suitcase under the bed where she'd shoved it last night, hoping Terry wouldn't notice. Perhaps the suitcase still offered the best way out. What had she got left, what was there to stay for? She felt comfortable with Terry, that was true; she had never made any pretence with him. But that was a long, long way from love. You couldn't build anything on that ... could you?

She stretched her legs and wiggled her toes, feeling the unborn child stirring inside her, making its presence felt: a presence she was – dared she say it – slowly getting used to.

You're the most wonderful woman in the world.

Perhaps, she said, testing the waters, feeling trepidation, *perhaps I really am.*

She listened. No snort of derision. No disparaging comments.

There had been nothing now for days.

Her mother's ghost wasn't there. Her mother's ghost had gone.

THIRTY-THREE

'MUM, MUM! WHERE are you? The results!'

It was past Amanda's bedtime – it was past everyone's bedtime – but one had not liked to leave her behind when even Dean had expressed an interest in coming to the count. Amanda had been especially enthusiastic, too, these last few days: a late convert to the cause. She had made a placard, *Vote For My Mum*, had paraded round the village with it. Gwen had been resigned to her fate by then. The damage was already done. Amanda's placard would not make much difference. One had always known that people had misgivings, but those misgivings would now harden into indisputable truths. *Gwen Collier is getting too big for her boots. Who does she think she is, putting herself forward for the parish council? Not to mention that Exhibition, and flaunting herself on the local news! She needs cutting down to size, there's no two ways about it.*

Gwen faced facts. What little standing she had ever had in the village was gone for ever. Her struggle to be respectable – to be *accepted* – was just as futile as her fight against dust and dirt and the unstoppable creepy-crawlies.

'Mum!' Amanda was pulling at her sleeve.

'Yes, I'm coming!' Gwen allowed herself to be led out of the little lobby where she had gone for a moment's peace and back into the main room, a vast chamber in the leisure centre in town: some sort of sports hall, one presumed. It was packed this evening. (Evening? It was almost morning: would be, by the time they were finished.) A great concourse of people was milling about. There were officials (Basil was in his element), candidates, the press, hangers-on. Tellers were sitting at long lines of tables. The untidy mounds of ballot papers tipped from box after box had been sifted, sorted and arranged into nice, neat piles. But the process was taking for ever; and it didn't help that votes were being counted from across the entire district. The parish election was just a sideshow to the more important district council seats. That Terry-person was here. (What was his surname again? She could never remember. She must ask Dean). He was up for re-election, standing in one of the town wards. Lydia was with him. (Were they a couple or not? One liked to be clear about these things. But it would never last, either way: it just wouldn't ... would it?) Lydia looked more striking than ever this evening, positively blooming. That was what pregnancy did for you (it couldn't be down to Terry, he was far too dull). The way she was dressed, too: it put one's neat grey skirt and smart blouse rather in the shade. Could one really get such clothes from a *charity* shop, the wonderful flowing skirt, the shimmering, flared blouse? With all that dark hair, Lydia looked startlingly exotic, like a flamenco dancer—

Gwen took a breath. *I am gabbling,* she thought. *I must slow down, take one step at a time. Oh, how I wish I was tucked up in bed*!

Basil was now taking to the makeshift stage at one end of the hall. He looked rather resplendent in his best suit. Very stiff and formal, of course: *pernickety,* one might say, if one had been the sort of person who used such words (one wasn't, thank goodness). Amanda was right: he was ready to give out the results.

All round the district first, in alphabetical order. People began clapping, cheering. (Was there any need for it? Wasn't it rather like *gloating*? One could not imagine Basil doing it. Basil was a stickler. One tended to overlook his magnificent sense of decorum.) Flash bulbs were going off, reporters were busy scribbling. Wasn't that girl over there the one from the local paper, the girl Imelda Darkley had sent flying on the day the Exhibition opened? Nearby was Imelda herself. One couldn't really miss her. Those shoulder pads on her sturdy frame put one in mind of that bull-headed monster, the name of which escaped one (Dean would know). Imelda's hair was done up, too, soaring high like a vast conical mountain (that mountain in Brazil, the one with Jesus on top: where was Dean when one wanted him?), and her habitual green wellies had tonight been swapped for shiny flat shoes. (One wasn't the sort of person who used words like *grotesque*; one never passed comments on the size of people's feet.) Margaret Pole was, of course, in attendance, as was old Smithson who'd decided to stand after all, deferring his retirement once again.

'Yoo-hoo, Gwen! Over here! Isn't this exciting, ha ha ha!'

The Stasi came bulldozing through the crowd, waving and shouting (one wished her voice wasn't *quite* so piercing). Her husband followed in her wake, fiddling with the collar of his shirt. He looked distinctly uncomfortable in his ill-fitting suit, not a patch on Basil.

'I haven't had so much fun in ages!' cried the Stasi. 'It shouldn't be long now until— But wait a minute, this must be Terry's result!'

The first of the town wards. Basil's lugubrious tones. 'Armitage, Mr Terence Alan....' Of course, that was the name: Armitage! To hear Basil announce it so courteously, one would never guess the choice epithets he had for Terry: *buffoon, demagogue, that man.*

So, Terry had scraped home. Did he look pleased? Relieved? Well, not really. He only had eyes for Lydia. Such an odd combination, really, those two. Would she take him for walkies and fondle his ears?

Oh, you are cruel, Gwendolen: so cruel!

'And now....' Basil, solemn, impartial.

'This is us, Gwen! Oh, I can't bear it, ha ha ha!'

The Stasi was gripping her arm, jumping around like an excited child. All that pulling of pints had given her some strength. One wished she would—

But one couldn't think straight. One's mouth was dry. One's heart beating. One just wanted to get it over with.

'Collier, Mrs Gwendolen Elizabeth....'

There it was: the first name to be announced. Bottom of the list.

Gwen let out a long breath. So. How did one feel? Relieved, naturally: relieved that it was all over. But.... Well, would it have been too much to ask to have come *second* from last? One would have liked a sop to one's tattered pride. Really, though: what else could one have expected? (...*newcomer ... couldn't keep her husband ... married twice...does her best, poor dear....*)

250

'Your face, Gwen, ha ha ha! Anyone would think it was a catastrophe!'

'But last place....'

'First, Gwen: you came first. He's reading them top down. You got more votes than anyone, you got over two hundred and – oh, there's my name! He just said my name!'

She will rip my sleeve, break my arm, if she grips much tighter, thought Gwen. *What did she mean, first? She must be mistaken. But then she so often is. She does tend to get hold of the wrong end of the stick.*

The Stasi let go of her. For the moment, all Gwen could think about was how much her arm was hurting. She rubbed the place where the Stasi's fingers had gripped, watching as the Stasi became involved in a fierce contretemps with her husband.

'I don't know if I'm in or not.'

'You should have been listening.'

'I *was* listening.'

'Not properly.'

'Yes I was! Were you listening? No you weren't, or you'd know if I'd got in.'

Whack, crack! Gwen flinched, holding her arm close to her chest, as the Stasi launched a few deadly strikes on her husband.

Over the loudspeakers, Basil's voice had developed a tone of peroration. '... Pole, Mrs Margaret: fifty-eight votes. And Darkley, Lady Imelda Ann: forty-three votes. That concludes....'

Gwen shook her head. The result was topsy-turvy, it couldn't be right. If it had been anyone but Basil one would have assumed there had been a miscalculation somewhere, but Basil didn't make mistakes.

Lydia appeared at her side, all dazzling smiles (one almost expected her to start clicking some castanets).

'I believe congratulations are in order,' she said, 'for both of you.'

'Who'd have thought I'd get more votes than you, Lydia, ha ha ha! But it's a shame we didn't all get on. It would have been like old times, the old Exhibition committee back together.'

'Unfortunately,' said Lydia, 'I was pipped by Smithson.'

She did not sound unduly upset, but Gwen was dismayed. 'Oh, Lydia, are you sure?'

'Quite sure. Basil was most definite.'

'But it's not *right*! It's not *fair*! None of this would have happened without you! We wouldn't even be here!'

'I'm a troublemaker, Gwen. A snake in the grass. That is how people see me, anyway. I was never going to be popular.'

'But you were going to change things! You were going to make a difference!' (*You were going to change things for me, make a difference in my life.*)

'I've done my bit. I have other fish to fry. This, for instance.' She laid a hand on her stomach. 'And a new painting. I thought, after my masterpiece was burned, that I wouldn't have the heart to ever paint again, but already I feel ideas and inspiration bubbling up inside me. My next painting will have a snake in it. I have developed quite a liking for snakes. The parish council I leave to you, Gwen. You must continue our good work in shaking up the village and making people think.'

'Me?' Gwen trembled. She could almost feel the weight of expectation pressing down upon her. How would she cope, when she couldn't even keep her own house clean, when no one in the village respected her?

'You will be elected leader, I have no doubt,' Lydia continued, 'now that Lady Darkley has been ousted.'

'*Me!*'

'Of course. Who else? Don't you realize, Gwen, how popular you are? I've never heard a bad word against you. It's rather heartening, I think, in this cynical age, that people still sometimes get their just deserts.'

Gwen could hardly hear Lydia above the noise in the hall – or was it a buzzing in her ears? She felt dizzy, come to that, and she couldn't breathe. It was suffocating in here.

'I must just ... some air ...'

She desperately needed a moment to herself, but as she made her way through the crowd, smiling people greeted her on every side, and her hand was shaken again and again. 'Well done, Gwen! Congratulations! So very glad!' It was like Waitrose on a bad day, familiar faces at every turn: one sometimes felt that one would never reach the checkout, and even when one did, one couldn't help wondering, as one waited in the queue, what they were all saying to one another up and down the aisles. 'There she goes: Gwen Collier ... her husband ran off with another woman ... her house is full of dust, teeming with creepy-crawlies ... she tries so hard, but ...'

Don't you realize, Gwen, how popular you are? I've never heard a bad word against you.

A fresh wave of dizziness overtook her as she reached the lobby. There was a side door open for smokers. Gwen stepped thankfully through it, gulped in the cool night air. Not so cool, actually: it had been a glorious day, and another was forecast for tomorrow. The night sky was clear, stars glinting above the black silhouettes of Basil's monstrosities.

Gwen moved away from the gaggle of smokers, wanting to snatch a moment's peace and quiet, to make sense of everything, but even here she was not alone. There was someone in the shadows, over there by the railings where people chained their bicycles – two people, in fact. Was it...? Yes it was: Dean. And Imelda's granddaughter. Such a nice girl, so quiet and polite. Was Dean ... was he actually *kissing* her? Well, well. One had begun to think he would never get round to....

But it was obviously a night for wonders. Over two hundred votes! Was it really possible that so many people had—

There was a sudden stir amongst the smokers. They fell back, were swept abruptly aside as if by a mini tornado. It could only be one person: Imelda Darkley, swooping out from the leisure centre like a Fury, looming up taller even than the monstrosities, blotting out the stars.

Gwen quailed.

'Are you coming, Calabria?' Imperious as ever.

'No, Grandma. Dean will take me home.'

'Very well. As you like.'

Imelda went charging off across the road to where her four-by-four was parked on double yellow lines. Strange to say, as one watched her, she didn't look half as tall and imposing as one thought. She looked, in fact, rather small and insignificant, an old shrunken figure climbing into an absurdly large car. It seemed incredible to think that this was the same woman who, until barely an hour ago, had been eternal chair of the parish council, queen of the village, suzerain of the country round. Her reign had lasted as long as one could remember. But, all at once, she had been reduced to this: to going home alone in the dark, with only forty-three votes to her name. One could almost feel a bit sorry—

'Tears, Gwendolen?'

Gwen turned as the sound of Lady Darkley's car faded into the night. She found herself face to face with Basil, Amanda at his side.

She wiped her eyes. 'Silly of me....'

'*Silly*, Gwen, is not a word that could ever be applied to you.'

He was looking at her strangely, almost warily. Getting used to having a wife who was on the parish council. Beginning to wonder if he'd ever get his dinner – sorry, supper – on time ever again.

And yet it wasn't quite that sort of look. Why did it make one think of Westminster Bridge?

'Well, Councillor Collier: it's all over. Your chariot awaits. Where am I to take you?'

She smiled automatically, the same old reticent smile, the one she wore like a comfy cardigan. But then something unexpected happened. It was as if the smile had suddenly come to life, as if it was taking over. She could feel it growing and spreading, a wide smile, an all-embracing smile; a smile like a butterfly stretching its wings.

She paused for a moment, savouring this strange new sensation, and then, 'Take me home, please, Basil,' she said.